Richard Marsh

Under One Flag

Richard Marsh

Under One Flag

1st Edition | ISBN: 978-3-75241-665-7

Place of Publication: Frankfurt am Main, Germany

Year of Publication: 2020

Outlook Verlag GmbH, Germany.

Reproduction of the original.

Under One Flag

By

Richard Marsh

A PET OF THE BALLET

I

She was regarding, ruefully, the condition of her white satin shoes. They were articles which the ladies of the ballet had to provide for themselves. Twice she had sewn on fresh uppers, and now both uppers and soles had gone. Clearly it was a case in which a new pair would have to be bought. And yet, this week, money seemed shorter than ever. She wondered if skilful patching would not make them do till treasury. And, while she wondered, there was a knock at the door.

"Come in."

Polly Steele was the only visitor who ever came her way. She took it for granted that it was Polly now—though why Miss Steele should be so ceremonious as to knock she did not stop to think. She was continuing to consider the question of the possibility of repairing the shoes when a voice behind her caused her to spring to her feet with a start.

"Pardon—Miss Lizzie Emmett?"

Standing in the doorway was an individual who was dressed in a fashion in which gentlemen in the immediate neighbourhood of Hercules Buildings were not accustomed to dress. His clothes were beautiful, he wore patent leather shoes, his tie was a marvel, he carried a glossy silk hat in a well-gloved hand. He became his costume—so tall and so slender; with a little beard cut to a point; a charming moustache, the ends of which curled gracefully upwards. The vision was such an unexpected one that Lizzie, forgetful, for the moment, of her manners, stared at the stranger with bewildered surprise. "I'm Liz Emmett." The stranger bowed and smiled.

"In that case, Miss Emmett, I believe that I have the honour of being the bearer of a little parcel for you. I trust that the contents may have the pleasure to meet with your approbation—also the source from which it comes."

He advanced into the room—the poor, scantily-furnished, untidy, tawdry little room!—holding out to her a small, neatly-fastened package. She took it with what was almost an air of sullen indifference, evincing neither curiosity nor satisfaction. "I don't know you." Again a bow and a smile.

"That is my misfortune, which I hope is on the high road towards amendment. My name is Philippe Rossignol. It may be that the day is not far distant when mademoiselle will come to look upon me as a friend—as a very good friend indeed—eh?"

There was something in the fellow's obsequious bearing which savoured of impertinence—something which it seemed as if the girl resented.

"I shouldn't think that you'd ever be a friend of mine. You don't look as if you was my sort."

The smile became more pronounced, and also more insulting.

"Not your sort? I pray that I have not so much ill fortune."

He paused, as if for her to speak. She spoke.

"I don't care for foreigners. Can't abide 'em. Never could."

The man drew himself up as if she had struck him. The smile lingered about his lips, though something very different was in his eyes. He was silent, as if considering what to say. His words, when they came, ignored her unflattering remark.

"The abode of mademoiselle is a little difficult to discover, unless one happens to know just exactly where it is."

"No one asked you to discover it, as I know of, so I don't see what odds that makes to you."

The girl's insistent rudeness seemed to occasion the stranger not only surprise, but something else as well, something approaching to curiosity. He observed her with more attention, as if she suggested a problem to his mind which was of the nature of a puzzle. She was young, strongly built, healthy. Beyond that, so far as he could see, she was nothing. She had neither face nor figure. Her movements were ungainly, her features were, emphatically, plain. Her dress was not only poor—worse, it was in execrable taste. She seemed to have decked herself in as many colours as she conveniently could, none of them being in sympathy with her complexion. Her manners were those of a woman of the people, her voice was a female Cockney's. Metaphorically, M. Rossignol shrugged his shoulders; to himself he said,—

"What there is attractive in her is for him to decide; for my part, I would rather that it were for him than for me. It is a folly even for a fool, even such a fool as that!"

Aloud he bade the lady farewell. "I have the pleasure of wishing

3

mademoiselle a very good day."

As he backed towards the door he favoured her with a bow which could scarcely have been lower had she been an empress. She let him go without a word or sign of greeting. It was only when he had vanished, and the sound of his footsteps had ceased upon the stairs, that she found her tongue.

"Greasy foreigner, nasty, sneering beast! Coming shoving his nose in here as if he was somebody and me the dirt under his feet. I'll show him! If he'd stayed much longer, a-trying it on with me, I'd have give him one for himself, and helped him to the door. What's this, I'd like to know." She glanced down at the package she was holding, as if suddenly remembering it was there. She read the address which was on it. "'Miss Lizzie Emmett, 14 Hercules Buildings, Westminster.' He's got my address all right, though how he's got it is more than I can say. What's inside? Feels as if it was something hard." She made as if to open it. Then in a fit of sudden petulance she threw it from her, so that it landed on the bed which was at her back. "I'm not going to trouble myself about his rubbish. I never set eyes on him in all my life before—who's he, I'd like to know. If ever he shows himself inside my place again, I'll start him travelling." She resumed her consideration of the vexed question of the shoes. "I can't get no more till Saturday, so they'll have to do, and that's all about it. I'll fake 'em up with cardboard, same as I did once before, and if anybody notices it, why, they'll have to."

Seating herself on the only chair the room contained she began to cut, with a pair of scissors, pieces out of the lid of a cardboard box, which was yellow on one side and white on the other. She was not deft with her fingers, nor quick. The job promised to be a long one, and not remarkable for neatness when done. As with hunched shoulders she pursued her task of cobbling, for a second time there came a knock at the door.

"Now who's that? If it's that bloke back again, he'll get what for." This, *sotto voce*; then, aloud, "Is that you, Polly?"

It was not Polly, as the voice which answered showed.

"Does anyone live here named Emmett?"

The visitor this time was a woman. Lizzie eyed her with as much surprise as she had eyed the man; certainly she was every whit as much out of place in Hercules Buildings as he had been. Like him, she was tall and slender, and beautifully dressed. Lizzie's feminine gaze, taking in the details of her costume, dimly realised its costliness.

"May I come in?"

"If you like you can."

4

Apparently the stranger did like. She closed the door behind her, standing, for a moment, to regard Miss Emmett. Then her look wandered about the room. She wore a big hat, to which was attached a veil which was so thick as almost to entirely obscure her features. But one realised, from something in her attitude, that what she saw filled her with amazement.

"I think that I may have made a mistake."

"I shouldn't be surprised but what you had."

"Is it a Miss Lizzie Emmett who lives here?"

"Yes—Liz Emmett—that's me."

"You!" The astonishment in the speaker's voice was unequivocal, and not complimentary. One understood that she was studying Lizzie from behind her veil as if she could scarcely believe her eyes. Her speech faltered. "Excuse me, but are you in the profession?"

A hint of defiance came into Lizzie's tone. She was beginning to suspect that her visitor might be something in the district-visiting line.

"I'm in the ballet at the Cerulean Theatre—that's what I am!"

The stranger seemed to shiver as she heard; as if the answer removed from her mind the last traces of doubt, leaving her, instead, with a feeling of uncomfortable certainty. Turning towards the tiny fireplace, she began to trifle with the odds and ends which were on the mantelshelf. Then, once more confronting Lizzie, with a deliberate movement she raised her veil.

"Do you know me?"

"I can't say as how I do."

"I am Agnes Graham."

Lizzie was moved to genuine emotion. She rose from her chair in a flutter of excitement. She became more awkward than ever.

"Think of me not knowing you! I ought to, seeing how often I've seen your picture. I beg your pardon, Miss Graham, I'm sure, but won't you take a chair?"

"Thank you, for the present I'll stand." She eyed the other steadfastly; it seemed as if the more she gazed the more her wonder grew. "I'm afraid that I have come to you on a foolish errand, and that you will laugh at me before I've done, if you don't do worse."

"Laugh at you, Miss Graham. That I'm sure I won't."

"May I ask, Miss Emmett, if you know anything of my private history?"

"Me!" The inquiry might have conveyed a reproach, Lizzie's denial was uttered with so much earnestness. "I don't know nothing at all about you, miss, except what's in the papers."

"Except what's in the papers!" Miss Graham smiled, not sunnily. "In that case you know more about me than I do about myself. Still, I am disposed to inflict on you a fragment of personal history. You might not think it, but, in spite of what is in the papers, I'm a dreamer."

"Indeed, miss? I'm a dreamer too."

The words were spoken so simply that it seemed difficult to suspect the speaker of a second intention. Miss Graham, however, shot at her a sudden doubting glance. Her tone became harder.

"I trust, for both our sakes, that our dreams do not run on the same lines. I have always dreamed of a home; of a harbour at last; of peace at the end; of a time when I shall be able to take my seat among the best, with a mind at ease. It may sound odd, but I have always looked forward to making a good marriage."

"I should think, miss, that you might have done that over and over again."

"I might, but I haven't. But lately I have thought that I might. I am sick of the stage, sick to death!"

She gave a little passionate gesture. In her voice there was a ring of sincerity.

"I shouldn't have thought, miss, that you would ever have been sick of the stage."

"You wouldn't have thought! What do you know of it? You!" She cast a look at Lizzie which was as scornful as her words. Then glanced at the empty rust-worn grate. Then again met Lizzie face to face. "I will be as frank with you as I would ask you to be frank with me. I have dreamed—I use the word advisedly!—I say that I have dreamed of being Countess of Bermondsey."

"Countess of Bermondsey! I'd like to lay, miss, that you could be anything you please!"

Miss Graham's lips were drawn close together.

"Are you laughing at me?"

"Laughing at you! Me, miss! I shouldn't think of doing such a thing."

"Then may I ask you to be as candid as myself? Before this my dream might have been something more solid than a dream, if it had not been for you."

"For me!"

Lizzie was open-eyed and open-mouthed.

"Pray don't let us play the actress off the boards. Don't you think we might confine that sort of thing to our hours of business?"

"But I don't understand you, miss. Do you mean that you might have been the Countess of Bermondsey if it had not been for me?"

Miss Graham's eyes were as keen and cold as the other's were hot and eager.

"I see that a denial is trembling on your lips. Pray don't trouble yourself to utter it. Is that the sort of person you are? I assure you that, in this case, at least, you make a mistake; for unfortunately I speak from knowledge." She stopped, then resumed with a strain of passion in her voice which, almost with every word, became more strenuous. "The Earl of Bermondsey, as, doubtless, you are aware, although for reasons of your own you may feign ignorance, has, for some time, been a friend of mine. I had reason to believe that he might become more, until, recently, the outward tokens of his friendship waned. I looked for the reason. I found it. He has, lately, become an assiduous patron of the Cerulean Theatre. This morning I taxed him with it. He offered no denial. I asked him for the lady's name. He floundered—as you may be aware his lordship is an adept at floundering—and, as he floundered, a piece of paper fell from his pocket on to the floor. I picked it up. On it was a lady's name and her address. I asked if she was the attraction at the Cerulean. He owned that she was. He said things of her," the speaker's voice quivered, "which I do not care to recount at second hand to you. 'Lizzie Emmett, 14 Hercules Buildings, Westminster,' was on the paper, and it was of you those things were said."

"Me!"

The actress moved slightly away from the fireplace, speaking with a strength of feeling and an eloquence of gesture which, had she been capable of such efforts on the stage, would have gained her immortality.

"It may be sport to you—I daresay it is, there was a time when I used to think that sort of thing was sport—but it is death to me. Death! He has as good as promised that I shall be his wife. I have staked everything upon the fulfilment of his promise. Nothing can compensate me for his breaking it. I won't try to make you understand why—you mightn't understand me if I tried! But if he does, I'll go under—under! If you only knew what I've endured since he's begun to tire, you'd pity me. I'm here to ask you to pity me now. We're both women—be generous—I'll be sworn it's not of much

7

consequence to you—be good to me. If you'll only send him back to me, help me to be his wife, there's nothing I won't do for you, in reason or out of reason. I swear it. I'll put it down in black and white in any form you like!" With trembling hands she caught hold of Lizzie's shabby sleeve. "But don't be cruel to me—don't be cruel!"

Lizzie shrunk away from her.

"You're making a mistake, Miss Graham, a big mistake!"

"Don't say that, for pity's sake, don't say that! Show mercy to me, as one day you may want some other woman to show mercy to you."

Lizzie withdrew herself still farther from the other's eager pleading.

"You've got it all wrong, I'm not the girl you're taking me for. I don't know no Earl of Bermondsey, nor yet no Earl of anything, and I don't want to."

"Why should you deny it?"

"Because it's the truth. I'm straight, I am, and I always have been, and I always mean to be, and if any of your toffs came playing it off on to me he'd get a bit more than he quite wanted."

The girl's tone and manner carried conviction even to her hearer.

"Is it possible that he is known to you under some different name? Tell me, what friends have you?"

The singularity of the request did not seem to occur to Lizzie. The reply came as promptly as if the question had been a commonplace.

"Friends? Do you mean fellows? The only fellow that ever was a friend to me, and he's only a sort of a one, is Joe Mason, what's carpenter up at the theatre; he's no earl. Ask yourself the question—do I look the sort of girl an earl would take up with?"

Miss Graham felt that she did not—had felt so all along; not although the earl was possessed of such peculiar tastes as was the one in question.

"You might look different on the stage—one can make oneself look like anything there."

"I might and I mightn't. As far as I know no one ever took me for a beauty even on the stage, not even Joe Mason."

The girl's eyes twinkled with laughter, as if the bare possibility of such a thing struck her as comical. Her visitor returned to the fireplace. She made a little troubled movement with her hands.

8

"I wish you would be frank with me. You must know something of him, even if you don't know him, else how came your name and address to be in his pocket, and why should he claim your acquaintance?"

"It beats me fair, it does. I never gave it him, that's certain. There's a muddle somewhere."

"Is there anyone else of your name at the theatre?"

"If there is I never heard of it, and I've been there now getting on for two years. There's no one else of that name in the ballet, that I do know."

"Have you ever acted for him as a go-between? Just think! I'll tell you what he looks like. He's quite young, only twenty-two; short, rather stout, light hair parted on the side, no moustache, red face, blue eyes; and when he's at all excited he speaks as if he had a plum in his mouth."

Lizzie shook her head.

"If he's like what you say he's not a beauty, but, so far as I know, I never set eyes on him; and as for being a go-between, either for him or for anybody else, I'd scorn to do it."

Agnes Graham's glance returned to the empty grate. She seemed to be reflecting.

"I believe you. You sound honest, and you look it. But that there's a mystery somewhere I'm persuaded. I'm in a desperate strait, and I want you to do something for me. I'll pay you for it well."

"I don't want your pay."

The other went on unheeding.

"I want you to use your eyes, and to find out who it is at the Cerulean he is after. That there is someone I have the best of reasons for knowing. When you have found out I want you to tell me. And if you won't do it for pay, do it out of kindness."

Lizzie hesitated.

"I'm not fond of spying, and I'm not fond of them as is, but as he don't seem to be using you well, if I do find out who he's playing it off with—though, mind you, I don't see how I'm going to—still, as I say, if I should happen to find out, why, I'll tell you, straight!"

"Thank you."

Agnes Graham held out her hand, in order that, by grasping it, the girl might ratify the bargain. And she did.

When she was again alone, Liz Emmett was lost in wonder. As she had said, she also was a dreamer and, as became a dreamer, had her heroes and her heroines. Theatrical heroines hers, for the most part, were; not, that is, the creations of the dramatist's fancy, but their flesh-and-blood enactors. The popular actress was the ideal creature of her waking visions. Who, on the contemporary stage, was more popular, in her own line, than Agnes Graham? There was a time when Lizzie had been more than half inclined to bate her voice when uttering her name. Even to this hour she had regarded her with a kind of reverence. Now this idol, whom the public voice had set upon such a lofty pedestal, had actually been to visit her; had come unceremoniously into her room and filled it with her presence, with, for purpose, such an errand.

The errand was not the least strange part of this strange happening. Agnes Graham, famous as she was beautiful, in the theatrical firmament a bright particular star, had supposed that she, Lizzie Emmett, was her rival for the heart, and possibly the hand, of an earl; a belted earl, as she remembered to have seen it printed somewhere. The thing was most confounding. How could such a notion have got into the air?

Lizzie, taking down the oblong shilling mirror from the nail on which it hung, surveyed her face in it relentlessly. She was conscious of her imperfections, and indifferent to them. She had supple limbs, was fairly quick upon her feet, sufficiently smart at rehearsals, equal to the average *figurante*. She was aware that, when so much was said, about all was said. She had neither good looks nor cleverness, was no scholar, nor wished to be, had a rough tongue, a quick temper, and a clumsy, if a willing, hand. And Agnes Graham had imagined that she had out-distanced her in the affections of a belted earl! Was ever idea more ludicrous? As the ridiculous side struck Lizzie she began to laugh; she continued laughing till her merriment threatened to become hysterical.

As it approached a climax she caught sight of the package which she had thrown upon the bed. She checked herself.

"Then there was that foreign bloke. I wonder what rubbish is in that paper of his."

Putting down the looking-glass, she took up the parcel. She cut it open with her scissors with a contemptuous air. Inside was a leather case. She paused to examine it. She had seen others like it in the windows of jewellers' shops. Pressing a spring, the top flew open. As it did so she gave a sort of gasp. On a bed of satin reposed a necklace of shimmering crystals. They gleamed and glistened like drops of dew. The pupils of her eyes dilated. She spoke in a whisper.

"Diamonds? They can't be diamonds?" She had seen diamonds in shop windows and on other women. "They can't be real."

Suddenly she gave utterance to an exclamation which the squeamish would have called an oath and a vulgarity. Presently she joined to it a snatch from the slang of the streets.

"This cops the biscuit."

She was staring, with wide-open eyes, at a strip of pasteboard which was in the centre of the necklace, so that it was surrounded by a stream of light. It was a gentleman's visiting-card. On it was engraved "Earl of Bermondsey." She glared at it, as if she fancied that her seeing sense must be playing her tricks. Her voice, when she spoke, was vibrant; in it there was a curious ringing.

"Well, if this don't take the blooming barrowful, straight it does. 'Earl of Bermondsey'! If that ain't the bloke she was a-talking of. If this ain't a case of Queer Street, I'm a daisy!"

She picked the card up between her finger and thumb gingerly, as if she was afraid it might burn her. She turned it over; on the reverse something was scribbled in pencil. Not being skilled in reading illegible handwriting, it was with difficulty she deciphered it: "With Mr Jack Smith's compliments."

"And who may Mr Jack Smith be, I'd like to know, when he's at home. Anyhow, one thing's certain sure, this little lot ain't meant for me. I don't know nothing about no Jack Smith, nor yet about no Earl of Bermondsey neither, and I don't want to; and as for oily foreigners, I can't abide 'em. I'll just take the entire boiling to Miss Graham. Perhaps she'll be able to twig the bloke's little lay; it's more than I can."

II

Lizzie Emmett had already departed some time when fresh visitors made an unceremonious entry into her empty room. The door was opened and, without giving any premonitory notice of her intention, a girl came in.

"Lizzie!" she cried. Then perceived that there was no one there. "Well, if Lizzie isn't out!" She slightly raised her voice. "Tom, Lizzie's out, but she's not gone far, because she hasn't locked the door. You can come in—I'll give you leave. We'll wait for her."

There entered the room, with something of a shuffle, a man with a rough, untrimmed brown beard. He was big and broad, also, it seemed, a little shy; attired, obviously, in his best clothes. He seemed ill at ease in them, as if, somehow, they deprived his limbs of their wonted freedom. He gripped the brim of his brown billycock with both his large red hands. There was on his good-natured face a mixture of amusement with confusion, as though he was in possession of some happiness of which he was, at one and the same time, proud yet ashamed.

The girl looked him up and down, as if searching for something wrong in his costume or his bearing.

"Now you've got to behave yourself."

He shuffled from one foot to the other. And he grinned.

"Don't I always behave myself?"

"You've got to behave yourself extra special well, you're in a lady's room." He looked about him, his grin continually expanding. The girl, propping up the mirror which Lizzie had left upon the table against a box, began, by its aid, to fidget with her hat, talking as she did so. "Tom Duffield, you're on your good behaviour; as I might say, you're on appro. If I'm going to be your wife you've got to do something to show that you deserve it, so don't you seem to forget it." The man laughed, for so big a fellow, with curious softness. "It's all very well for you to laugh, but perhaps it is not all so cut and dried as you quite think. You're going to take two ladies out for a holiday to Kew Gardens, Mr Duffield, by the boat, so just you behave to them in a way that'll show you'll do credit to me as a husband." He laughed again. She faced him. "Well, and what might you be laughing at?"

He shuffled with his feet.

"Nothing—at you."

"That's a nice thing to say, upon my word. If you think I'm nothing, or that I'm going to be treated as nothing, you'll soon find that you're mistaken, and so I tell you. Don't stand fidgeting there like a great gawk; go and get some sweets—chocolates—good ones, none of your cheap truck, mind, and some fruit—grapes; Lizzie'll be ready by the time you're back."

The man put on his hat. He went, without a word, to do her bidding, with the obedience and the silence of a well-trained dog. Indeed, on his face, in his eyes, even in his bearing, there was something which was dog-like. The girl stared for a moment at the door through which he had gone.

"He's useful if he's not ornamental."

She returned to the mirror. Not impossibly it suggested to her that exactly the contrary might have been said of herself—she was ornamental if she was not useful. Even stronger than the man's resemblance to a dog was hers to a humming-bird. Like it, she was small; like it, too, she was exquisitely, daintily fashioned, almost too fragile for human nature's daily food. She seemed singularly out of place in that poor, tawdry chamber. Fitted, rather, for a gilded cage, or at least for some shrine of elegance and glitter. Everything about her was in proportion, tiny, and, if she was a little overdressed—if, for instance, in the details of her costume there was too much colour, the accentuation became her peculiarly exotic beauty. Her attitudes, her gestures, her little tricks of movement, all were bird-like; one felt, so free from grossness was her frame, that she scarcely was a thing of earth at all.

She preened herself before the poor apology for a looking-glass as if there was nothing in the world which could be better worth her doing. In it her pretty black eyes flashed back their enjoyment of the situation; they loved to see themselves imaged in a mirror; nor were they ashamed to confess their pleasure. If, on her cheeks, there was the suspicion of a bloom which was not Nature's, it was not there because either youth or health was failing; when one earns one's living behind the floats one's roses fade. The blood-red line of her lips was real enough, as also was the rose-pink of her delicate nostrils.

She had scarcely been alone a minute, and with so small a looking-glass had had no time to examine all that there was of herself that would repay examining, when she heard the sound of footsteps coming up the stairs. She listened.

"Who's that?" Her small white teeth gleamed between her scarlet lips. "It's that silly Tom come back again. Now, what's he forgotten? Perhaps he's met Liz, so they've both come back together." The steps were but a single pair, hardly a woman's. There was an audible uncertainty in the way in which they negotiated each separate tread which suggested that the road was unfamiliar. "It's that Tom! Now, what's he want, I wonder?" Someone tapped at the door. "That doesn't sound like Tom. Someone, I expect, for Lizzie. Bother!" Then aloud, "Come in."

The abuse which had been on the tip of the girl's tongue, ready to be hurled at the offending Tom, gave place to something very different indeed. She appeared, for the moment, to be overcome by something which was akin to consternation, to have lost her presence of mind, her readiness of speech. Nor, possibly, was her confusion lessened by the fact that the newcomer seemed to be, every whit, as embarrassed as she was. He was a young man, except, perhaps, in a legal sense, nothing but a boy. Not a very intellectual nor healthy-looking boy either. For a person of his age he was unpleasantly stout;

so stout as almost to merit the epithet of bloated. His cheeks were puffy, so also was his body. That the redness of his face was not the ruddiness of physical vigour was demonstrated by the obvious fact that the mere exertion of climbing the staircase had made him short of breath. Although his dress was that of a man of fashion he scarcely seemed a gentleman. Not only was he *gauche* and clumsy, there was about him an atmosphere of coarseness which was redolent rather of the tap-room than the drawing-room. One perceived, instinctively, that the society in which he would be most at home would be that of the *convives* of the bar.

That the girl knew him was evident—as evident as that he knew her. He looked at her with something in his eyes which was not spiritual; she at him as if she would infinitely have preferred his room to his company.

She was the first to speak.

"Well, you've got a cheek! Upon my word! What do you mean by coming here?"

There was a curious quality in his voice as he replied, which almost amounted to an impediment in his speech.

"When you gave me your address last night, Miss Emmett, I told you I'd look you up. You didn't suppose I gave you a fiver for it unless I meant to use it."

The girl continued to look at him for still another second. Then a burning flush set all her face in flames. She turned away trembling, as if she were positively frightened. She murmured to herself,—

"Here's a pretty kettle of fish! The brute! If I hadn't clean forgotten all about it! Whatever shall I say?"

He came farther into the room.

"I hope you've received my little present, Miss Emmett, and that you like it."

She angrily confronted him.

"My name's not Emmett, so don't you think it."

"Not Emmett!" He winked. "Of course not. Still, as it's been good enough for me to find you with, it's near enough, for me. If it comes to that, my name's not Smith."

"I don't care what your name is, and the sooner you get out of this the better it'll be for you."

"Don't be cross, my dear. I only want you and I to understand each other."

"I don't want any of your understandings. I don't want to have anything to say to you. My friend's just stepped out; if he comes back and finds you here he'll throw you down the stairs quicker than you came up them."

"Your friend?" An ugly look came into the young man's eyes. "So you've got a friend."

As she met his glance the girl's face hardened.

"What do you mean? You think yourself too clever. I'm not the sort you take me for. When I say my friend I mean the young man to whom I'm engaged to be married, so don't you make any error."

"On my honour, I believe that you look prettier by day than you do by night."

"Don't try any of your nonsense on with me. Are you going to get out of this?"

"You might at least thank me for the pretty present which I sent you!"

"Don't talk stuff to me about your presents, you've sent me none of them."

A look of inquiry came into the young man's face, and of annoyance.

"Hasn't Rossignol been yet? Do you mean to say you haven't had it?"

"Had what? Oh, stow this, do! Do you think I don't know what kind of chap you are? You're a barber's clerk, that's what you are. You've got a pound or two in your pocket, and you go gassing about and pretending you're a don, and talk about sending presents as if you'd got the Bank of England at your back, when, I lay odds, it breaks you to pay for your clothes. We girls come across lots of your sort, so we come to know your trade mark, don't you see."

"I do assure you that in my case you're wrong, Miss Emmett."

"Don't I tell you that my name's not Emmett? When you said last night that you'd give me five pounds for my name and address I saw that you were fool enough for anything, so I gave you the first that came, and that happened to be a friend of mine's, and I'm in her place now, waiting for her to come back with my young man, so that's how you've chanced to find me here."

Her companion eyed her as if he were endeavouring to ascertain from her countenance whether or not she was speaking the truth.

"If what you say is true, then I shouldn't be surprised if your friend has got the present I sent to you."

"Oh, has she? Then she's welcome. I daresay fifteen pence would pay for it." With an exclamation as of alarm she ran to the door. "There's my young man. If you don't go, I'll call out to him. If there's anything you want to say to me you can say it to-night at the theatre. Now, are you going?"

"Honour bright, if I come to the theatre will you let me speak to you?"

"Of course I will. Haven't I always done. Hark! there's my young man coming along the pavement, I know his step. Go, there's a good chap, you don't want to get me into trouble."

"Will you give me a kiss if I go?"

"What, here, now? What do you take me for? Do you want me to get my head knocked off my shoulders? If my young man caught me at any of those games he'd do it as soon as look at me, and yours too. We'll talk about that sort of thing to-night, at the theatre. Can't you go when I ask you?"

It appeared that he could, because he did. She shut the door behind him the instant he was through it, keeping fast hold of the handle with her hand. She listened to his descending footsteps with an expression of satisfaction not unmingled with anxiety. As they died away she sighed—a sigh of unequivocal relief.

"That was a near thing, it ought to be a lesson to me, it's given me quite a turn." In spite of its artificial bloom, her pretty, dainty face had assumed a sudden pallor, a fact of which her candid friend, the mirror, at once informed her. "I declare that I look quite white; that sort of thing's enough to make anyone look white." She repaired her loss of complexion with the aid of something which she took from her pocket. "It's a mercy Tom wasn't here, or even Lizzie. She's a queer sort, is Lizzie, and she might have wanted a lot of explanation before she could have been got to see the joke of my giving him her name and address instead of mine. Of course I only did it for a lark. If I'd thought he meant to do anything with it I wouldn't have given it him for a good many fivers, though the coin was useful." There came from between her lips a little ripple of laughter almost like the burst of music which proceeds from a song-bird's throat. "What fools fellows are! He's no toff, anyone can see it with half an eye, he's only a clerk or something got hold of 'a little bit of splosh' and trying to do the swagger. He's said his last words to me, anyhow; Saturday, the theatre'll see my back for good and all. And until then I'll take care that Tom comes and does the dutiful." She stood in an attitude of listening. "That is Lizzie. It's lucky that Mr Jack Smith was off the premises before she came."

Lizzie came boisterously in, her cheeks red with the haste she had made, her eyes glistening with excitement.

16

"Polly Steele!" she exclaimed. "You here!"

The other girl bestowed on her one mischievous glance, then returned to the mirror.

"It looks like it, doesn't it? You don't happen to have seen Tom, I suppose?"

"Tom? Tom Duffield?"

"That's the gentleman. I've got a bit of news for you, my dear. Tom and I have made it up."

"Made it up?" She looked at the speaker inquisitorially, then read her meaning. "Oh, Polly, I'm so glad!"

"I thought you would be. He doesn't seem sorry."

"When was it? Last night at the theatre I didn't seem as if I could get a word with you."

"No? I wonder how that was." Polly eyed her friend, her face alive with mischief. "It was this morning, my dear. He came round while I was at breakfast, and he went on so, and he seemed so set on it, that I couldn't find it in my heart to keep on saying no. So the banns are to be put up on Sunday, and we're to be married a month to-day."

"Oh, Polly!"

"And Saturday'll be my last appearance on any stage. Tom's going to allow me forty shillings a week until we're married; and of course I shall have my meat for nothing—he won't hear of my keeping on at the theatre. He's making money hand over fist at that shop of his; sold ten beasts last week and I don't know how many sheep. You should hear him talking! I shall be riding in my carriage before you know where you are."

Lizzie was leaning against the mantelshelf as Agnes Graham had leaned, and, as the famous actress had done, was looking down at the empty grate.

"I'm glad you're leaving the theatre. I was beginning to get worried about you."

"Worried about me! Whatever for?"

Again Miss Polly's countenance was instinct with impish roguery.

"Oh, you know very well what I mean, my lady, so no pretending. You're too pretty for the theatre, and that's the truth."

"Why, I thought a theatre was just the place where pretty girls are wanted."

"Maybe. But pretty girls don't want a theatre, leastways, not if they can help it, they don't." Lizzie spoke with sudden animation. "But talk about your news! What do you think's come my way?"

"A set of diamonds?"

There was mockery in Polly's tone, and in her eyes.

"You may laugh, but that's just what it was—leastways, a diamond necklace."

"Lizzie!"

"Yes, as fine a one as ever you saw—better than Maggie Sinclair's, and they say hers is worth a thousand."

"It wasn't meant for you."

"Wasn't it? There it was upon the parcel as plain as print, 'Miss Lizzie Emmett, 14 Hercules Buildings, Westminster,' and inside there was the fellow's card—'With Mr Jack Smith's compliments.'"

"What? Lizzie! Where is it?"

"It's where it ought to be—with her as Mr Jack Smith ought to marry."

"Whatever do you mean?"

"Why, Polly, it's like a story, just like it is in the books. Who do you think's been here this morning? In this very room?"

Polly drew back, as with a sudden accession of timidity.

"Not Jack Smith?"

"Jack Smith! I'd have Jack Smithed him if he'd shown his nose inside my place. Someone as is worth a good few Jack Smiths—Agnes Graham!"

"Agnes Graham!"

"Yes, you may stare, but it's truth, she came into this very room. And I've just come from her place. And what do you think she done as I was coming away? Kissed me—yes! straight. It seems as this here Jack Smith he's as good as promised to marry her, and she's been driving herself half silly because he's been carrying on with a girl at our show—yes! And this morning, as they was having a few words, something fell out of his pocket. She picked it up. On it was my name and my address. She asks him if that was the girl. He says it was—like his blamed impudence! So she comes round to me and asks me not to sneak away her bloke."

"Asks you?"

"Yes, queer start, ain't it? I'm the sort to sneak away anybody's bloke! I'd give a bit to know how he got hold of my name and address."

"It does seem odd!"

"Odd ain't the word for it. There's something what's a little more than odd about it, as it seems to me. And who do you think Jack Smith is?"

"Some barber's clerk or other, I suppose."

"Barber's clerk! Why, he's the Earl of Bermondsey!"

"Who? Lizzie! You don't mean that!"

"I do, it's gospel truth! His name was printed on the card; 'With Mr Jack Smith's compliments' was wrote on the back. Miss Graham told me it was him, she knew his writing directly she set eyes on it. He's been passing himself off as Jack Smith to some girl or other up at our place, and going on no end."

Miss Steele, her face turned away from Lizzie, was drumming on the table with the fingers of her left hand.

"Did you say that he was going to marry Miss Graham?"

"It seems that he as good as promised that he would, but now she's afraid that he'll take up with this other girl what he's been carrying on with."

"What makes her think so?"

"Don't I tell you that he about equal to up and told her so."

Miss Steele was silent.

"Does she think"—there was a tremulous break in her voice—"that he would marry the other girl?"

"That's what she's afraid of, though, if I was her, I'd let him. If I was Miss Graham I wouldn't marry him, not if he was a hundred times the Earl of Bermondsey. Don't you remember what we was reading about him only the other day—how he'd just come into his money, and what a lot of it there was? And houses, and parks, and forests, and I don't know what? My truth! He's only a kid, and a pretty sort of kid he seems to be; one of them fools what's worse than the clever ones, just because they're fools. I shouldn't be surprised if this girl what he's been carrying on with—I'll find out who she is before this night is gone, and if she gave him my address I'll mark her!"

"Perhaps she only did it for a joke!"

"A nice sort of joke! What do you think? I'll spoil her beauty, the nasty cat! I shouldn't be surprised, if she played her cards cleverly, but what she got him to take her to church."

"I wonder!"

"The Countess of Bermondsey! That's a mouthful, ain't it?"

"The Countess of Bermondsey!"

As Miss Polly Steele echoed her companion's words she was still standing against the table, her little slender figure drawn as upright as a dart. Her cheeks were flushed, her eyes were sparkling, her lips were parted; one could see how her bosom rose and fell as her breath came in quick, eager respirations. Something had filled her with a strange excitement which each moment was mastering her more completely.

It was Lizzie who first heard the ascending footsteps.

"Hullo!" she cried. "Here's Mr Duffield."

A sudden peculiar change had taken place in the expression on Polly's countenance; it had become hard, even angry, her gleaming teeth had closed upon her lower lip. Lizzie admitted the returning lover.

"Morning, Mr Duffield." She looked at him with what was intended to be archness. "Polly has been telling me all about it. I wish you joy."

He laughed, as though she had perpetrated a capital joke.

"Thank you, Miss Emmett. We mean to have a bit if we can get it, don't we, Polly?" He was laden with paper parcels. He advanced with them towards the little silent figure which was standing at the table, his good-humoured face one mighty smile. "I've brought the whole shop full. Here you are, old girl. You'll want a cart to carry them."

She struck out at him with her clenched hands, dashing the parcels he was holding out to her in confusion on to the floor. She was in a flame of passion.

"I don't want your rubbish! And how dare you call me old girl? Who do you think you are, and what do you think I am? Keeping me waiting here, dancing attendance on your pleasure, and then insulting me; if you ever try to speak to me again I'll slap your face."

She pushed past him towards the door.

"Polly!" cried Lizzie, staring at her in a maze of wonder.

Miss Steele shook her fist so close to Lizzie's face it grazed her skin. Rage transfigured her. Her voice was shrill with fury.

"You great, ugly, stupid idiot! You've done more harm this morning than you'll ever do good in all your life! Let me pass!"

20

At the door she turned to shake her fist at Mr Duffield.

"Don't you dare to follow me!"

She vanished, flying down the stairs three or four steps at a time, in a whirlwind of haste, leaving her lover and her friend in speechless amazement, as if the heavens had fallen.

A CHRISTMAS MIRACLE

"Bank holidays are admittedly common nuisances; they are neither Sundays nor week-days; they disorganise everything, both public and private life; and what is Christmas Day but a bank holiday, I should like to know! Here am I actually having to make my own bed and prepare my own breakfast; goodness only knows what I shall do about my lunch and dinner. And this in the twentieth century."

It was a monstrous fact. Granted that to a certain extent I had to thank my own weakness, still, Christmas Day was to blame. When, about a month before, Mr and Mrs Baines had begun to drop hints that they would like to spend Christmas Day with relatives at some out-of-the-way hole in Kent—it was three years since they had spent Christmas Day together, Mrs Baines told me with her own lips—I was gradually brought to consent. Of course I could not remain alone with Eliza—who is a remarkably pretty girl, mind you, though she is a housemaid—so I let her spend Christmas Day with her mother. They all three went off the day before—Eliza's home is in Devonshire—so that there was I left without a soul to look after me.

I allow that to some small extent the fault was mine. My bag was packed—Baines had packed it with his own hands, assisted by his wife and Eliza, and to my certain knowledge each had inserted a Christmas present, which it was intended should burst upon me with the force of a surprise. I had meant to spend Christmas with Popham. It seemed to me that since I had to spend it under somebody else's roof it might as well be under his. But on the morning of the twenty-fourth—Tuesday—I had had a letter—a most cheerful letter—in which Popham informed me that since one of his children had the measles, and another the mumps, and his wife was not well, and his own constitution was slightly unbalanced owing to a little trouble he had had with his motor—he had nearly broken his neck, from what I could gather—it had occurred to him that Christmas under his roof might not be such a festive season as he had hoped, and so he gave me warning. Obviously I did not want to force myself into a hospital, so I wired to Popham that I thought, on the whole, that I preferred my own fireside.

But I said nothing about my change of plans to Mr and Mrs Baines or Eliza, for it seemed to me that since they had made their arrangements they might as well carry them out, and I had intended to go to one of those innumerable establishments where, nowadays, homeless and friendless creatures are guaranteed—for a consideration—a "social season."

Eliza started after breakfast, Mr and Mrs Baines after lunch. I told them that I was going by the four o'clock and could get my bag taken to the cab without their assistance. When the time came I could not make up my mind to go anywhere. So I dined at the club and had a dullish evening. And on Christmas Day I had to make my own bed and light my own fire.

A really disreputable state of affairs!

I never had such a time in my life. I was bitterly cold when I first got up— it had been freezing all night—but I was hot enough long before I had a fire. The thing would not burn. There was a gas stove in the kitchen, I could manage that all right, to a certain extent—though it made an abominable smell, which I had not noticed when Mrs Baines had been on the premises— but I could not spend all Christmas Day crouching over half a dozen gas jets. Not to speak of the danger of asphyxiation, which, judging from the horrible odour, appeared to me to be a pretty real one. I wanted coal fires in my own rooms, or, at least, in one of them. But the thing would not behave in a reasonable manner. I grew hot with rage, but the grate remained as cold as charity.

I live in a flat—Badminton Mansions—endless staircases, I don't know how many floors, and not a Christian within miles. I had a dim notion, I don't know how I got it, but I had a dim notion that a person of the charwoman species ascended each morning to a flat somewhere overhead to do—I had not the faintest idea what, but the sort of things charwomen do do. Driven to the verge of desperation—consider the state I was in, no fire, no breakfast, no nothing, except that wretched gas stove, which I was convinced that I should shortly have to put out if I did not wish to be suffocated—it occurred to me, more or less vaguely, that if I could only intercept that female I might induce her, by the offer of a substantial sum, to put my establishment into something like order. So, with a view of ascertaining if she was anywhere about, I went out on to the landing to look for her.

"Now," I told myself, "I suppose I shall have to stand in this condition"—I had as nearly as possible blacked myself all over—"for a couple of hours outside my own door and then she won't come."

No sooner had I shown my unwashed face outside than I became conscious that a child—a girl—was standing at the open door of the flat on the opposite side of the landing. I was not going to retreat from a mere infant; I declined even to notice her presence, though I became instantly aware that she was taking the liveliest interest in mine. I looked up and down, saw there were no signs of any charwoman, and feeling that it would be more dignified to return anon—when that child had vanished—was about to retire within my own precincts, when—the child addressed me.

"I wish you a merry Christmas."

I was really startled. The child was a perfect stranger to me. I just glanced across at her, wishing that I was certain if what I felt upon my nose actually was soot, and replied—with sufficient frigidity,—

"Thank you. Your wish is obliging. But there is not the slightest chance of my having a merry Christmas, I give you my word of honour."

My intention was to—metaphorically—crush the child, but she was not to be crushed. I already had my back to her, when she observed,—

"I am so sorry. Are you in any trouble?"

I turned to her again.

"I don't know what you call trouble, but on a morning like this I am without a fire and it seems extremely probable that I shall have to remain without one."

"No fire!" Even from across the landing I was conscious that that child's eyes were opened wider. "Why, it's freezing. Haven't you any coals or wood?"

"Oh, yes, I've plenty of coals and wood, but what's the good of them if they won't burn?"

"Won't burn? Why ever won't they burn?"

"I don't know why they won't burn—you'd better ask 'em."

I am altogether without a clear impression of how it happened. I can only say that that child came across the landing, and, as I returned into my own quarters, she came after me—quite uninvited. We moved to the dining-room, the scene of my futile efforts. She regarded the recalcitrant grate with thoughtful gaze. It began to be borne in on me that she was rather a nice-looking child, with brown hair, and a great deal of it, and big brown eyes. Presently she said,—

"I have seen people make a fire."

Which was an absurd remark. I snubbed her.

"I don't know that there's anything remarkable in that. I also have seen people make a fire."

"One would never think it to look at that grate."

24

"What's the matter with the grate?"

"It's too full of everything. To make a fire you begin with paper."

"Haven't I begun with paper? There are at least six newspapers at the bottom of that grate; it's stuffed full of paper."

"That's just it; I believe it's stuffed too full. And I feel sure that you don't want to start with a whole forest full of wood. And it looks to me as if you had emptied a whole scuttle full of coals on the top of all the rest."

"I have."

"Then how ridiculous of you. How can you expect it to burn? I think I can show you how it ought to be."

She showed me. I ought not to have let her; I do not need to be told that, but I did. I held the scuttle while she put back into it nearly all the coal; then she removed about five-sixths of the wood and nine-tenths of the paper, and started to lay that fire all over again. And she kept talking all the time.

"Have you had your breakfast?"

"I emphatically haven't."

"I haven't had any either."

It struck me that there was a suggestiveness about her tone.

"I'm afraid I can't ask you to share mine."

"Why? Haven't you any food?"

"Oh, I daresay there's food, but—it wants cooking."

"Well, let's cook it! Oh, do let's cook it! I should so love to cook my own breakfast; I never have; it would be just like a picnic."

"I don't know that I care for picnics; I'm too old."

"I've seen people older than you are." I felt flattered; I am not so very old after all. "What have you got? Have you any eggs?"

"I shouldn't be surprised if I have some eggs."

"Then, to begin with, we'll say eggs. How shall we cook them?"

"Boil them."

"Couldn't we fry them? I'm rather fond of fried eggs."

"So far as I'm concerned I'm sure we couldn't fry them."

"I'm afraid I might make rather a mess of it. Then we'll say boiled eggs.

What else—bacon?"

"I imagine that there may be bacon."

"Then we'll say eggs and bacon; that'll be lovely. Don't you like bacon?"

"I don't object to it—occasionally—if it's properly cooked."

"How do you like it cooked?"

"I haven't a notion. I've never even seen anyone cook bacon."

"I don't think I have either. But we'll see what we can do. And cocoa?"

"No cocoa. I doubt if there's any in the place. And we won't say coffee. I don't believe there are more than half a dozen people in the world who can make good coffee. And I feel convinced that I'm not one of them."

"I don't care for coffee. We'll say tea—and toast."

"I think I could make some toast, if pressed."

"I'm glad you can do something. You see; now the fire's going to burn. Where's the pantry? Let's go and look what's in it."

The fire certainly did show signs of an intention to behave as a fire ought to. I don't know how she had done it, it seemed simple enough, but there it was. Feeling more and more conscious that my conduct was altogether improper, not to say ridiculous, I led that child from the dining-room, across the kitchen, to the receptacle where Mrs Baines keeps her store of provisions. She looked round and round and I knew she was not impressed.

"There doesn't seem to be very much to eat, does there?"

The same thing had struck me. The shelves seemed full of emptiness, and there was nothing hanging from the hooks. Still, as coming from an entire stranger, the remark was not in the best of taste.

"You see," I explained, feebly enough, "it's Christmas."

That child's eyes opened wider than ever; I was on the point of warning her that if she went on like that they would occupy the larger part of her face.

"Of course it's Christmas. Do you suppose that I don't know it's Christmas? That's just the reason why you should have more to eat than ever. Some people eat more at Christmas than they do during all the rest of the year put together."

This was such a truly astonishing statement to make that, unless I wished to enter into a preposterous argument, I had nothing to say. I also realised that it did not become me to enter at any length, to a mere child—and she an utter stranger!—into the reasons why, at Christmas, it had come to pass that my larder did not happen to be so well filled as it might have been. I merely endeavoured to pin her to the subject in hand.

"There are eggs and bacon and bread, and I believe there's tea—all the materials for the morning meal. I don't know what else you require."

"That's true—that's quite true. There are eggs in three different baskets; I expect one basket's for cooking eggs, one for breakfast eggs and one for new-laid. We'll have new-laid. How many shall we have? Could you eat two?"

"I have been known to eat two; especially when, on occasions like the present, breakfast has been about two hours late."

"Then we'll have two each. Then there's the bacon; fortunately it's already cut into rashers, but—how shall we cook it? I know!" She clapped her hands. "I'll fetch Marjorie!"

"Marjorie!" As she uttered the name I was conscious of a curious fluttering sensation, which was undoubtedly the result of the irregular proceedings. I had known a person of that name myself once, but it was absurd to suppose that the fluttering had anything to do with that. "Who's Marjorie?"

"Marjorie's my sister, of course." I did not see any of course about it, but I had too much self-respect to say so. "She's ever so fond of cooking; she's a splendid cook. I'll go and get her to cook that bacon."

Before I could stop her she was off; the child moved like lightning. What I ought to have done would have been to slam my front door and refuse to open it again. Who was Marjorie? Extraordinary how at the mere mental repetition of the name that fluttering returned. Her sister? She might be a young woman of two or three-and-twenty. I could not allow strange persons of that description to cook my bacon, with me in my dressing-gown and soot upon my nose.

I am practically persuaded that I was nearly on the point of closing the front door, with a view—so to speak—of not opening it again during the whole of the day, when that child returned, with another child a little taller than herself. This child had black hair, dark blue eyes, and was as self-possessed a young person as I ever yet encountered; grave as a judge—graver! She looked me straight in the face, with her head inclined just a little forward.

"I beg your pardon. It seems curious that I should call on you without even knowing your name, but my sister Kathleen told me that you were in rather a trouble about your breakfast, so I thought I would come and see if I could help you."

"That's—that's very good of you. Will—will you both of you breakfast with me?"

I wasn't one quarter so self-possessed as she was; indeed, I was all of a quiver.

"Kathleen tells me that she has already consented to do so, and I should be very pleased to join her. Now, Kathleen, where is that bacon you spoke about?"

They went into the pantry and took matters into their own hands as if the place belonged to them and as if they had been cooking my breakfasts for years. I positively felt in the way, and hinted as much—with an inclination to stammer.

"Perhaps—perhaps you'll be able to do without my assistance."

The young woman was quite clear upon that subject, and did not hesitate to say so.

"Thank you; I would much rather be without your assistance. I don't care to have men meddle in domestic matters."

She spoke as if she had been fifty instead of perhaps twelve. I wondered if she had her sentiments from her mother; I could have sworn she had them from someone.

"Then in that case I might—I might have a wash and—and put myself into another coat."

She looked me up and down with something in her air which was not suggestive of approval.

"I'm sure you might. You don't look at all tidy; not in the least like Christmas Day. Only please be ready in five minutes."

28

I was, so was the bacon; everything was ready in that five minutes. I do not know how they did it, those two children, but they did. There was the table laid, places for three, and we three sat down to an excellent meal. Marjorie served the bacon. I have tasted a good deal worse, mind you, and the plates were hot! Kathleen poured out the tea, and I ate and drank and looked on, and wondered how it all had happened. Presently Marjorie asked a question.

"Have you had any Christmas presents yet?"

"No, I can't say that I have, not just yet, but—my goodness!" An idea occurred to me. "A most extraordinary thing; do you know, I was positively forgetting to give you two people your Christmas presents."

Both looked at me, their faces notes of exclamation. Marjorie spoke.

"You can't really have presents for us—not really. I daresay half an hour ago you didn't know we were in the world."

"Can't I? Such an observation simply shows the limitations of your knowledge."

I rose from the table; I left the room. When I returned I had a parcel in either arm.

"Now if those two parcels don't contain the very Christmas presents you want, then all I can say is, I have misjudged your wants entirely and beg to apologise."

You should have seen their countenances! their looks of wonder when inside each parcel was discovered a doll, the very finest and largest article of the kind that could be procured, although I say it. Of course they had been meant for Popham's girls, but more dolls could be bought for them and sent on afterwards. In the meantime those two young women were in a state of almost dangerous agitation.

"Why," cried Marjorie, "mine has black hair and blue eyes!"

"And mine has brown hair and brown eyes!"

"You dear!"

They said this both together. Then they precipitated themselves at me, and they kissed me—absolute strangers! Then the dolls had breakfast with us. Each sat on a chair beside its proprietor, and I, as it were, sat in the centre of the four. I have seldom assisted at a livelier meal. We laughed and we talked, and we ate and we drank, and we fed the dolls—those dolls had both a large and an indigestible repast. I felt convinced they would suffer for it afterwards. And in the midst of it all I heard a strange voice; at least it was strange to me.

"I beg ten thousand pardons, but I couldn't think what had become of those children—I thought I heard their voices. What are they doing here?"

I looked up and there, standing in the open doorway, was a lady; a young lady, a charming, and, indeed, a pretty young lady. Those two young women flung themselves at her as they had flung themselves at me; only, if anything, more so.

"Mamma! mamma! just look at our dolls! Aren't they beautiful? And when you lay them down they shut their eyes and say good-night."

The lady was their mamma; exactly the right sort of mamma for them to have. I explained, and she explained, and it was all explained. By a most amazing coincidence she was in almost the same plight as I was. She was a Mrs Heathcote; had recently come with her two girls from India; had taken the flat opposite mine in the expectation of her husband joining her by Christmas Day, instead of which his ship had been delayed in the Suez Canal, or somewhere, somehow, and he could not possibly reach her for at any rate a day or two. And on the previous day, Christmas Eve, her cook had behaved in the most abominable manner, and had had to be sent packing, and her sympathetic friend, the housemaid, had gone with her, so that on Christmas Day Mrs Heathcote was positively left without a soul to do a thing for her; precisely my condition. She had gone out to see if temporary help could be procured, and during her absence those two daughters of hers had slipped across to me. She had found no help, so that she had to deal with precisely the same problem which confronted me. She had breakfast with us—and the dolls!—Marjorie explaining that it was she who had cooked the bacon, and in an amazingly short space of time we were all of us on terms of the most delightful sociability.

I insisted that they must all go out with me to lunch at a restaurant. It might not seem to promise much entertainment to have to go for a meal to a place of the kind on Christmas Day, but the girls were delighted. It is my experience that most children like feeding in public, I don't know why, and when pressed their mother was willing, so I was charmed.

"Now," I observed, "that it is settled we are to go somewhere, the question is—where?"

"May I choose?" asked Mrs Heathcote.

"My dear madam, if you only would, you would confer on me a really great favour. On the subject of the choice of a restaurant I consider a lady's opinion to be of the very first importance."

That was not, perhaps, the whole truth, but on such matters, at such moments, one need not be a stickler. She smiled—she had an uncommonly pleasant smile; it reminded me of someone, somewhere, though I could not think who. She rested her elbows on the table, placing her hands palm to palm.

"Then I say Ordino's."

When she said that I had a shock. I stared.

"Excuse me—what—what did you say?"

She smiled again.

"I suppose you'll think I'm silly, and I daresay you've never heard of the place, and I myself don't know where it is, and anyhow it mayn't be at all nice—mind I'm not giving it any sort of character. But if the place is still in existence, since it is Christmas Day and we are to lunch at a restaurant, if the choice is left to me, I say again—Ordino's."

"May I ask if you've any special reason for—for choosing this particular place?"

There was an interval of silence before she answered. Although I had purposely turned my back to her I had a sort of feeling that there was an odd look upon her face.

"Yes, I have a special reason, in a sort of a way. When we've lunched perhaps I'll tell it you. If the lunch has been a very bad one then you'll say—quite rightly—that you'll never again rely upon a woman's reason where a restaurant's concerned."

It was—I had to hark back into my forgotten mental lumber to think how many years it was since I had entered Ordino's door. I had told myself that I would never enter it again. And yet here was this stranger suddenly proposing that I should visit it once more, on Christmas Day of all days in the year. Why, the last time I fed there—the very last time—it was a Christmas Day.

I should write myself down a fool were I to attempt to describe the feelings with which I set about that Christmas morning's entertainment. We lunched at Ordino's. It was within half a mile of where I lived, and yet I had never seen or passed it since. The street in which it was had been to me as if it were shut at both ends. If a cabman had wanted to take me down that way I had stopped him, even though it meant another sixpence.

It had scarcely changed, either within or without. As the four of us trooped inside—six with the dolls, for the dolls went out to lunch with us—I had an eerie sort of sensation that it was only yesterday that I was there. The same window with the muslin curtain drawn across; the same small room with the

31

eight or ten marble tables; the same high desk, and if it was not the same woman who was seated at it then she was a very decent imitation.

"What a queer little place it seems."

Mrs Heathcote said this as we stood looking about for a table.

"Yes, it does seem queer."

It did—for a reason I was not disposed to explain. I chose the same table—that is, the table next to the desk in which the woman sat. As might have been expected, we had the place to ourselves, and the whole services of the one waiter. I fancy that the establishment provided us with a tolerable meal; the cooking always had been decent at Ordino's. Judging from the way in which the others despatched the fare which was set before us, the tradition still survived. So far as I was personally concerned I was scarcely qualified to criticise. Each mouthful "gave me furiously to think;" I thought between the mouthfuls; never before had I had a meal so full of thinking. My guests were merry enough; those two young women were laughing all the time.

At last we came to the dessert. "Madam," I began, "have you been badly treated or well?"

"Excellently treated, thank you. I think it has all been capital, only I'm afraid you haven't had your proper share."

"Oh, yes, I have had my proper portion and to spare. Is it allowable to ask you to gratify my curiosity by telling me for what special reason you chose Ordino's?"

She toyed with a pear which she was peeling.

"You will laugh at me."

"There will be no malice in my laughter if I do."

"Then the story is not mine."

"Whose then?"

"It's about my sister—Marjorie."

I gripped the edge of the table, but she did not notice, she was peeling her pear. Her daughters were occupied with their dolls. They were teaching them the only proper way in which to consume a banana. Judging from his contortions the one waiter seemed to find the proceedings as good as a play.

"You have a sister whose name is Marjorie?"

"Oh, yes, she is all the relations I have."

"Marjorie what?"

"Marjorie Fleming." Then I knew that a miracle had happened. "My eldest girl is named after her." I might have guessed it; I believe I did. "She's the dearest creature in the world, but she hasn't had the very best of times."

I said nothing, having nothing to say. I waited for her to go on, which presently she did do, dreamily, as she peeled her pear.

"Do you know that it was in this place—I suppose in this very room— perhaps at this very table, that her life was spoilt one Christmas Day."

"How—how spoilt?"

It seemed as if my tongue had shrivelled in my mouth.

"What is it that spoils a woman's life?"

"How should I know?"

"I thought that everyone knew what spoils a woman's life—even you cynical bachelors." Cynical bachelors! I was beginning to shiver as if each word she uttered was a piece of ice slipped down my back. "Different people write it different ways, but it's all summed up in the same word in the end—a lover."

"I thought that it was a lover who is supposed to make a woman's life the perfect thing it ought to be."

"He either makes or mars it. In my sister's case he—marred it."

"A woman's life is not so easily spoilt."

"Hers was. All in a moment. It was years and years ago, but it's with her still—that moment. I know, I know! Poor Marjorie! The whole of her life worth living is in the land of ghosts."

My heart stopped beating. The sap in my veins was dried. It seemed as if the world was slipping from me. All Marjorie's life worth living was in the land of ghosts? Why, then, we were in the land of ghosts together!

"She told me the story once, and only once, but I've never forgotten it— never; a woman never does forget that kind of story, and I'm sure Marjorie never will. I know it's just as present to her now as if it had only happened yesterday. Dear Marjorie! You don't know what a dear sister my sister is. Although, in those days, she was only a young girl, she lived alone in London. Our father and mother died when we were children. She was full of dreams of becoming a great artist; they are gone now, with the other dreams. She had a lover, who was jealous of her artist friends. They had lovers' tiffs. They used often to come to this place. They came here together one

Christmas Day, of all days in the year. And it is because of what happened on that Christmas Day that Ordino's Restaurant has been to me a sort of legend, a shrine which had to be visited when occasion offered. They quarrelled. Marjorie told me that she never could remember just how the quarrel began, and I believe her. Quarrels, especially between a man and a woman, spring out of nothing often and often. They grew furiously hot. Suddenly, in his heat, he said something which no man ever ought to say to any woman, above all to the woman whom he loves. Marjorie stood up. She laid on the table the locket he had just given her—a Christmas gift—with, in it, his portrait and hers. And she said, 'I return you your locket. Presently, when I get home, I will return all that you have given me. I never wish to see you, or to hear from you, again.' And she went towards the entrance, he doing nothing to stop her. As she opened the door she saw him stand up and give the locket, her locket, to the woman who sat at the desk, as that woman is sitting now, and he said, in tones which he evidently intended that she should hear, 'Madam, permit me to beg your acceptance of this locket. Since it is associated with someone whom I wish I had never met, you will do me a great favour by relieving me of its custody.' Marjorie waited to hear no more. She went out, alone, into the street, that Christmas Day, and she has never seen him since or heard if he is alive or dead."

I was speechless. I could only sit and stare at the ghosts who stared at me.

All at once "the woman who sat at the desk," as Mrs Heathcote had put it, came down from her place and stood beside us.

"Madam," she exclaimed, in what struck me, even then, as tones of singular agitation, "it is a miracle, a true miracle. You must forgive me, I could not help but listen; my parents have told me the story many and many a time. It all happened as you have said. It was to my mother the locket was given. She wished very much not to take it, but the young gentleman, he was very excited, and at last, to avoid a scene, my father said to her, 'At least in your keeping it will be safe; worse might befall it than to be left in your hands. These foolish young people will make it up again. Presently they will return; you will be able to give back the locket to its proper owner.' But they did not return, neither the one nor the other, never, not once! At last my mother died; the locket came to me. She wished that when I was in the desk I should always carry it as she had done, for she believed that, at last, there would arrive a day when one or the other would return and the locket would be restored. Madam, here is the locket. I entreat you to permit me to beg you to return it to your sister, to whom it properly belongs."

The speaker held out something which I vaguely recognised as the locket of that eventful Christmas Day, which I had purchased with such loving thought and tender carefulness, and of which I had rid myself in such a storm of rage. Mrs Heathcote stared alternately at it and at the woman who for so long had held it, as a sacred charge, in such safe keeping, as if its sudden appearance had robbed her of her power of speech. I was conscious that someone had come into the place. Instantly those two young persons—who were still instructing their dolls in the proper manner of eating a banana—tore off towards the door, crying, at the top of their voices,—

"Father! father! Oh, mother, here's father!"

And all at once Mrs Heathcote went pushing past me, then I knew that she was in the arms of a man with a beard—I believe she was crying!—and exclaiming,—

"Robert, have you dropped from the skies?"

"No," he responded, reasonably enough, "I've merely dropped in from the overland route. I made up my mind I'd get at you somehow by Christmas Day, and I have. But before I was allowed to go to you, where I supposed you to be, I was made to come here. For some mysterious reason of her own that sister of yours, before she went anywhere else, insisted on visiting Ordino's Restaurant; for an explanation, if you want one, I can only refer you to Marjorie."

Marjorie! Behind him was a woman whose face, whose form, whose everything I knew. It seemed that "the woman who sat at the desk" recognised her also. She held out the locket.

"Madam, allow me to have the happiness to return to you your locket. That it is yours I am sure because of your portrait which is in it. You have scarcely altered at all since the day it was taken."

I snatched it from her.

"Give it to me!" I stormed. "Since, through all these years, it has been held in such safe keeping, Marjorie, won't you take your locket back again?"

She had never moved her eyes from off my face, just as I had kept mine on hers. She moved a little forward. And—then I had her in my arms and her cheek was next to mine, and the locket was in her hand, and—we both of us were crying—I admit it.... Oh, yes, it was a miracle of grace and healing, since by the grace of God the open wound was healed. For us—for Marjorie and me—the life worth living is no longer in the land of ghosts. We are living it now, together; dear wife! together.

And it is universally admitted that we are the best customers Ordino's Restaurant has. Those two young persons have been there again and again since then, with their dolls, whom they are still instructing in the proper manner of eating a banana. I should be afraid to estimate how many bananas they have themselves consumed in the process of instruction. And to think that that Christmas miracle all came about because that child intruded herself into my apartments—actually!—with a view of showing me how to make a fire!

In itself, was that not a miracle too?

OUR MUSICAL COMEDY

"I forbid you to do it!"

Of course when George said that, with such an air, and in such a tone, I should have been perfectly justified in making an end of everything. The idea of his actually ordering me, when we had been engaged scarcely any time at all, was really too much. But I remembered what was due to myself and—I think!—behaved beautifully. I was merely crushing.

"You will remember, if you please, that, at present, I am not your wife. And may I ask if you propose to speak to me like that when I am?"

"I trust that whenever I see you contemplating a false step I shall always use my influence to endeavour to persuade you not to take it."

"Persuasion is one thing—ordering is quite another."

It all began with the private theatricals in aid of the parochial charities. Almost for the first time since I had been in the place people seemed to have found out my existence. It was the rector's son—Frank Spencer—who was the actual discoverer. I really believe it was that fact which George did not like. Mr Spencer came and said that they were going to have theatricals and would I take part in them? I told him that I had never acted in my life. He declared that they could not do without me. I explained that I did not see how that could be, since I had not had the least experience, and, indeed, doubted if I should not make a complete spectacle of myself and spoil everything. He replied that it was ridiculous to talk like that—which I thought was rather rude of him, since he was sure that I should make a first-rate actress—though I could not even guess what made him sure; and everybody was certain that the whole thing would be an utter failure without me—then look how the parochial charities would suffer! I confess that I did not understand why everybody should take that view; though, on the other hand, I did not want the charities to languish on my account, and—well, I may as well own it—I rather liked the idea. I thought it was not half a bad one. Because I never had acted was no reason why I never should; at any rate, it occurred to me that it would be capital fun to try.

So when I informed Mr Spencer that I would consider the matter, I fancy that I rather conveyed the impression that my consideration might have a favourable issue.

Then the trouble began. George objected. When I wrote and told him that I was thinking of taking part in an amateur dramatic performance in aid of some most deserving charities, which were much in need of help, he sent me back a letter which rather surprised me. In the course of it he observed that there was a great deal too much of that sort of thing about—if that were so then certainly hitherto none of it had come my way; that not seldom amateur theatricals were but a cloak for something about which the less said the better —what he meant I had not the least idea; that they were generally exhibitions of incompetent vanity—which was not exactly a pleasant remark to make; that he could not understand how any sane person could wish to be connected with proceedings which, as a rule, were merely the outcome of a desire for vulgar notoriety. He concluded by remarking that while he had not the slightest desire to bias my judgment, of which, as I was aware, he had the highest opinion, at the same time he hoped that I would consider very carefully what he had said before arriving at a final decision.

Two days afterwards I met Mr Spencer, and he overpersuaded me. It is not to be denied that he had a most persuasive manner, and was, decidedly, not bad-looking; though, of course, that had nothing to do with it. It was the moving fashion in which he depicted the lamentable condition of the Coal Club, and the Clothing Club, and the Soup Kitchen, and that kind of thing, which induced me to promise to do all that I could for the Good Cause.

Still, when later Mr Spencer informed me that it was suggested that *A Pair of Knickerbockers* should be one of the pieces, and I had read it, and understood that it was proposed I should play Mrs Melrose to his Mr Melrose, I admit that I was taken aback. It was at this point that George came on the scene. When he heard, there was quite a storm.

"Do you actually propose to appear upon the public stage attired in a pair of knickerbockers?"

"Do you call the Assembly Room at the 'Lion' the public stage?" I asked.

"I do, since anyone will be admitted who chooses to pay at the door."

"I'm sure there's nothing wrong in the piece or the rector wouldn't allow it to be played."

"The rector! You're not engaged to the rector, you're engaged to me, and I forbid you to do it."

It was then I made that crushing retort about not being his wife yet. Still, at the bottom of my heart I felt that there was reason in what he said. I doubt if any girl ever has looked well—really well!—in knickerbockers, and I was sure that they would not suit me. I had not the faintest intention of appearing either in public or private in any garment of any kind whatever which I knew would make me look a fright. So I made a great show of my willingness to meet George's wishes on every possible occasion, and promised that I would not act in *A Pair of Knickerbockers*. He was delighted, and—well, we had rather a nice time.

When I told Mr Spencer of my decision I quite expected that he would not like it. On the contrary, he did not seem to mind in the least; indeed, he seemed to be almost relieved.

"That decides it!" he exclaimed. "Your refusal is the last straw; it brings me to the sticking point; now I have made up my mind."

Then he made of me a confidant.

It appeared that he was a dramatist; he had written a play. It was most interesting. He had sent it to the manager of every theatre in London, and to a good many out of London too, and not one of them would bring it out. Which showed that there was something in it.

"Because," as he explained, "it's notorious that a man who's an outsider, and by that I mean one who wasn't born on the stage, or doesn't own a newspaper, or fifty thousand a year, or a handle to his name, has no more chance of getting a decent play accepted than he has of flying to the moon. If this play of mine was piffle, or the usual kind of stodge, then it might have a chance of being produced. The mere fact that it has not been produced, and probably never will be, proves that it is out of the common ruck."

He looked so handsome as he said this, and so full of scorn for the people who were incapable of seeing merit when it stared them in the face, that I felt a wave of sympathy sweep over me.

"Not that it matters," he continued. "In this world nothing matters."

It seemed rather a sweeping assertion. But I understood the bitterness which called it forth. So, with one fleeting glance out of the corner of my eye to let him know that there was one who comprehended, I suffered him to go on. And he went on.

"However, where there's a will there's a way, and when a man's set on gaining his end it's hard to stop him—if he is a man! There's more roads lead to Rome than one. My play shall see the light in the same fashion that many a work of genius has done before. Who knows how and where Shakespeare's first play was produced? We'll act it at the 'Lion.'"

"How splendid!" I exclaimed.

"Mind you," he added with a modesty which did him credit, "I don't say that my play's a work of genius."

"But I'm sure it is."

He shook his head.

"Frankly, it's not. In fact, it's a musical comedy in one act."

"But a musical comedy may be a work of genius."

He regarded me with what I felt almost amounted to an air of mystery.

"Did you ever know a musical comedy that was?"

"Yours may be an exception to the rule."

He suddenly seemed to make up his mind to adopt an air of perfect frankness.

"I know whereabouts my piece is as well as anyone living, and I give you my word it's not a work of genius. It's a kind of a go-as-you-please sort of thing; you'll see what I mean when you've read it."

I did see; or, rather, it would be more correct to say that I did not see. I told him so when we met again.

"I found it so difficult to make out what it's all about; it seems so vague. Nothing that anybody does seems to have any connection with anything that anybody else does."

The way in which he received my criticism was charming; he did not show the slightest sign of being hurt.

"You think that's a fault?" he said.

"It does appear to be rather a disadvantage. You know when people go to the theatre they like to have some idea of what they're looking at."

"I suppose they do. The fact is, that that's where the trouble was—I got stuck. When anyone had been doing anything I couldn't think what they ought to do next, so I started someone else doing something else instead. That's why I said it was a kind of a go-as-you-please. You observe I call it *A Lover's Quarrel*. Don't you think it's rather a good title?"

"It's not a bad title. But I don't understand which the lovers are supposed to be, or where the quarrel comes in."

"Perhaps not. You see the title was used in a sort of general sense." A bright idea seemed all at once to strike him. I was beginning to suspect that that was a kind of thing which did not strike him very often. "I tell you what —you've got the dramatic instinct—couldn't you give me a hint or two? What I want is a collaborator."

I felt convinced that he wanted something.

"Of course, I'm quite without experience. I think you're rash in crediting me with a dramatic instinct. I'm not sure that I even know what you mean. But I'll look through it again and see if I can be of any use."

"Do! and, mind you, do with it as you like; turn it inside out; cut it to pieces; anything! I know you'll make a first-rate thing of it. And I tell you what, we'll announce ourselves as joint authors."

In a weak moment—he certainly had very seductive eyes!—I yielded what amounted to a tacit consent. I read his play again, and came to the conclusion that while, as it stood, it was absolute rubbish, it yet contained that of which something might be made. I re-wrote the thing from beginning to end. What a time I had while I was in the throes of composition! and what a time everyone else had who came within a mile of me! I was scarcely on speaking terms with a single creature, and when anyone tried to speak to me I felt like biting them.

When it was finished Mr Spencer was in ecstasies.

"It's splendid! magnificent! there's nothing like it on the London stage!" I admit that I thought that that was possible. "There's no mistake about it, not the slightest shred of a scintilla of doubt, we've written a masterpiece!"

The "we" was good, and as for the "masterpiece," it was becoming plainer and plainer that Mr Frank Spencer was one of those persons who are easily pleased; which, as that sort is exceedingly rare, was, after all, a fault on the right side.

"Everybody," he went on, "will be enraptured with it; they won't be able to help it; they're absolutely bound to be."

I wished I felt as certain of that as he did. Indeed I doubted so much if rapture would represent the state of mind of a certain gentleman that, in the daily letter which I always wrote to him, I never even hinted that I was engaged on a work of collaboration; though, for a time, that work filled my mind to the extinction of everything else.

"Now," continued my co-author, "the thing is to cast it, and, mind you, this will want casting, this will; no round pegs in square holes. We don't want to have a fine play spoilt by anyone incapable; everyone will have to be as good as we can get."

Although he spoke as if it would be a task of the most delicate kind—and, for my part, I did not see how, in the neighbourhood of West Marden, we were going to cast it at all; yet, in actual practice he seemed to me to make nothing of the matter. When he came with what he called the "proposed cast" I was really amazed.

"Do you seriously mean, Mr Spencer, that these are the people whom you suggest should act in our play?"

"Certainly. I've thought this thing out right to the bed-rock, and I assure you that we couldn't do better. Of course, you must remember that I shall do a good bit myself. I fancy you'll be surprised when you see me act. I haven't much voice, but it isn't voice, you know, that's wanted in this sort of thing; and though I can't say that I'm a regular dancer I can throw my feet about in a way that'll tickle 'em. And then there's you—you'll be our winning card; the star of the evening. You'll carry off the thing on your own shoulders, with me to help you. The others, they'll just fill in the picture, as it were."

"I do hope, Mr Spencer, that you won't rely on me too much. I've told you, again and again, that I've never acted in my life, and have not the faintest notion if I can or can't."

Putting his hands into his trouser pockets he tried to patronise me as if he were a wiseacre of two hundred instead of a mere child of twenty.

"My dear Miss Wilson, I know an actress when I see one."

"You have an odd way of expressing yourself. I hope that you don't mean that when you see me you see an actress; because I assure you that I trust that you do nothing of the kind."

I wondered what George would think and say if he heard that hare-brained young simpleton accusing me of looking like an actress.

"You give my words a wrong construction. I only meant to express my profound conviction that in your hands everything will be perfectly safe."

"I can only say, Mr Spencer, that I hope you're right, because when I think of some of the people whose names you have put upon this piece of paper I have my doubts. I see you have Mrs Lascelles to act Dora Egerton, who is supposed to be a young girl, and who has to both sing and dance. I should imagine that Mrs Lascelles never sang a note; her speaking voice is as hoarse as a crow's. And as for dancing, why, she must weigh I don't know what, and is well past forty."

"There's nothing else Mrs Lascelles could act."

"Nothing else she could act! Act! I'm perfectly convinced that she can't act anything."

Mr Spencer winked, which was a reprehensible habit—one of several which I was meaning to tell him I objected to.

"She'll take two rows of reserved seats."

"Indeed, is that her qualification? Then am I to take it that the qualifications of all the rest of the people whom you have down on your piece of paper are of a similar kind?"

His manner immediately became confidential; he was very fond of becoming confidential. It was a fondness which I was commencing to perceive that it might become advisable to check before it went too far. There were moments when I never knew what he was going to say. I felt that he might say anything.

"You see, between ourselves, on the strict QT, it's like this; if we want to make the show the howling success it ought to be, what we've got to do is to see that everyone in the cast represents money."

"I don't understand."

I did not.

"Oh, yes, you do; only—I know!" He winked again; there was positively an impertinent twinkle in his eye. "You can see as far through a brick wall as anybody, when you like, only sometimes you don't like. What we've got to do is to fill the Assembly Rooms with money, and with more money, mind you, than the room holds. And the way to do that is to get the people to act whose names I have got down on that piece of paper."

"I still don't follow you. However, since you are managing the affair I suppose it's no business of mine. You are responsible for its success, not I."

"Exactly; you've hit it! I am responsible, and you may take it from me that in a little matter of this sort I know my way about. It's going to be a success— a bumper."

In spite of his confidence, when we came to actual business, things did not begin auspiciously.

By way of a commencement, he read the piece to the people who were going to act it. He said that dramatists always did do so, and that it was necessary to do everything in regular order. The reading took place at Mrs Lascelles's house, The Grange. I had not been in the house before, and from the manner in which she received me I inclined to the opinion that she would just as soon I had not come into it then. As I looked round the room I could not but feel that, for the performance of a musical comedy, Mr Spencer had gathered together a truly curious company. I began to wish that I had had no hand in the collaboration. Before he had finished the reading that wish took a very much more definite form.

He was not a good reader; that fact forced itself upon one's attention before he had got through three lines. But had he been the finest reader in the world it would not have made a great deal of difference. A more dreadful set of people to read a musical comedy to one could not by any possibility imagine. The jokes—especially as he read them!—did not strike even me as being very good ones, and sometimes they were a little frivolous. What does one expect in a musical comedy? Had they been the finest jokes conceivable it would not have mattered. I do not believe there was a person present who could have seen a joke at all, even with the aid of a surgical operation. Each time there was a touch of frivolity the faces of the audience grew graver. And as for the songs! Everybody knows the kind of songs one does hear in musical comedies. The words are not suggestive of either Shakespeare or the musical glasses. I had planned mine on the same lines. There was one chorus which struck me as rather catchy.

> "It tickled me so I had to smile;
> I told the girl she was full of guile.
> She said, 'What ho!'
> I replied, 'Oh, no!
> To put salt on my tail you must walk a mile!'"

I do not pretend that that's poetry, or anything but nonsense. You expect nonsense in a musical comedy. But when Mr Spencer had read two verses, Mrs Parker, who is the wife of the chairman of our local bench, rose from her chair with an expression of countenance calculated to sour all the milk for miles around, and observed—in such a tone of voice!—

"Excuse me, Mr Spencer. I must go. When I received your invitation I did not expect this kind of thing."

"What kind of thing?"

Mr Spencer looked up with a start. It was rapidly becoming more and more obvious to me that he was one of those young men who are incapable of seeing even as far as the tips of their own noses. He had been stammering and stumbling on in apparently sublime unconsciousness of the sort of reception which our masterpiece was receiving. The singularity of Mrs Parker's bearing seemed to take him entirely by surprise.

"May I ask, Mr Spencer, what you call the—stuff you have been reading?"

"Stuff? You mean the piece? It's a musical comedy."

"Indeed. I haven't noticed any music yet, and as for comedy—there is none. It appears to me to be a mere tissue of meaningless vulgarity. Where did you get it from?"

"Miss Wilson and I wrote it together—that is, she did the greater part of it.

In fact, Miss Wilson practically wrote it all."

Which was true enough, but he need not have put it quite so emphatically just at that moment.

"Miss Wilson?" Mrs Parker put up her glasses and she looked at me. How she looked! "I have not the pleasure of Miss Wilson's acquaintance, but I cannot help thinking that she might have been better employed."

Then she went. Fancy my sensations!

Mr Spencer must have been pachydermatous. He seemed unable to feel either on his own account or on mine. Candid criticism of that ultra-candid sort was to him like water on a duck's back. Directly Mrs Parker was out of the room he turned to Mrs Lascelles.

"I don't think it's so bad, do you?—considering!"

"Considering." She said this with an accent for which I could have thrown something at her. That wretched boy only smiled. It seemed to be his *role* in life—to smile. Mrs Lascelles was good enough to add a sort of saving clause. "I daresay it will be better on the stage than it is off."

Mr Spencer jumped at the opening.

"Of course! On the stage it will be simply ripping! It's meant to be acted, not read; no good play ever reads well. The better it is the worse it reads."

"This one doesn't read well, does it? In any case I think you made a mistake in asking Mrs Parker to take part in a piece of the kind."

"It was a mistake, wasn't it?"

That young man beamed as if he were congratulating himself on having done something exceedingly clever. In return, Mrs Lascelles observed him with an air which was not exactly beaming.

"Frankly, Mr Spencer, I don't see much of a part in the piece for me."

As a matter of fact there was no part; there was just a song and a dance and nothing else. But I, personally, was convinced that that was too much. That extraordinary young man, however, put the matter in a way which staggered me.

"You see, Mrs Lascelles, it's like this: your part at present is simply outlined—the outline has to be filled in. That's the advantage of a piece like this, you can do that so easily. What I want is your idea of what you'd like the part to be, and then I'll write it up. See what I mean?"

I did not see what he meant. Under the circumstances I think I was to be congratulated on having been able to hold my peace—till later.

The reading limped to a finish. Then came the chorus. So far as I was able to gather, not a creature thought anything of the play, and they thought still less of the parts which had been allotted them. Mr Spencer scattered promises like leaves in autumn. It made my ears burn to listen to him. I was not so pliable. For instance, Major Hardy came up to me to make some truly sensible remarks.

"Candidly, Miss Wilson"—everybody was candid, it was in the air—"my idea was that we should represent *Hamlet*. I don't know if you are aware that I am by way of being a Shakespearian scholar. I have formed my own notion of the Prince of Denmark. I fancy that I might give shape and substance to that notion if I were allowed to read the part. I should have to read it. Between ourselves, my memory is so imperfect that I could never hope to get anything off by heart. You will therefore see that it is something of a jump to the—eh —kind of thing we have just been listening to. So far as I understand it is proposed that I should play a negro minstrel. Now Mrs Hardy would never permit me to black my face—never! She'd be afraid that it wouldn't come off again. On some points she is extremely nervous. Could the part not be transformed into that of a Highland piper? I have the kilts, and I have the pipes, and I can do some remarkable things with the bagpipes when I am once fairly started. Sometimes it takes me a little time to get into my stride, apt to make two or three false starts, don't you know; wind goes wrong or something, but really, people seem to find that the most amusing part of it."

I informed him that the character could not be "transformed" into a Highland piper; that as for bagpipes, they were out of the question. I had heard of his "pipes." He was fond of playing on them in remote portions of his grounds; people had mistaken them for foghorns. In fact, I tried to convey the impression that I was not to be trifled with. From the look which came on his face I fancy that, to a great extent, I succeeded.

What does anyone suppose was the first remark which Mr Spencer addressed to me when at last we were alone together?—with all the assurance in the world!

"Went off magnificently, didn't it? I told you it would; with a regular bang!"

My attitude, when confronted by this amazing observation, was one of polar frigidity.

"I noticed the bang; it was one of those bangs which accompany a final explosion. Of course, I need scarcely observe that, so far as I am concerned, the whole affair is at an end."

46

"Miss Wilson! you're joking! You're not going to let them see that you're afraid of them?"

"Afraid! Mr Spencer, you use the most extraordinary language. Why should I be afraid? I beg to inform you that I am afraid of nothing, and of no one."

"I'm sure of it! All you have to do is to show a bold front and you'll do as you like with the lot of them."

"So far I've not observed much of the bold front about you. You kowtow to everyone as if you liked nothing so much as being trampled on."

"That's diplomacy; bound to be diplomatic. This sort of thing always begins like this."

"Does it? Then I wish you'd told me so at the beginning. I hate diplomacy."

"Miss Wilson, you have the dramatic instinct—"

"Mr Spencer, I wish you wouldn't talk nonsense. I believe you say that to everyone. I heard you tell Mrs Lascelles that when she appears on the stage she'll hold the audience in the hollow of her hand."

"So she will. She's going to appear in short skirts. When they catch sight of her they'll kill themselves with laughing."

When he said that a dreadful suspicion flashed across my mind that he was making fun of us all, including me; having a joke at our expense. I had little doubt, after what I had seen and heard that afternoon, that he was perfectly capable of such disgraceful conduct. I did not hesitate to let him know at once what I suspected.

"Mr Spencer, is it your intention that we shall all of us make laughing-stocks of ourselves for your amusement? Because, if so, I beg to state that I, for one, decline. I heard what you said to Mrs Lascelles; I heard you tell her that she would make the hit of the piece."

"So she will; a hit's made in all kinds of ways."

"Do you dare to tell me that all the while you were intentionally leading her on to making a complete idiot of herself?"

No eel that ever lived could compare with that young man for slipperiness. He always had an explanation handy—the more impossible the position the readier the explanation was.

"It's like this. If people are bent on making fools of themselves, and will only bite your nose off if you try to stop them, what are you to do? I tell you that the burden of the piece will be on your shoulders and mine before the night comes round, and we'll carry it off. But it's no good telling people that now, it has to be managed. Let's wait till they've got themselves into a fine old hole, and all the tickets are sold. All the country-side will crowd to see them make fools of themselves. Then, when they've muddled themselves into a state of semi-idiocy, they'll come and beg us—as a favour—to do what they wouldn't let us do at any price if we were to propose it now. You leave it to me. I've perhaps got a funny way of my own of doing things, but I've a knack of getting where I want at the end. You keep your eyes wide open and you'll see some sport."

He closed one of his eyes that very moment and winked at me again. It was clear enough that he was a reprehensible young rascal, and all the while there was a doubt at the back of my head as to whether he would not wind up by landing me in a disagreeable situation. But, as I think I have already said, he had such a way about him, and such a plausible air, and he really was so good-looking, that he actually succeeded in persuading me—after all that had already happened—to continue my connection with that miserable play.

We had the first rehearsal. Oh, dear, it was dreadful! Not only were we all at sixes and sevens—no one knew anything of his or her part, or had the faintest notion what to do—but not a creature seemed to have an idea of how to put matters even a little into shape. As for that Spencer boy, he was worse than useless. It seemed to me that he took either an imbecile or a malicious pleasure in making confusion worse confounded. As for order! Everybody was talking together, and as no one could get anyone to pay the least attention to what he or she was saying, by degrees some of them began to sulk.

"You ought," I yelled to Mr Spencer when, for a moment, I succeeded in catching him by the coat sleeve, "for the first rehearsal to have called the principal performers only; we shall never get on like this."

Although the piece was only in one act there was a long cast, and a tremendous chorus, besides no end of people who were just supposed to dress up and walk on and off. "Get half the parish on the stage, and the other half is bound to come and laugh at them"—that was Mr Spencer's idea. The consequence was that that ridiculous little platform at the "Lion," which was going to be the stage, was so crammed with people that there was scarcely room to move, so that the proceedings almost resembled a scrimmage in a game of Rugby football.

Miss Odger, who was standing by, heard what I said, although Mr Spencer apparently continued oblivious of my presence. Quite uninvited she answered for him.

"And pray, Miss Wilson, who would you describe as the principal performers? I suppose you, of course, are one."

She certainly was not another, she was only in the chorus.

"Anyhow, Miss Odger, one would hardly speak of the members of the chorus as principals, would one?"

"Is that so? I had no idea. In my ignorance I thought we were all supposed to be equal. Since we are all doing our best I did not know that some of us were to be treated as inferiors. May, did you?"

She turned to Miss Taylor, who, I was aware, hated the sight of me, as her answer showed.

"Didn't you know, my dear, that Miss Wilson not only wrote most of the piece, but proposes to act most of it too? I daresay she will let Mr Spencer do a little, but the rest of us, I imagine, are only to form a kind of background."

"If that is the case the sooner it becomes generally known the better. Miss Wilson will find that she will be at liberty to do it all by herself, though she may have to do it without the background."

It was no use my attempting to match myself against them at saying disagreeable things there, even had my dignity permitted it, which it did not. I simply walked away.

That rehearsal, which really never was a rehearsal at all, ended in something like a general squabble. Everybody went away on pretty bad terms with everybody else. I doubt if one single creature left that room in a good temper, except Frank Spencer. He seemed absolutely radiant. I should not have been a scrap surprised to learn that, directly the last of us was out of sight, he had to hold his hands to his sides to keep himself from bursting with laughter.

The next day, as regards my share in the proposed entertainment, there came the final straw in the shape of a visit from his mother. Such a visit! Mrs Spencer was an individual to whom I never had felt drawn. A little, fussy woman, with a fidgety manner, who was always tangling herself up in her own sentences. When she was announced, what she wanted with me I could not guess. It was with indescribable sensations that I gradually learnt.

"Miss Wilson," she began, "you are an orphan." I admitted it. From the way in which she was regarding me she might have been expecting me to deny it. "Therefore, much should be excused you. Providence does not wish us to press hardly on the motherless." I did not know what she meant, or why she was nodding her head as if it were hung on springs. "My dear young lady,

I would ask you to excuse me if, on this occasion, I speak in a manner calculated to show you that I appreciate your situation, if I ask you to regard me as if I were your mother." I stared. I could not at all fancy Mrs Spencer as my mother. But that was only the beginning. What she proceeded to say next took my breath away. "I know my boy. I know his faults. I know his virtues. He has many fine qualities." Had he? I could only say I had not noticed them. "But it has not been always altogether fortunate for him that he is such a universal favourite—especially with young women." She looked at me in a style which made me go both hot and cold. "He has generous instincts; noble impulses; a natural inclination to do only what is right and proper. But—alas! —he is of a pliant disposition, as clay in the hands of the modeller; easily led astray."

"Is that so? I am bound to admit that your son has not struck me as being a very vertebrate creature, but I don't see what his peculiarities have to do with me."

"Miss Wilson, I don't like to hear you talk like that. I don't like it."

"Mrs Spencer!"

"It shows a callous disposition, especially in one who is, apparently, so young."

"What do you mean?"

"You know what I mean perfectly well. Your own conscience is telling you, as you sit there, that you have taken advantage of his simplicity to induce my boy to do what he never would have done if he had been left alone."

"Mrs Spencer! This is monstrous!"

"It is no use your jumping up from your chair in that excitable manner and raising your voice. I am here to do my duty as a mother, and as the wife of the rector of this parish. Already your machinations have created a scandal, and you have set the whole place by the ears. Can you deny that you have entangled my son in a dreadful business, the end and aim of which is to perform in public a stage play for which you are responsible?"

"I presume that you are aware that you are alluding to Mr Frank Spencer's own musical comedy."

"It is not straightforward of you to attempt to take up such an attitude, Miss Wilson. Is it not a fact that for the play—which Mrs Parker informs me is of an absolutely impossible kind—"

"Oh, Mrs Parker was your informant, was she?"

"Certainly. She was never more shocked in her life. To think that she

50

should have been invited—actually invited!—to listen to such dreadful stuff!"

"It was your son who invited her; it was he who read the dreadful stuff, of which he is part author."

"Miss Wilson, it is unworthy of you to try to put the blame upon my boy, who is a mere lad."

"He's older than I am."

"In years, but we do not count by years only. I insist upon your telling me if for that dreadful play you are not principally, and practically, solely responsible?"

"I certainly have tried to make sense of your son's nonsense."

"And you really propose to perform it in public?"

"For the benefit of the parochial charities."

"For the benefit of the parochial charities!" You should have seen the expression which was on her funny little face as she repeated my words. "Miss Wilson, you dare to say such a thing! When you are perfectly well aware that neither the rector nor I would ever permit a farthing of any money obtained by such means to be devoted to such a purpose!"

"This is the most extraordinary thing I ever heard. Don't you know that the inception of the whole affair is your son's? He came and begged me to take part in an entertainment in aid of the parochial charities; he forced me to read his wretched play—"

"Oh, Miss Wilson! Miss Wilson! How can you talk to me in such a manner!" She actually wrung her hands, or seemed to. "Your painful behaviour compels me to ask if it is a fact that you are engaged to be married?"

"I am, though I do not see what that has to do with the matter under discussion."

"Then, under such circumstances, do you think it right and proper to encourage my poor boy?"

"Encourage your poor boy! I!"

I thought when she said that, that I should have had a fit.

"He is always with you; it is common talk. He is continually at your house—"

"Do you imagine that I invite him?"

I believe that I screamed at her.

"He has a photograph of yours in his cigarette-case; another in his pocket-book; another in his desk; a fourth on his bedroom mantelpiece."

"That's where my photographs have vanished to! Now I understand! Let me inform you, Mrs Spencer, that if, as you say, your son has my photographs, he has stolen them. Yes, stolen them—without asking my permission, and without my knowledge—like any common thief."

I do not deny that I lost my temper, but who, under the circumstances, would not have done? We had a brisk discussion. When we parted it was with a mutually-expressed hope that it was to meet no more.

Soon afterwards I went out to get some stamps. Old Bunting, who keeps the general shop and the post-office, received me with what he perhaps meant for an ingratiating simper.

"I hear, miss, that we're to have lively doings up at the Assembly Rooms; real old-fashioned ballet dancing and all sorts of things."

"I don't know what you mean, Mr Bunting."

I did not.

"Regular music-hall performances, so I'm told; short skirts and no end. It seems a bit unusual for ladies and gentlemen to go in for that kind of thing, but you'll have the place crammed to the doors, I promise you so much."

When I left Bunting's almost the first person I encountered was Mr Frank Spencer. I had it out with him then and there.

"Mr Spencer, will you at once return those four photographs of mine which you have stolen, or will it be necessary to communicate with the police?" He had the assurance to pretend to look surprised, but then he had assurance enough to pretend anything. "Your mother informs me that the whole idea of a performance in aid of the parochial charities is an invention of your own; on your father's behalf she repudiates it altogether. How dare you attempt to drag me into such a thing? As for that miserable musical comedy of yours—"

"Of ours."

If I could believe my senses there was still a twinkle in his eye.

"Of yours; you will give me your word of honour that you will destroy it at once, or I promise you that you shall hear from my solicitors."

"Really, Miss Wilson, I think it's rather hard of you to assail a fellow tooth and nail like this."

"You think I'm hard on you, do you? Here comes someone who, I fancy, you will find is of a different opinion." For who should come sailing into sight but George. Although I had not the faintest notion where he had sprung from, on the whole the sight of him was not unwelcome. "George," I began, "Mr Spencer has stolen four of my photographs. I want him to return them to me at once."

"So this is Mr Spencer." George looked him up and down in a style which was not exactly flattering. "I am sure, Mr Spencer, that it is unnecessary for me to emphasise Miss Wilson's request."

"Quite. Here are two of the photographs in question." He took one from a cigarette-case, and a second from a pocket-book, as his mother had said. That boy's audacity! "I will see that the other two are forwarded directly I reach home."

I still addressed myself to George.

"Mr Spencer appears desirous of associating me with a scrawl which he calls a musical comedy. Will you request him to see that the manuscript of the thing is entirely destroyed?"

"You hear, Mr Spencer?"

"Perfectly. I will do better than Miss Wilson asks. I will send the 'scrawl' in question with the two photographs. She will then be able to do with it what she pleases. While apologising for any inconvenience which Miss Wilson may have been occasioned, I would beg to be allowed to add that I think that Miss Wilson is disposed to regard me with almost undue severity. She forgets how hard up for amusement a fellow may be in a place like this. My idea was to get her to join me in playing off a joke on the aboriginals which wouldn't be forgotten for years. I can only express my regret that she should have taken up the point of view she has."

The impertinent young rascal walked off with his head in the air, and a look on his face which nearly suggested that he was the injured party. And, of course, George proceeded to lecture me.

"So this is your idea of taking part in amateur theatricals on behalf of the parochial charities!"

"It's not my idea at all," I retorted. "You know very well it isn't."

But he refused to admit that he knew anything of the kind. He would keep on making the most uncalled-for observations, instead of showing me the sympathy of which I stood so much in need. We almost quarrelled.

Mr Spencer sent back the photographs and the musical comedy. I tore that into shreds and burnt them every one. But I did not hear the last of it for ages. It created quite a schism in the place. All sorts of people were offended; I have not the faintest notion why. Although some of them even went so far as to attempt to lay the blame on me. I have been the victim of a good deal of injustice in my life, but that really was the most unjustifiable injustice of all.

STAGGERS

A grey, watery sky, through which there are occasional glimpses of the sun. A sloping and a muddy field. A large crowd. I suppose it is attributable to the proximity of the village; but I had no idea that there would be such a gathering. A long line of vehicles in the adjoining lane—principally dogcarts. Most of them seem to be as full as they can hold, occasionally fuller. Philipson informs me that the occupants of these vehicles intend to follow the hunt by road; he adds that they will probably see more of it than we shall. His observation occasions me surprise. If it be possible to hunt in a comfortable dog-cart, along decent roads, in a civilised manner, why should he have induced me to spend a guinea on the hire of an animal which, I am convinced, is of uncertain temper?

I was aware that meets were popular functions, but I had no notion they were so popular as this. It may be owing to the fact that we are only about twenty miles from town, but the place is inundated by what can only be described as an actual rabble. Men and boys, and even women and girls, line the hedges, many of them without hats, or, in the case of the latter, bonnets. The inhabitants seemed to have turned out *en masse*. They escorted us from the station much in the fashion in which a crowd escorts a regimental band through the streets of London, only they got in our way much more than the crowd is ever allowed to get in the way of the band. There was no footpath in the lane, and I am sure that sometimes as many as half a dozen people were under my horse's feet at once. A strong feeling of sociability seems to reign among the spectators; and, as several of them are shouting to each other right across the field, the noise is considerable. Some of the remarks which fall upon my ears can scarcely be regarded as flattering by the enthusiastic sportsmen present who are members of the hunt. Among all these people the horsemen seem to be in an insignificant minority. Yet there are quite a number of them, too.

In a cleared space in the centre of the field is a cart. It looks very much like the carts which are used to convey bulls through thoroughfares in town. Only, unlike those, this is roofed over. It is also more elegantly fashioned. The wheels, which are tolerably clean, are painted bright scarlet, while the cart itself is chastely decorated in two shades of green. Some little distance behind it, in the charge of the huntsman and two whippers-in, are the hounds. I am bound to say that those sagacious animals appear to me to be taking less interest in the proceedings than one might reasonably expect.

Presently an elderly gentleman, who weighs, perhaps, seventeen or eighteen stone, and who is attired in magnificent apparel, as befits the Master of the Hunt, gets out of the carriage in which he has driven to the ground, and scrambles on to the back of a horse which promises weight-carrying power rather than speed. "Ready, Jenkins!" he cries. A respectable-looking individual, in a long green coat, which he wears ostentatiously unbuttoned in front, goes to the rear of the deer-cart, and, presumably, unfastens the door. A hush, as of expectation, follows. Nothing, however, happens. The man in the green coat seems to be having an argument with something inside the cart.

"Twist his tail!" shouts a voice in the crowd—decidedly a boy's.

"The brute won't uncart," says Philipson.

I immediately have visions. I think of the tales I have read of the cruelties which always attend stag-hunts; of the poor, frenzied, frightened creature tearing madly, blindly, beside itself with terror, to escape the merciless pursuit of the ferocious, eager hounds. Only a short time ago I had read somewhere a piteous account of a stag which, in its agony, had broken its heart and died. And they called it sport! I had half a mind to express myself on the subject, there and then, strongly; to declare that I, for one, would not take part in such an orgy of senseless cruelty. I had my hand upon the rein, and was about to turn my horse's head stationwards, resolute to forfeit the guinea which I had paid for its hire rather than continue to be a constituent fraction of such a ruthless throng, when the deer uncarted. I fancy that the man in the green coat punched it in the ribs, or adopted some similar means of persuasion. But the animal certainly did get out of the cart.

In appearance it was not all my imagination had pictured it. It was undoubtedly a deer, but of what kind I have no notion. I am no sort of an authority on the subject, but I apprehend that this one was of a breed which does not run to size. When one thinks of a stag one thinks of antlers; if that stag had antlers, then they were in what may be described as an apologetic state. I protest that I saw nothing of them. What struck me most was the animal's demeanour. Whether it was paralysed by fear, or by forebodings of the horrible fate that was in store for it, is more than I can say. When it got out of the cart, it walked about a dozen feet, then stopped to crop the grass. "Hi-hi-hi-i-i!" shouted the crowd, unnecessarily, it seemed to me. Even the hounds showed signs of interest. Some of them began to bark quite noisily. Everyone was excited—except the deer. It looked up, as if actuated by a certain indifferent curiosity, went on about another dozen feet, then stopped to crop the grass again. The excitement was increasing. At this rate of progression the creature would be out of the field by the time "the shades of night were falling." The man in the green coat, coming to the front of the deer-cart, took down the whip which was beside the driver's seat. With the whip in his hand he walked after the deer. When he had got within a foot or so of it, he cracked the whip in the air with the report of a pistol-shot. The deer looked up, as if surprised and even pained at such conduct. The man cracked the whip a second time. The deer seemed annoyed. Kicking up its heels like a skittish colt, it ambled down the slope and over the hedge.

Immediately the whole place was in a turmoil. The vehicles in the lane began to move. A large proportion of the crowd streamed across the field with the apparent intention of seizing the deer by the heels before it had a chance of getting away. The hounds barked; men shouted; boys whistled. It was a scene of pleasing confusion. In a few seconds, I take it, the word to start was given, the huntsman blew his horn, and the hounds, barking as if with the intent to split their throats, went rushing after the people, who already were rushing after the deer. The hunt was off. I, also, was nearly off, because, in the muddle, which was the most marked feature of the moment, a man in pink cannoned against me, and almost succeeded in laying my steed and its rider low. "Look out where you're coming to!" he exclaimed, as he went pushing past me—which struck me, then, as being the most unreasonable remark I had ever had addressed to me.

When I had had time to regain my own and my horse's equilibrium, I perceived that Philipson, some little distance off, was being borne away in the seething crowd of riders. Looking back towards me he waved his whip. "Come on!" he cried. I came on. It was about time I did. Everyone, with one accord, was making for the gate which was in the corner of the field, and as I, unwittingly, was in the direct road to it, perfect strangers were addressing me with that absence of restraint which we look for only in the case of our lifelong friends. The process of getting through the gate reminded me not a little of the crowd which one sees outside the pit door of a popular theatre. Everyone seemed anxious to get through first, and everyone seemed to be under the impression that everybody else was doing his best to hinder him. I daresay it took me five minutes to reach the other side of it. When I did, I quite expected that Philipson would have been with the hounds, a mile away. However, somewhat to my surprise, I found him awaiting me, like a true friend, but a little wanting on the point of temper.

"You've been a nice time!" he observed.

"It hasn't been my idea of a nice time," I ventured to observe.

It hadn't.

"We may as well go home," he went on further to remark, "for all the chances we have of seeing any sport to-day."

If that indeed were so, we, at least, had not the galley to ourselves. We all scampered across the field, scattering as we went. Through another gate, across one or two more fields, until at a sudden dip in the ground we found ourselves confronted by a wire fence. We had not seen a sign of the hunt. Obviously the fence was unsurmountable. We moved along in search of a gate. When found, it proved to be locked, and of diabolically ingenious construction. To open it was beyond our powers. One man proposed pulling up a yard or two of the fencing, but as he made no attempt to put his own proposal into execution, we let it pass. The language employed was unprintable. We separated, Philipson and I going off in search of a hedge—or of what, I believe, is called upon the stage a "practicable" gate; Philipson, on the way, being more voluminous on the subject of wire fencing than I ever thought he could have been.

We discovered ourselves, at last, to be in a lane, though we had not the faintest notion of where we were, or of where the hunt was either. However, we trotted on, as if we still entertained hopes of being in at whatever it may be which, in "stagging," takes the place of death. Suddenly we reached a point at which another lane turned into ours. As we did so, three men in pink came tearing along it as if they were riding for their lives. At sight of us they almost pulled their horses back upon their haunches.

"Where are they?" demanded the man in front.

Philipson was able to supply him with but scanty information.

"Haven't seen them since they started," he remarked.

"Confound it!" cried the man.

Off rode the trio, as if the hounds were at their heels. We followed at a milder pace. We had not gone far before we heard the sound of wheels approaching from behind us. Looking back, we perceived that three dog-carts were advancing in Indian file. Judging from the rate at which they were coming, one might have been excused for supposing that, being without the fear of pains and penalties for furious driving, they were matched against time. They slowed when they reached us.

"Where are they?" inquired the driver of the leading vehicle—if he was not a publican, then I am prepared to assert that he was a butcher.

"Haven't the faintest notion," replied Philipson.

The driver of the second cart struck in. There could not be the shadow of a doubt as to what he was—"Vet" was written large all over him.

"It's all right, push along, Jim! He's making for the cinder-heaps, I tell you; I know he is. When the wind's like this, he always makes for there."

Two girls were in the hindmost cart—probably relations of one or other of the gentlemen in front. The one who was acting as Jehu waved her whip impatiently.

"Yes, do let's hurry on! What's the good of hanging about?—we're only wasting time!"

The procession re-started. I do not remember to have ever seen vehicles careering along what, I presume, was a public highway, at such a rate before. You could hardly see the wheels go round. From a purely spectacular point of view it was exhilarating—really!

"Do you call this stag-hunting?" inquired Philipson, his eyes fixed on the rapidly retreating dog-carts.

"No," I said, "I don't."

I was unable to tell what prompted his inquiry. It seemed an uncalled-for one just then. But I could but answer it.

We jogged on for, perhaps, another mile without, it seemed, getting nearer to anything, or to anywhere, when an astonishing thing took place. We were still in the lane, and, judging from appearances, we bade fair to continue in the lane during the remainder of the day. All at once, without giving us the slightest warning of its approach, something, springing over the hedge upon our right, alighted on the road only three or four yards in front of us. It stared at us, and we at it. Not impossibly, we were the more surprised of the two. Certainly it was the first to recover its presence of mind. Swerving to one side, it cleared the hedge upon our left with a degree of agility which did it credit. It was only after it was over that we realised what it was.

"It's the deer!" cried Philipson.

"It's the deer!" I echoed.

We watched it moving across the field at a pace which, though it appeared leisurely, a little observation showed us was much faster than it seemed. While we hesitated, wondering what, under the circumstances, would be the proper thing for us to do, the whole pack of hounds came through the hedge over which the deer had first appeared. Without condescending to notice us, dashing helter-skelter through the hedge in front of them, they continued the chase.

"Come on!" shouted Philipson.

And I came!

Forcing our horses through a gap in the hedge, we found ourselves in a position which, from a sportsman's point of view, was as pleasant as it was unexpected. A glance over my shoulder showed me that we were not alone. Three or four horsemen, who seemed to be racing, were close behind us, while a not inconsiderable field tailed off in the distance. For what seemed three-quarters of an hour but what, probably, was more like three minutes, we enjoyed something like a burst. Our horses were comparatively fresh; the going was easy; the quarry, at the start, at any rate, was well in view. We passed over field after field—they were divided from each other by apologies for hedges; although, so far as I am aware, my steed did not pretend to be much of a jumper, the animal took them in its stride. It seemed as if the blood was growing warmer in my veins. I felt that this sort of thing really was worth paying a guinea for; that, if this was "stagging," you might give me as much of it as you chose. On we went, with such determination that I did not even slacken rein when a row of hurdles rose right in front of me. I went at them with the *sang-froid* of a steeplechaser. My horse negotiated the obstacle in gallant fashion, clearing it with his forelegs and bringing it down with his hind. Philipson, who was somewhat in the rear, with a want of spirit of which I had scarcely thought him capable, steered for the gap which I had made. Taking full advantage of the opening I had given him, he crept up to my side.

"This is something like!" he gasped.

"Magnificent!" I answered.

I but voiced the feelings of my heart—it was magnificent. The ground, which was open pasture, descended in a gentle slope for fully half a mile. Far away, and getting farther and farther, was the deer. Although it still seemed to be travelling at its leisure, plainly enough it kept away from the hounds with ease. A hundred yards behind they followed it like a single dog. You could not have covered them with the proverbial pocket-handkerchief, because they were scattered pretty widely, both to the right and to the left, and behind and in front; but evidently they were animated by a common purpose, to get on even terms with their quarry.

"This is too hot to last!" gasped Philipson.

I was becoming conscious of that fact myself. Horses jobbed out at a guinea a day are not supposed to be Derby fliers; nor are they guaranteed to keep on at top speed for an indefinite distance. Away we raced—it was, literally, racing; but, the further we went, the more clearly I realised that something was going wrong with my animal's works. I should have to ease up soon or stop entirely. The stag, and the hounds, and the country together, settled the question for me in a fashion of their own.

We had come down a reasonably graduated incline, I know not how far, and I know not how long, when I suddenly perceived that the graduation of the incline was ceasing to be reasonable. From a mere slope it was becoming transformed into a positive declivity. Instead of falling, say, one in a hundred, it was beginning to fall one in ten, and, so far as I could perceive, bade fair, ere long, to fall one in something less than two. Indeed, not more than a couple of hundred feet in front of us, unless appearances were deceptive, the ground dropped away into what looked uncommonly like a sheer precipice. At any rate, the deer and hounds, passing over it in their wild career, had disappeared from view as if by magic. Philipson and I reined up our horses as short as we could. I do not fancy that either of the brutes objected. As we did so, several other men came up one after another from behind; the legitimate hunt they were, who had followed from the first, and whom we had all but robbed of their laurels. They reined up almost in a line with us.

"Pretty steep bit here," said a man upon my left.

A man upon his left replied to him.

"Beastly! That's an old quarry ahead; you can get down it, but it isn't easy. There's the railway in front; there's a devil of a fence, and a devil of a hedge to tackle before you reach it. Then ditto, ditto on the other side, then a brook, then a plantation of young trees which want thinning, and which is not so well adapted to horse exercise as the maze at Hampton Court."

The speaker's knowledge of the country proved to be correct—at least, as far as Philipson and I investigated it, which was as far as the old quarry. It might have been possible to get down it—indeed, the speaker proved that it was by going down it himself, and inducing three other idiots to go down with him; but precipice-climbing on horseback had not been the sort of experience we had been in search of when we went "stagging." Philipson and I refrained. We remained up above with several other sensible persons, and watched those enthusiastic "staggers" tearing—with no slight expenditure of labour—bars out of the strongly and carefully-constructed fence, the property of the railway company. Then, with their pocket-knives, they commenced to cut a gap in the thickest six-foot hedge, an appurtenance of the same corporation. When we had seen so much, Philipson and I had seen enough. We induced our horses to retrace their steps uphill.

The descent had been delightful, the ascent was not so pleasant. If it was half a mile down, it was, certainly, three miles up. Nor was the sum total of our satisfaction heightened when, after sundry divagations, we found ourselves in what bore a singular resemblance to that unending lane which we had originally—and so gladly!—quitted.

"It strikes me," remarked Philipson, as he looked to the right and to the left of him, "that I've been here before. I seem to know this lane."

I seemed to know it, too. But it was no use making the worst of things. I endeavoured to put a fair front upon the matter.

"I dare say if we keep on we shall get somewhere soon."

"I hope we shall," said Philipson, in what struck me as being a tone of almost needless gloom.

We did keep on—that I do earnestly protest. Not very fast, it is true—our horses, for reasons of their own, seemed to object to hurry. I said nothing, and as Philipson, if possible, said still less, conversation languished. We had pursued the devious twistings of that eternal lane for what seemed to be ten miles, and which, possibly, were nearly two, when an exclamation from Philipson roused me to a consideration of the surroundings.

"Hallo!—I say!—what's that?"

"What's what?"

I followed, with my eyes, the direction in which he was pointing with his outstretched hand. He had stayed his horse, and was raising himself in his stirrups with what seemed to be positive excitement. His interest seemed centred in a flock of sheep which browsed unconcernedly in the meadow on our left. At the first glance I thought that they were sheep, "and nothing more." A moment's inspection, however, disclosed the fact that among them was a creature of another species, a little larger than themselves, but not much, and of a different shape and colour. Like them, it grazed, "the world forgetting," if not "by the world forgot," and seemed to be so very much at its ease, and so entirely at peace with all the world, that some seconds elapsed before ocular demonstration succeeded in convincing me that it might be a relation to the noble animal which a large number of enthusiastic sportsmen were ardently pursuing.

"It is a deer?"

The words came from me in the form of a query. For some reason the inquiry seemed to nettle Philipson. He seemed to think that there could be no possible room for doubt.

"Of course it's a deer. What's more, it's the deer."

"No!"

That did seem to me to be almost inconceivable. How came the creature there? Why did it not betray more symptoms of anxiety? Did it suppose that it was out for a holiday, the programme of which included refreshments by the way? Was it possible that it could already have forgotten its wild flight from the red-hot ardour of the heated chase? What had become of the hounds, and the hunt, and the array of dog-carts, and the excited pedestrian throng? Were we two all that was left of them?

While such questions passed through my brain, for which I in vain sought answers, we sat on our horses on one side of the hedge, while on the other the proud monarch of the woodland cropped the sweet grasses with the humble sheep, for all the world as if he were one of them. Plainly, we were more interested in him than he in us; the close proximity of men caused him no annoyance.

Philipson volunteered an observation.

"I fancy we'd better stop here till the cart comes along. Someone ought to keep an eye on him. The last time I was out the deer was lost. I believe it was over two months before he was found again."

It occurred to me that Philipson was proposing that we should act towards this denizen of the forest glades very much as if we were a couple of policemen—we were to guard, not to hunt it. The responsibility which Philipson was desirous that we should assume was not, however, forced upon us. Before I could say "Yes" or "No" to what struck me as being his somewhat singular proposition, who should come trotting along the lane but the Master of the Hunt himself. He was alone. One perceived that he had not unduly spurred his willing beast. Philipson nodded. He jerked his thumb over the hedge.

"There's the deer."

"Eh?" The Master pulled up. He looked where Philipson pointed. He saw that the thing was so. "What the dickens is it doing there?" That is what I wanted to know. He was a portly man. The peculiar behaviour of the deer seemed to fill his soul with indignation. His face put on an extra tinge of ruddiness. "Where're the hounds?"

"I expect the stag threw them off in the forest; we quitted when we crossed the line and made for it—didn't think it was good enough."

I thought that Philipson's words were neatly chosen; they conveyed the impression that we had been in the hunt from the beginning, all the way, to the point alluded to.

"Where's the cart?"

"Haven't a notion. My friend and I thought that we would keep an eye upon the stag till we had news of it."

Although he did not say so, the Master appeared to think that it might be advisable that he also should keep an eye upon the stag. His interest in the creature's safety was certainly likely to be of a more personal kind than either Philipson's or mine. I take it that stags are animals of intrinsic value, not to be regarded as things to be lightly trifled with, deserving of as much care and consideration as, say, the domestic cow. So we sat, all three in a row; pretty silent, on the whole; staring over the hedge at the monarch of the woodland, as he enjoyed an adventitious meal.

Presently a boy came into the field through a gate at the side. I imagine he was a shepherd boy—I have no positive proof to adduce of the fact, but such is my impression. I noticed that he cast at the flock what I felt was an interested glance, and, as he did so, observed the stranger in their midst. It was enough for him that there was a stranger; he did not stop to inquire who he was or what had brought him there, but on the instant he obeyed what I suspect to be the natural instinct of the natural boy. I believe that I was the only one of the trio who had noticed his approach—as yet he had not noticed us at all. Had I foreseen his fell design, I should, undoubtedly, have given tongue; but by the time I had so much as an inkling of his intention it already was too late, the deed was done. It is possible that he was under the impression that the intruder was, uninvited, taking a gratuitous meal, and that he resented both his impertinence and his dishonesty. Anyhow, stooping down, he picked up a stone and hurled it at the deer with that force and that directness of aim with which boys can throw stones. The missile struck the animal a resounding blow, I should judge, in the neighbourhood of the ribs, at a moment when it was not expecting anything of the kind. It leaped high in the air in the first flush of its surprise; then, without staying to make inquiries, it bolted across the field and over the hedge at a pace which was very much in excess of anything which I had seen it display in the presence of the hounds.

I conceive that the Master was to the full as amazed as the deer had been, and also, when he understood what had happened, as indignant. He looked after the vanished animal as if totally at a loss to comprehend the cause of its curious conduct—no doubt he had known that deer before—then he brought his head round slowly, scouring the landscape as he did so, till the boy came within his line of vision. Having sighted him, he glared as at some monstrosity, his cheeks purpling, and the blood-vessels becoming more and more distinct. Philipson explained.

"The young beggar threw a brick at him—nice young rascal!"

The Master shook his clenched fist at the boy across the hedge. I never before saw an elderly gentleman in such a passion.

"You somethinged somethinged something, what do you mean by

throwing your somethinged somethinged bricks at my blankety blankety deer?" Even the casual reader must have read something about the remarkable language which occasionally exudes from the lips of gentlemen, in moments of excitement, on the hunting-field. The Master flavoured the atmosphere with examples of that sort of language then. "If I get hold of you, I'll twist your somethinged somethinged head off your blankety blankety shoulders!"

If there had been a handy gate, it is probable that the Master would have used it to pursue that boy, and, regardless of consequences, when caught, have given him something for himself. But there was no gate just there. The hedge was well established and closely grown. The Master's horse was not the kind of quadruped to force its way through such an obstacle, or to surmount it by a jump, especially with its owner on its back.

The Master's stentorian tones were the first intimation the boy had received that there had been spectators of his action. When he heard that strident voice, and was saluted by that flow of language, and recognised the Master's "pink," no doubt he realised the full enormity of his offence. As he did so, like the deer, "he stood not on the order of his going, but went at once," rushing pell-mell through the gate by which he had entered, and passing from our sight.

"I'd give five pounds," declared the Master, "for a chance of breaking every bone in the scoundrel's body!"

As I was hoping that he did not mean exactly what he said, Philipson, who kept his eyes open, diverted our interest into a new channel.

"Hallo! There's the hounds!" he cried.

Turning round, as Philipson had done, sure enough, in the field behind us, there were the hounds. At least, there were some of them. Each individual member of the pack was wandering about in a desultory fashion, doing nothing in particular, apparently not a little bored, and wondering what it was that had brought it there.

"What are those dogs doing there by themselves? Where's the hunt?" inquired the Master.

That was the question. So far as could be seen, not a person was in sight. Since the deer had come in one direction, and now a portion of the hounds had come in another, perhaps, shortly, the hunt might appear in a third. One never knew. There seemed to be little or no connection between the various parties. That this was so seemed to occur to the Master. The reflection excited him. It moved him to action. There was a gate into that field, a decrepit gate, which hung loosely on its hinges. Pushing it open, the Master bustled into the meadow, holloaing and shouting with much zeal, but to little purpose. The hounds did not seem to understand him in the least, or to know him either. But when he rode right into their midst, and commenced to strike out at them indiscriminately with the lash of his hunting-whip, they began to bark at the top of their voices, and, as the poet has it, to make "the welkin ring." If clamour was what he was aiming at, then he succeeded to perfection—the "music of the pack" was deafening. But if, as I rather fancy, he entertained some dim idea of whipping the dogs on to the trail of the stag, then the result was ignominious failure. They barked and jumped about, and jumped about and barked, and he lashed them and shouted, but, beyond that, nothing and nobody got any "forwarder."

The performance might have continued until one side or the other had had enough of it—the probability being that the Master would have been the first to tire—had not the deer, finding that the hounds did not come to it, saved them trouble by coming to them. That sagacious animal—I was beginning to suspect that it was a sagacious brute, and at least as well acquainted as anyone else with the rules of the game—put in a fresh, and, as usual, wholly unexpected appearance on the scene. Philipson, as his habit seemed to be, had his eyes the widest open.

"By Jove! There's the deer!"

There was the deer, in the very next field to the one in which the Master, with ideas of his own, was whipping the hounds. And, what was more, there were some of the hunt as well. Nor were they entirely unprovided with dogs; they were being shown the way by, so to speak, their share of the pack—some six or eight hounds. On they came in gallant style. The stag, leaping the hedge, found himself confronted by the major portion of the pack. When he saw the dogs, the dogs saw him. Then there was music! In an instant the Master and his antics were forgotten—they went for their quarry with a tumultuous welcome. With perfect ease he doubled on his tracks, and, leaping back over the hedge, returned at an acute angle to the course he had come. The Master went spluttering after him. Philipson and I did our best to get a share of the fun.

The scene was changed like a transformation scene in a theatre. A moment or two before, the place had been deserted, and not a soul had been in sight. Now people came hurrying from every quarter, as if they had been concealed behind unseen wings and waiting for the signal to appear. Half a dozen horsemen and a line of dog-carts came scurrying along the lane. You would have thought they had been flying for life, the dog-carts in particular. Horsemen and horsewomen seemed to spring up out of the ground on every side. On a sudden, the entire hunt appeared to be gathered together almost as it had been at first. Everyone went pounding away across the turf, crashing through the hedges—preferentially selecting the gates, however, when they could find them—as if, whatever they might have been doing hitherto, they meant business at last.

Certainly, there is something contagious in such surroundings. I found that there was, and my horse did, too. Just now the animal had appeared dead tired, and I should have said also a little lame. But when the flurry began, and eager riders, on all sides, went pressing hastily forward, moved by a common mastering excitement, my wearied guinea's-worth, forgetting its fatigue, became as lively as the best of them. The revival of the interest had also freshened me. Away we went, my steed and I, as light-heartedly, apparently, as if it had been the first move we had made that day.

We had another burst—though I am bound to admit that in a singularly short space of time both the deer and the hounds were out of sight. They had gone before, not improbably, so far as I was concerned, for good. But as a large number of people, who were undoubtedly as much out of the hunt as I was, went pounding eagerly on, I went pounding too. Philipson was on my left. It was more than doubtful if he would catch a glimpse of the stag again that day—it would be entirely owing to the benevolence of that intelligent creature if he did. Yet on his face was mirrored a stern, concentrated purpose, which might have suggested to a stranger that he had at last made up his mind to hunt the quarry, single-handed, to its final doom.

That burst did not continue long—fortunately. I was becoming conscious that a good many people seemed to be getting in front, and that my horse was exhibiting no marked anxiety to occupy a post of honour, when, having edged my way through still another gate, I found myself on the high road. Soon the road began to bear a striking resemblance to a street. Shortly I found myself, in company with a number of other individuals, clattering down what was obviously the leading thoroughfare of a country town.

Among the inhabitants our advent created the liveliest interest. We might have been royalty, from the way in which they stared at us. Someone looked out of every door and window. Numbers of persons lined the pavements. As I passed one house I heard a woman shrieking up the stairs,—

"Bill, 'ere's the 'unters; come and 'ave a look at 'em."

I suppose Bill came. Encouraging remarks were addressed to us by miscellaneous spectators, principally boys.

"You're all right, mister, 'e's gone down there; if you 'urries up, you'll get a sight of 'im."

I do not know if the observation was directed to me; if it was, I could have assured the speaker that neither my horse nor myself had the slightest intention of "hurrying up" to catch a sight of anyone.

About a hundred yards farther down we found ourselves in the midst of what looked very like an actual riot. Although the street was very wide just there, it was rendered almost impassable by a motley concourse of vehicles, horsemen and pedestrians. On one side of the street was a butcher's shop. Towards this butcher's shop all faces were turned. From it there proceeded an amazing din—there were sounds of dogs barking, of men's voices, and of one voice in particular.

I turned to Philipson in search of an explanation. The explanation which he proffered, although succinct and to the point, took me somewhat by surprise.

"Stag's taken shelter in the butcher's shop."

It seemed to me to be a curious shelter for a stag to choose—a butcher's shop! And so, judging from his words, which, in an interval of comparative silence, were distinctly audible, the butcher seemed himself to think.

"Don't let any of your dogs come into my place, or I'll cut their somethinged throats for them. Your deer—if it is your deer—has done me ten-pounds'-worth of damage. You pay me that ten pounds, and then I'll talk to you; but not till then. You know who I am; there's my name and my address!"—the speaker pointed with his cleaver to the name over his shop-front—"and if you want anything from me, you know how to get it. There's the law for me as well as for you! But don't let any of you chaps—I don't care who he is—try to set foot in my premises, or he'll be sorry, and so I tell you."

The butcher seemed to be very angry indeed, which, if the deer really had done him ten-pounds'-worth of damage, was not to be wondered at.

Philipson and I did not wait to see the discussion ended. We adjourned to an inn and there refreshed. A roaring trade that inn was doing. The stag's behaviour did someone good. And very sociable were the customers. I gleaned from them several interesting scraps of information. It appeared that that was not the first time a stag had sought refuge in that particular butcher's shop; and since the enterprising tradesman invariably demanded compensation for damages which he alleged the creature had done him, dark suspicions were entertained as to the means which he adopted to get him there.

As I journeyed homewards, on the whole I was disposed to conclude that chasing a carted stag, under certain given conditions, might be made a not unamusing pastime—with about it a flavour of something Gallic, perhaps. They have some odd notions of sport on the other side of the Channel.

The stag-hunter's pleasure depends, it seems to me, entirely on the intelligence of the particular stag whose services happen to be retained for the day. If, being ill-tempered, or obstinate, or stupid, the moment it is uncarted it runs straight on, and keeps straight on, then, I should say, the probability is exceedingly strong that no single member of the hunt will ever catch sight of it again till the hunt is over. If, on the other hand, the creature is generous, not to say charitable—as our stag was!—and wanders about looking for disconsolate "staggers"—as our stag did!—then, I take it, the affair may be managed—by the stag!—in such a manner that everyone concerned may be justified in thinking that he has done something worth his talking about.

MY WEDDING DAY

The night before my wedding day I could scarcely sleep a wink—that is, to speak of. I suppose it was partly the excitement; because, of course, I could not help thinking—and there were so many things to think of. "Now, Maud," said mamma, when she was bidding me good-night, "don't you girls stop up talking. You get between the sheets as soon as you're upstairs, and go to sleep at once." But she might as well have talked to the moon. Of course, Eveleen came in to have what she called a "few last words"; from the way she said it there might have been going to be a funeral instead of a wedding. I had not previously suspected her of being sentimental; but that night she was positively depressing. And so horridly hopeful. She hoped that George would make a good husband, and that we should be happy, and that I should never regret what I was doing, and that it would all turn out for the best, and that marriage would suit me, and that I should not go into a rapid decline, like Aunt Louisa did, and that George would not quarrel with mamma, and that he would not estrange me from all my relations and friends, and that whatever happened I should always remember she was the only sister I had; she kept on hoping that sort of thing till I had to bundle her off.

To crown all, when at last I was between the sheets, who should come creeping into the room like a ghost but mamma herself, though it must have been frightfully late; and her manner was positively sepulchral.

"When you were a small child," she began, "I always used to come and kiss you before you went to sleep; have you forgotten?" Of course I had not forgotten. "So I have come again to kiss you, for the last time."

"Dear mother, I'm not dying to-morrow; at least, I hope not."

"That depends on what you mean by dying"—which was a cheerful thing to say! "I trust, my dear daughter, that events will prove you have chosen wisely, and that you will have every happiness; my own married life has not been without its trials. Only, in the midst of your own happiness, do not forget that you have a mother, and that you are still my child. God bless you!"

As she stooped over to kiss me I felt her tears fall on my cheeks. That finished me. After she had gone I had a good cry—the first I had had for years and years. I was more than half disposed to jump out of bed and run after her and promise that I would never leave her—never! never! never!—but—I managed not to. Still I was anything but comfortable, lying all alone in the dark there. Because I could not shut my eyes to the fact that mamma had said things to George, and that George had said things to mamma, and that papa had said things to both of them; and everybody knows how that sort of thing grows, till a breach is made which may never be bridged over. Then there was my dress. Three times I had had to have it altered; till, finally, in desperation, I had made up my mind to have an entirely new bodice made. I could not go to the altar screwed up so tight as to be in continual terror of my seams bursting, or else being suffocated. George would be furious if anything did happen. The new bodice was something of a fit. But it had not yet come home, though Mme. Sylvia had promised—pledged what she called her professional reputation—that it should come before ten o'clock to-morrow morning. Still, I could not help owning to myself that I had scarcely any faith in the woman; and suppose it did not come? My wedding dress!

The horror of such a prospect was too much for me. I believe it frightened me to sleep, if you could call it sleep. Because then I dreamt—such dreams! They were really dreadful nightmares. I know that in one of them George was throwing mamma out of the window and I had on scarcely a rag, and papa, laughing like a maniac, was cutting my wedding dress into tiny shreds and Eveleen was shrieking; when, in the very midst of it, I woke with a start—a frightful start—to find that someone was gripping my shoulder with a clutch of steel, and that a voice was saying to me in the pitchy darkness,—

"Maud, wake up!—wake up! There are burglars in the house; they are in the drawing-room stealing your presents!"

Roused out of sleep by a thunder-clap like that, it was not surprising if I were disposed to wonder where I was and what had happened.

"Who is it?" I inquired. "And what's the matter?"

"It's Eveleen! And as for what's the matter, they're not my presents, so it's not of the slightest consequence to me what becomes of them, though I should not be in the least surprised if they're all of them gone by now. Do wake up!"

Before I really knew it I was not only wide awake, but I was stealing along the pitch dark passage in my night-gown, with Eveleen's hand in mine. Sure enough, as we leaned over the baluster, we could see, through the open door, that there was a light in the drawing-room, where all my wedding-presents were laid out for inspection.

"What are you doing in there?" I cried. "Who are you?"

Looking back they seemed rather foolish questions to have asked. It was, perhaps, because she felt this strongly that, without the slightest warning, Eveleen burst into the most appalling shrieks and yells.

"Help! help!—murder!—thieves!—burglars!—help-p!"

I had never suspected her of having such powerful lungs. It was partly owing to the surprise occasioned by the discovery, and partly to the thrill which the noise she made sent right through me, that I was induced to do the most daring—and also the rashest—thing I ever did do. Without giving Eveleen the least hint of my intention, I flew down the stairs and dashed into the drawing-room in my night-gown, just as I was. What would have happened if the burglar had stayed and attacked me is too terrible for thought. Fortunately, he did nothing of the kind. Just as I tore through the door the light in the room went out; I heard a scrambling noise, as if somebody was stumbling against furniture and knocking over chairs. Then I saw a blind lifted and a figure leaped through the open window. I believe I should have leaped after him if Eveleen had not stopped me. I had already lifted the corner of the blind when she shouted,—

"Maud! What are you going to do?"

"I can see him running across the lawn, and I believe he's taken all my presents!"

"If he has, whatever good do you suppose you'll be able to do by jumping through the window after him?"

"There he is! He's going through the gate! He'll escape!"

Eveleen, coming rushing across the room, flung her arms around me and held me tight.

"Come back!" she cried; which were hardly the correct words to use, since, as a matter of fact, I had not actually gone.

Then papa and mamma and the servants came hurrying in, and there was a fine to-do. That burglar had apparently supposed that those wedding-presents had been laid out for his inspection. Anyhow, he had gone carefully over them and selected the very best. As Eveleen rather coarsely—and also ungratefully —put it, the things he had left behind were hardly worth having. He had taken Aunt Jane's turquoise bracelet, and Uncle Henry's pearl necklace, and Mrs Mackenzie's diamond brooch, and, indeed, nearly every scrap of jewellery, and the silver tea-service, and the dressing-case—George's own present to me —and five cheques, and all sorts of things; though, of course, in the excitement of the moment, we could hardly be certain what he had taken; but I may say at once that it turned out to be worse even than we feared. When, at last, a policeman did appear upon the scene, he was anything but sympathetic. From his manner we might have left my presents lying about on purpose, and the window open too. He was the most disagreeable policeman I ever did encounter.

Anyone would easily imagine that after such an interruption there was no more sleep for me that night. But mamma insisted upon my going back to bed. Extraordinary though it may seem, I believe I was no sooner between the sheets than I was fast asleep. And that time I had no dreams. I was visited by no premonitions of what was to happen to me on what I had meant should be the happiest day of my life. My existence had been uneventful up to then. Scarcely anything worth speaking of had occurred, except my meeting George. It appeared that Fate had resolved to crowd into a few hours the misfortunes which might very well have been spread over the nineteen years I had been in the world. Everything went wrong; some evil spirit had been let loose that day to play on me as many cruel pranks as it possibly could—I feel sure of it. Stealing my wedding-presents was only the beginning. I had worked and schemed, planned and contrived, so that everything should go smoothly and be as nice as it could be. Instead of which anything more tragic could hardly be conceived.

To begin with, Eveleen, who seemed destined on that occasion to act as a bird of ill-omen, awoke me, for the second time, out of sleep with a piece of information which was really almost worse than her first had been. Indeed, for a moment or two, when I realised all that it meant, it seemed to me to be an absolutely crushing blow. She waited till she was sure that I had my eyes wide open; then she let fall her bombshell.

"Maud, I have another pleasant piece of news for you. Bertha has the measles."

"Eveleen," I exclaimed, starting up in bed, "what do you mean?"

"Exactly what I say. And as Constance slept with her last night she will probably have them also, so that you will, at any rate, be two bridesmaids short. Read that."

She handed me a letter which she had been holding in her hand. Seating herself on the side of my bed, she watched me with an air of calm resignation while I read it. It was easy enough for her to be calm; it was different for me. I had arranged for four bridesmaids. Bertha Ellis was to be one; her cousin, Constance Farrer, was to be another. Bertha had had for some days what we had thought was a cold; during the night it had turned into measles—at her time of life, because she was as old as I was. And Constance had actually slept in the same bed with her. So, as Mrs Ellis had written to point out, it was altogether out of the question that either of them should be present at my wedding.

"Now," I demanded, "perhaps you will be so good as to tell me what I am to do."

"I suppose it would be too late to get anyone to take their places?"

"At the eleventh hour—practically at the church door? And who is to get into their dresses? They are both of them so ridiculously small."

"You would have them like that in order to make you look tall. It seems as if it were a judgment."

"How can you say such awful things? Why don't you suggest something?"

"The only thing I am able to suggest is that you should do without them and put up with Ellen and me.

"You know very well that I only asked Ellen Mackenzie because I knew that her mother was going to give me a diamond brooch—and now it's stolen. It's not alone that she's hideous, but she won't harmonise with me in the very least; and, anyhow, having only two bridesmaids will spoil everything."

"Then there's nothing for you to do except postpone the wedding, unless you know of some establishment where they hire out bridesmaids of all shapes and sizes on the shortest notice."

"If it were your wedding day I wouldn't talk to you so heartlessly. How can you be so unkind?"

"Pray, Maud, don't start crying. Red eyes and a red nose won't improve either your appearance or anything else. You are perfectly aware how your nose does go red on the slightest provocation."

Talk about the affection of an only sister! Mamma came in just as I felt like shaking Eveleen.

"Oh, mamma," I burst out, "Bertha Ellis has the measles, and Constance Farrer is almost sure to have them, so I shall be two bridesmaids short, and I had set my heart on having four."

Mamma was, if anything, less demonstrative in the way of sympathy even than Eveleen.

"Be so good, Maud, as not to excite yourself unnecessarily. You will have need of all your self-control before the day is over. Anything more unreasonable than your father's conduct I cannot imagine. He insists on going to the City."

At that both Eveleen and I jumped up.

"But, mamma, he's to give me away at half-past twelve!"

"That makes not the smallest difference to your father. It seems that there's some absurd foreign news which he says will turn that ridiculous City upside down, and he simply insists on going."

I was beginning to put some clothes on anyhow.

"Then he sha'n't!—I won't let him! Mamma, you mustn't let him!"

"It's all very well for you to say that, and goodness knows I have done my best; but you might as well talk to a wooden figure-head as to your father when he is in one of his moods. He's gone already."

"Gone! Mamma!"

"He said that if he was not back at twelve he would meet you at the church door at half-past; but you know how he may be relied upon to keep an appointment of that kind; especially as he went out of his way to inform me— not for the first time—that the whole business is a pack of rubbish."

There are fathers, no doubt, who take the tenderest interest in everything which concerns their children; especially when they have only two, and both of them are daughters. But if my father has any tenderness in him he manages to conceal the fact from the knowledge of his family. And as for interest, I doubt if he takes any real interest in either of us. When George was coming to the house about seven times a week mamma dropped a hint to papa to sound George as to what was the object of his dropping in so often. But papa could not be induced to take it.

"Don't you try to induce me to ask the man if he intends to make a fool of himself, because I won't do it." That was all that papa could be induced to say.

When, after all, without any prompting from anyone, George put to me the question on which hinged so much of my life's happiness, it was ever so long before anyone said a word about it to papa. As to referring George to him, as some daughters, more fortunately situated, might have done, I knew better. At last, one evening, when I was alone with him in the drawing-room after dinner, I managed to find courage enough to tell him.

"Papa, I think you ought to know that I am engaged to be married."

He looked up from the book which he was reading.

"What's that? Rubbish!"

He looked down again. It was a promising beginning.

"It may be rubbish, but it is a simple fact. I am engaged to be married."

"How old are you?"

"I should have thought you would have known my age. I was eighteen last birthday."

"In another ten years it will be time enough to think of nonsense of that sort."

"Ten years! I am going to be married in six weeks from to-day."

"Be so good as not to interrupt me when I'm reading with nonsensical observations of that kind."

That was the form my father's congratulations took. It may easily be imagined what trouble we had with him. He could not be brought to regard things seriously. It was not merely because he thought I was too young; if I had been fifty it would have been exactly the same. It was simply because he hated being bothered. And yet when, after repeated trials, it was driven home to his understanding that I was going to be married, and that George was a respectable person, he surprised me by the generosity which he all at once displayed. One morning, as he was leaving the breakfast-table to start for the City, he slipped a piece of paper into my hand.

"That's to buy clothes."

When I had looked at it, and saw it was a cheque, and the figures which were on it, I jumped up and ran after him into the hall, and kissed him.

"What's that for?" he demanded. I explained. Putting his hand on my shoulder he turned me towards the light and looked me up and down. Then he remarked, "Perhaps, after all, that young man's not such a fool as I thought him." It was the nearest approach to a compliment he had ever paid me.

What we had to endure from him on the great question of the wedding! His ideas on the subject were barbarian.

"Let us all go in a four-wheeler—we can put the young man on the box—and drive round the corner to the nearest registrar. It will all be done in a business-like manner inside ten minutes."

That was his notion of what a wedding ought to be. I need scarcely say that mine was entirely different. I had made up my mind to have a really pretty wedding. May Harvey had been married the year before. Hers was a pretty wedding; I had resolved that mine should be prettier still. Mamma, Eveleen and I arranged everything. By degrees we persuaded him, if not exactly to agree, then at least to wink at what was going to happen. On one point I was firm—that he should give me away. He promised that he would. But when he began to realise what a pretty wedding really meant he became restless and more and more trying, and he said the most horrid things. And now on the very day itself he had gone off to the City! If I could have relied on his returning at twelve, or even on his meeting me at the church at half-past, I should not have minded. But I was perfectly aware that if business was at all pressing he would think nothing of sending one of his clerks to take his place; on some absolutely essential matters I knew to my cost that he had not the slightest sense of propriety. As, however, all I could do was to hope for the best, there was nothing left but to appear resigned.

"I presume if my own father doesn't care enough about me to trouble himself to be present at my marriage it's not of the slightest consequence."

Just as I was about to sigh Eliza, the housemaid, appeared in the doorway, addressing mamma.

"If you please, ma'am, cook's going."

Mamma turned round to her with a start.

"Cook's going—where?"

"She's leaving the situation."

"Eliza! What do you mean?"

"If you please, ma'am, Mary and she have been having words about who it was left the drawing-room window open last night; and then Mary she said she believed as how it was cook's young man who broke in and stole Miss Maud's presents; and then cook, she said that after that she wouldn't stay with her in the same house not another minute; so she's gone upstairs to put her things together."

Off went mamma to interview cook. I turned to Eveleen, who was still sitting on the side of my bed with an air of complete unconcern, as if nothing whatever mattered. I always did say that she was almost too much like papa.

"It seems as if everything was going wrong—everything! Eveleen, what is the time?"

"Just past ten."

"Past ten! Has my dress come?" She shook her head with an air of the utmost nonchalance. If it had been her dress! "But Mme. Sylvia promised that I should have it before ten! And I've had no breakfast!"

"There is breakfast waiting for you downstairs."

"As if I wanted any breakfast! As if I could eat, feeling as I do! You know that I had arranged to commence dressing at ten! Eveleen, what am I to do?"

"You mean about the dress? It's only just past ten; it may come still."

"May come! Eveleen, do you want me to—to hit you? Eliza or someone must go at once and fetch it, finished or not."

"I daresay Eliza can go, if you think it necessary. If you take my advice you won't excite yourself."

"Won't excite myself! If it were your wedding and your dress you'd talk in a different strain."

"I should have made different arrangements."

"You would have made—" I bit my lip till it nearly bled; I had to do something to stop myself. "I know how nice you can be if you like; but I don't mean to quarrel with you, to-day of all days, if I can help it." As I was speaking Eliza reappeared in the doorway. "Eliza, I want you to get a hansom and to tell the man to drive you to Mme. Sylvia's as fast as he can. I'll give you a note to her. You're to bring my dress back with you. I'll write the note while you're putting on your hat. Do be as quick as you can."

"If you please, miss, Miss Mackenzie's downstairs."

A voice exclaimed behind Eliza,—

"Oh, no, she's not; she's here." There stood Ellen, in her bridesmaid's dress, all smiles. She came bustling into the room—in that bustling way she always has. "Well, my children, how are you? And how's the sweet young bride? You told me to be here by ten—ready dressed—and here I am. What do you think of it?" She turned and twisted herself about so as to show off her dress. "It's a bit tight under the arms and a shade loose in the back, but it's not so bad. Am I the first? Where are Bertha and Constance?"

I waved my hand towards Eveleen.

"Tell her—I can't!"

Eveleen told her everything, and I will say this for her, she made out things to be as bad as they very well could be. Ellen Mackenzie's face was a study. She is one of the plainest girls I know—her dress did not suit her at all; I knew it wouldn't; nothing ever does; and she seemed to grow plainer and plainer as she listened. But she was more sympathetic than any of my relations had been. She threw her arms round me, quite indifferent as to what might happen to her dress.

"You poor darling! To have had your presents stolen—and two bridesmaids down with the measles—and your father gone to that horrid City —and the servants quarrelling—and now no wedding-dress! As to that Mme. Sylvia, if I were in your place I should feel like wringing her neck."

"I shouldn't be surprised if I did wring it if my dress isn't ready by the time that Eliza gets there. Eliza, haven't you got your hat on?"

She had actually stood there looking on and listening, with her eyes and mouth wide open. But she was ready almost as soon as the note was—it was a note! And just as we had started her off, with strict injunctions to come back at once and bring the dress back with her, if she had to snatch it out of the dressmaker's hands, a person arrived who stated that he was a detective and had come to inquire into the burglary, and who insisted on seeing me. So we saw him all three of us together, and a most unpleasant interview it was. He asked me the most disagreeable questions, wanting to know what I valued the missing presents at, and how much they had cost, and if the jewellery was real, and unpleasant things of that sort. While we were in the very midst of it mamma came in in a state of painful excitement.

"Are you a policeman?" she demanded. "Because if you are I should like you to tell my cook and my parlourmaid that if they leave my house this day without giving me due and proper notice they will do so at their peril, and that I shall prosecute them both as sure as they are living." The detective stroked his chin and seemed disinclined to do as mamma desired. She went on, "My parlourmaid has been making the most unwarrantable accusations against my cook, in consequence of which she declares that she won't stay in the house another minute; and when I told my parlourmaid what I thought of her behaviour she announced that she should also go at once. They are both perfectly well aware that it is my daughter's wedding day, and that if they do go everything will be in a state of confusion; so I want you to speak to them and bring them to a proper sense of their duty."

The detective still seemed dubious.

"I am afraid, madam, that that sort of thing hardly comes within my jurisdiction. But if they are going I should like to ask them a few questions about this burglary before they leave the house."

Cook with her hat on, and Mary with hers in her hand, had been standing in the doorway all the while. Cook now came forward—battle in her eye; we always had had trouble with her temper.

"I'm quite ready to answer any questions that's put to me; but if anyone says a word against Mr Parsons, who's as honest and respectable a man as ever walked this earth, then I say they're liars."

Then came Mary, who, as we had all of us noticed, always had a way of hinting more than she actually said.

"What I say is true, and I'm not going to be frightened from speaking the truth by anyone. I say that Mr Parsons was hanging about this house last night till after twelve o'clock; and so he was."

There was a frightful scene. I believe, if the detective had not been present, that those two women would have attacked each other. When Eveleen and Ellen got me back into my own room my nerves were in such a state that I was trembling all over. It was past eleven. There were still no signs of Eliza or my dress. The carriage was to come to take me to the church at twelve; the wedding was to be at half-past; as we wanted to catch the afternoon train for Paris we had arranged to have it early. I was feeling both miserable and desperate, altogether different from what I had intended to feel.

"I shall go and fetch the dress myself," I said.

"Rather than you shall do that," exclaimed Eveleen, "I'll go myself." And she went, giving me a few words of advice before she departed. "Do control yourself, Maud, and don't give way. Everything will be all right if you keep calm. I promise to bring you your dress in twenty minutes, if I don't meet Eliza with it on the way."

It was all very well for her to talk about keeping calm, but I had reached a stage when something had to be done. So I threw myself on the bed and had a cry. Although Ellen did try to comfort me it was not the slightest use. Then, when she saw the state I was in, she started crying too. And while we were both of us at it in came mamma. She was almost in a worse condition than we were. Cook and Mary had both left, and the detective had gone without having done the slightest good, and everything was topsy-turvy. The refreshments for the reception which was to take place after the wedding were to come in from outside, and the waiters also; still, it was dreadful to be practically servantless. Mamma was in such a state of painful agitation that she almost drove me to hysterics. Then Jane, the kitchenmaid, came rushing in. Since Eliza had not yet returned, she was the only maid we had in the house.

"If you please, ma'am, the carriages have come."

"Carriages! What carriages?"

"To take Miss Maud and her bridesmaids to the wedding, ma'am."

"Wedding!" Mamma laughed; it was an awful sound. "Since it does not seem likely that there will be any wedding, it will hardly be worth their while to wait."

"Shall I tell them to go, ma'am?"

When the idiotic Jane asked that question I leapt right off the bed on to the floor.

"Mamma! Jane! How can you be so absurd?"

I was just going to give both of them a piece of my mind—because mamma's conduct really was ridiculous—when someone else came tearing up the staircase. It was Eveleen, followed by a smartly-dressed young woman carrying a large box—which I made a dash at—with Eliza in the rear.

"Here's your dress!" cried Eveleen.

The young woman began to explain.

"Mme. Sylvia sends her apologies, and hopes you will excuse her for having kept you waiting; but there has been an unavoidable delay owing to an unfortunate misunderstanding—"

Eveleen cut her short.

"We'll have the apologies and all that sort of thing afterwards. What you have to do, Maud, is to put on that dress in the shortest time on record, and let's hope it fits. You've been crying—so have you, mamma—and Ellen! You're three nice people. As for you, Ellen, nothing will get those marks off your face except clean water, and you'll have to wash."

Ellen's complexion takes a tremendous time; she uses all sorts of things for it, so that that was a bad blow for her. We all began to bustle. The young woman began to unpack the box, and I got quite ready to slip into the dress when it was unpacked. Suddenly there was an exclamation from Mme. Sylvia's assistant.

"My goodness! what is this?" She was holding up what looked as if it were some weird sort of a blouse made of all the colours of the rainbow; it was certainly not part of my wedding-dress. She stared and we stared. Then she dropped on to a chair with a groan. "There's been a mistake," she gasped. "In the hurry I've brought a dress which we have been making for Mrs Markham for a fancy-dress ball, and I'm afraid your dress has gone to her."

There are moments in life when, the worst having come to the worst, obviously the only thing left to do is to look it boldly in the face. I realised that one of those moments had come to me then. All hope was gone; nothing remained but to calmly face despair. I gave myself a sort of mental pinch, and walked quietly up to that young woman, feeling—and no doubt looking—almost dangerously cool. I picked up the parti-coloured garment, which was all that had been brought to me after all that strain and stress.

"This looks as if it might be some sort of fancy dress. Am I to understand that it is a fancy dress?"

I believe that that assistant was overawed by my manner.

"Yes; it's for one of our customers—a Mrs Markham—for a fancy-dress ball."

"And, pray, where is my wedding-dress?"

"I expect it has been sent to Mrs Markham in mistake for hers."

"And when may I rely on receiving it back from Mrs Markham?"

"Not before to-morrow, at the earliest; it has been put on a train at Euston —she lives in the North."

"Since I am to be married to-day, it will not be of much use to me to-morrow, will it? Put this article back in your box. Return it to Mme. Sylvia, and inform her, with my compliments, that she will hear from my solicitors. I should imagine that she will probably hear from Mrs Markham's solicitors also. Take Mrs Markham's fancy costume—and yourself—away as fast as you possibly can. Eveleen, I will be married in my going-away dress."

I have little doubt that they were all impressed by what, under the circumstances, seemed my almost preternatural calmness. Scarcely a word was spoken by anyone. Even mamma merely remarked that the assistants in Mme. Sylvia's establishment seemed to be as utter idiots as their principal; and that, for mamma, was nothing. I bundled her off to dress, and I made Eveleen and Ellen go too. I attired myself for my wedding, which was far from what I had intended to do. It had been arranged that I should be costumed by a sort of committee consisting of my four bridesmaids, with mamma acting as my supervisor. But since that arrangement had been made everything had been altered; and as now nothing remained but my going-away dress, I needed no assistance in putting on that. With a travelling costume a bridal veil seemed almost painfully out of place, so I resolved to do without that also. I wore a hat.

Just as I was putting the finishing touches to my hat there came a tapping at my bedroom door. When I cried, "Come in!" to my amazement who should enter but George's best man, Jack Bowles.

"Maud!" he exclaimed. "Whatever's up? Do you know it's nearly two, and George is almost off his head, and the parson's going to a funeral?"

I turned to him with what he has since assured me was the air of a tragedy queen.

"I am ready now. We will start at once."

He stared, as well he might.

"Like that?" he cried.

"Like this. You and I will drive to the church together, and I will explain everything to you as we go." I hurried with him down the staircase, calling to the others as I went; unseen, unnoticed, a quiver passed all over me as I recalled how, in the days gone by, with a prophetic eye, I had seen myself, a vision of snowy white, descend that staircase "with measured step and slow," surrounded by my bridesmaids. "Mamma, I'm going to drive to the church with Mr Bowles. You and Eveleen and Ellen had better follow in another carriage."

"My dear!" mamma's voice came back. "What do you mean? I'm not nearly ready yet."

"Maud!" Eveleen distinctly shouted.

But I waited for nothing; for no one. Hastening to a carriage with Mr Bowles, off we started. It was rather an invidious position; there had been passages with Mr Bowles which made my situation one of some delicacy. When George told me that he had asked him to be his best man, I felt that he was hardly the person I should have chosen for the part. However, I had not quite seen my way to acquaint him with the manner in which Mr Bowles had behaved at Mrs Miller's dance; to speak of nothing else. So there we were alone together perhaps for the last time in our lives. Possibly what had passed between us made him all the quicker to feel for me in the plight in which—as I explained to him—I found myself. He showed the most perfect sympathy. Even George could not have been nicer.

But, for me, disasters were not ended. I was to be the victim of another before the church was reached. It seems to me that motor cars are always doing something. As we were passing along the busiest part of the High Street one of them did something then. It skidded—or something—and took off one of our back wheels. Down dropped a corner of the brougham with a crash which sent me flying into Mr Bowles's arms. Presently, when, apparently uninjured, we found ourselves standing in the road, the centre of an interested and rapidly-increasing crowd, we realised that it might have been worse.

"The stars," I murmured, with a presence of mind which, now that I look back upon it, seems to have been really phenomenal, "are fighting against me in their courses."

"Poor old George," said Mr Bowles, who was always rather inclined to slang, "will be fairly off his nut."

All at once I espied papa coming along in a hansom cab. I called out to him. Stopping the cab he sprang out to us.

"What are you two doing here?" he demanded, in not unreasonable astonishment. Then he went on to offer exactly the kind of explanation I had expected. "Do you know, I've been so occupied that I quite overlooked the fact that I was due with you at half-past twelve. I hope it made no difference. Where's George?"

"He's at the church."

"At the church? What's he doing there?"

"He's waiting for me to come and be married."

"Waiting? How's that? Aren't you married already?"

"No; and—it—doesn't look—as if—I—ever—shall be."

"Jump into my hansom—you and Bowles—we'll soon see about that."

We jumped in, Mr Bowles and I, and we drove off to the church—to my wedding!—three in a hansom cab! If ever anyone had foretold that such a thing would—or could—have happened to me I should have expired on the spot.

When we reached the church—we did reach it!—we found that such of the people as remained were standing on the steps or in the doorway. George, who was nearly distracted, came rushing forward at the sight of me; the people actually cheered. It appeared that the clergyman—our vicar—who had been specially retained, had gone to a funeral; but a curate, of some sort, had been routed out from somewhere, and he performed the service. Just as it was begun in came mamma and Eveleen and Ellen. The instant it was over George and I tore off home, got my trunks—George himself helped to carry them—and rushed to Charing Cross just in time to catch the boat-train.

When it had started, and he and I were in a compartment alone together, I put my head on his shoulder and I cried—with joy. Everything had gone as wrong as it very well could have done; but we were married!

TWO OF A TRADE

"Fares, please!"

The omnibus conductor stood in front of a lady, young, and not ill-looking, and waited. As he waited he flicked his packet of tickets with the forefinger of his right hand. The lady addressed seemed to experience some difficulty in finding the sum required. She felt in a bag which was hanging at her waist. She dived into the recesses of a pocket which was apparently placed in an even more inaccessible position than a lady's pocket is wont to be. Without result. Her proceedings attracted the attention of all her fellow-passengers; and the 'bus was full;—indeed, her manœuvres were the cause of some inconvenience to her immediate neighbours. At last she delivered herself of a piece of information.

"I've lost my purse!"

The conducter eyed her stolidly. He was not so young as he had been. Possibly a long experience of 'bus conducting had brought him into intimate relations with ladies who did lose things; so that his sympathies were dulled.

"Lost your purse?"

He echoed her words as if the matter was not of the slightest interest to him.

"Yes;—that is, I had it when I came into the 'bus;—I'm afraid it has been stolen."

"Stolen?" echoed the conductor;—still with an air of complete indifference.

"Yes," said an old man, who was on the seat opposite, at the end farthest from the door; "and that man sitting by you is the man as took it."

Since Bruce Palliser was the only man sitting by her the allusion could only be to him. He turned on the speaker in surprise.

"Are you suggesting, sir, that I have stolen the lady's purse?"

"That's it; that's what I'm suggesting. Only it's more than a suggestion. I see you fumbling with the lady's skirt. I wondered what you was up to. Now I know."

A woman sitting on the other side of the purseless lady interposed.

"Here's a penny, if that's any good;—or, for the matter of that, here's twopence. It's not nice for any of us to be crowded in the same 'bus with parties who say they've had their purses stolen."

"I'm afraid it isn't," admitted the sufferer. "I'm very sorry, but—all my money was in my purse. If you would let me have a penny I should be very much obliged."

The penny was forthcoming.

"Do you make any charge?" inquired the conductor, as he handed over the ticket in exchange.

"No," rejoined the lady. "I do not."

"He's got it on him now," asserted the old gentleman in the corner. "If you'll hand him over to a policeman you'll find he has."

"I trust," exclaimed Mr Palliser, "that you'll afford me an opportunity to prove that what this person says is absolutely false."

The young lady stood up.

"Please stop the 'bus. I'm going to get out."

"You call a policeman," persisted the old gentleman. "You'll soon find where your purse is."

"But, madam!" cried Mr Palliser. The 'bus stopped. The young lady began to move towards the door. Bruce Palliser following, appealing to her as he did so. "Madam!—if you will give me your attention for a single instant!"

The young lady alighted. Mr Palliser alighted also. The 'bus went on.

"I see him take it," announced the old gentleman in the corner. "Put it in his pocket, I believe he did."

Bruce Palliser, standing in the roadway, tried to induce the young lady to give him a chance to establish his innocence.

"If you will permit me to explain who I am, I will make it quite clear to you—"

She cut him short.

"Have the kindness not to address me."

She climbed into a passing hansom. He had to spring to one side to avoid being cut down by a furniture van. By the time the van had gone the cab had gone also.

Later in the day he rushed into the station with just time enough to enable him to catch the train which was to take him home. He had already entered a compartment before he realised that a seat near the door was occupied by the young lady of the omnibus. The recognition was obviously mutual. Something in her attitude made him conscious of a ridiculous sense of discomfort. He felt that if he did not leave the carriage she would—although the train was about to start. Scrambling back on to the platform he was hustled into another compartment by an expostulating guard. When the train stopped at Market Hinton, and he got out, he observed that the young lady of the omnibus was emerging from the compartment from which he had retreated with so small a show of dignity. Apparently she also had reached her journey's end. He thought he knew most of the people who lived thereabouts, at least by sight. He had certainly never seen her before. Who could she be?

Stupidly enough he hung about the station, allowing himself to be buttonholed by an old countryman who was full of his sufferings from rheumatism—one of that large tribe with which every doctor is familiar, the members of which never lose a chance of obtaining medical advice for nothing. He was not in the best of tempers by the time that he reached home. Nor was his temper improved by the greeting which he received from Jack Griffiths, who had acted as his *locum* during his enforced absence in London.

"You're not looking any better for your change," declared Jack, who had an unfortunate—and exasperating—knack of seeing the pessimistic side of things. "You're looking all mops and brooms."

"I'm not feeling all mops and brooms—whatever state of feeling that may be. On the contrary, I'm feeling as fit as I ever felt in the whole of my life."

"Then you're not looking it; which is a pity. Because it's my opinion that you'll want all the stock of health you can lay your hands on if you're to continue to hold your own in Market Hinton."

"What might you happen to mean?—you old croaker!"

"It's easy to call me a croaker, sir, but facts are facts; and I tell you that that new doctor's making things hum—cutting the grass from under your very feet."

"What new doctor?"

"The new doctor. I wasn't aware that there was more than one. If there is then you're in greater luck even than I thought you were."

"Are you alluding to that female creature?"

"I am. I am alluding to Dr Constance Hughes, M.D. (London). Mrs Vickers is of opinion that she's a first-rate doctor."

"Mrs Vickers!—Why, she's one of my oldest patients."

"Precisely; which is perhaps one reason why she feels disposed to try a change. Anyhow she called Dr Constance Hughes in one day, when that medical lady happened to be passing; and I'm inclined to think that, if she could only see her way, she'd like to call her in again."

"Pretty unprofessional conduct! What does the woman mean by it?"

"Which woman? Dr Constance Hughes? She's nothing to do with it. She had to go in when they stopped her on the high road; but, from what I understand, when she learnt that Mrs Vickers was your patient she declined to call again. Than her conduct nothing could have been more professional. But it isn't only Mrs Vickers. I hear golden opinions of her on every side. And she drives some of the finest horses I ever saw."

"So I've been told. Thank goodness, so far I've seen neither the woman nor her horses; but if half they say is true, she knows more of horse flesh than of medicine."

"Then, in that case, she must be a dabster. Heaps of money, I'm informed; taken up the profession simply for the sake of something to do, and because she loves it. Bruce, Dr Constance Hughes is going to be a dangerous rival!"

Such, ere long, was to be Bruce Palliser's own opinion.

When, the following afternoon, he returned from his rounds, he learned that an urgent summons had come for him, earlier in the day, from Mrs Daubeny, one of his most influential patients. He hurried round to her. On his arrival at the house the maid who opened the door informed him that the other doctor was upstairs. As he had not come, and Mrs Daubeny was in such pain, they had sent for other assistance. While she was speaking, the maid conducted him upstairs. Opening a door, she ushered him in, announcing his appearance.

"Dr Palliser."

He found himself in a bedroom, with someone lying in the bed, and two women standing on either side of it. One of the women he recognised as Foster, Mrs Daubeny's housekeeper; and the other—as the lady of the omnibus. He stared at her in blank amazement. Although she had her hat on, her sleeves were turned up, and she was holding in her hand what he perceived to be a clinical thermometer. Foster went—awkwardly enough—through a form of introduction.

"Oh, Dr Palliser, I'm so glad you've come! This is Miss Hughes—I mean Dr Hughes. Mrs Daubeny has been so bad that if she hadn't come I don't know what we should have done."

Mr Palliser bowed; so stiffly that the inclination of his head only just amounted to a movement. The lady was as stiff. Although she looked him full in the face there was that in the quality of her glance which almost hinted that she did not notice he was there. She explained the position, in a tone of voice which could hardly have been more frigid.

"Mrs Daubeny has had an attack of acute laryngitis, rather a severe one. Fortunately, however, the worst is over; unless, that is, it should recur."

"I am obliged to you. I have had the honour to treat Mrs Daubeny on former occasions. I will see that all is done that is necessary."

The lady returned her thermometer to its case. She turned down her sleeves. She donned a sable jacket which Mr Palliser could not but feel was not unbecoming. With the curtest possible nod to the newcomer she quitted the room.

At his solitary meal that night, the more Bruce Palliser turned matters over in his mind the less he liked them.

"This is a nice kettle of fish! To think of her being Dr Constance Hughes! For all I know she may actually be of opinion that it was I who stole her purse —as that lying old scoundrel asserted—I should like to wring his neck! She wouldn't condescend to even give me a hearing; the vixen! She has a first-rate tale to tell against me, anyhow. Why, if she chooses to tell everyone that someone stole her purse, and that there was a man in the omnibus who declared he saw me take it, I sha'n't even be able to bring an action for slander; the thing is true enough. I ought to have dragged that old ruffian out by the hair of his head, and made him own then and there that he lied. I've half a mind to write to her and insist on her giving me an opportunity to explain. But she wouldn't do it; she's that kind of woman. I know it! I could see by the way she treated me this afternoon that she means to get her knife into me—and well in, too. A male rival is bad enough—I've had one or two passages-of-arms with old Harford—but a female—and such a female! I may as well announce my practice for sale while there's any of it left to sell. That woman won't leave a stone unturned to ruin me!"

During the next few days he was destined to hear more of Dr Constance Hughes than he cared for. She seemed to have impressed other people a good deal more favourably than she had him. Market Hinton is in the centre of a hunting country. The fact that she had quite a string of first-rate horses, and that she could handle the "ribbons" as well as any coachman, and had an excellent seat in a saddle, appealed to the local imagination in an especial degree. To be a "good sportsman" meant much at Market Hinton; of anyone who reached that high standard they could think no evil. Bruce Palliser found that, because Dr Constance Hughes had hunters who, with her on them, could hold their own in any country, and in any company, people were taking it for granted that her medical qualifications must necessarily be unimpeachable.

Old Rawlins, of "The King's Head," put the case in a nutshell.

"She drives a mare that would win a prize at any show in England; and it does you good to see the way she drives her. That mare wants some driving! I say that a woman who can handle a horse like she can handle that mare ought to be able to handle anything. She shall have the handling of Mrs Rawlins the next time she's ill; I'll have her sent for."

Bruce Palliser was to make the close acquaintance of the mare in question before very long, and in a fashion which did not tend to give him such a high opinion of the creature as Mr Rawlins possessed.

Just as he was preparing for dinner a call came to a patient who lived the other side of the town. His stable only contained one horse, and that had already done a good day's work. Taking out his bicycle he proceeded to the patient's house on that. He was not detained long. Glancing at his watch as he was about to return he perceived that if he made haste he would not be so very late for dinner after all, and would have a chance of getting something to eat before everything was spoiled. So he bowled along at a pace which was considerably above the legal limit. It was bright moonlight. Until he reached Woodcroft, the residence of Dr Constance Hughes, he had the road practically all to himself.

Woodcroft was a corner house. As he neared it he became suddenly conscience that a vehicle was coming along the road which bounded it on one side. As he came to the corner the vehicle swept round it. He had just time to see that it was a high dog-cart, and that Dr Constance Hughes was driving. For some reason the discovery caused him to lose his head. Forgetting that he was riding a free wheel, instead of jamming on the brakes he tried to back pedal. Before he had realised his mistake he was under the horse's hoofs, and the dog-cart had passed right over him.

Mr Palliser was conscious that the startled animal first reared, then bolted —or rather, tried to. Fortunately her master sat behind her in the shape of her mistress. Not only was she brought to a standstill, but, in less than half a minute, Dr Constance Hughes had descended from the dog-cart, and was kneeling at Mr Palliser's side.

Her first remark was scarcely sympathetic.

"You ought to have rung your bell," she said.

"I hadn't a bell to ring," he retorted.

"Then you never ought to come out without one, as you're very well aware. What's wrong?"

"Nothing's wrong."

He proved that there was nothing wrong by quietly fainting in the middle of the road.

"What's up?" was the first remark which he made when he returned to consciousness. "What's happened? Where am I? What on earth—"

He stopped, to groan with pain, and to recognise the futility of an attempt to sit upright. He lay still, looking about him with wide-open eyes. He was in bed—not his own, but someone else's. And in someone else's room; one, moreover, which was strange to him. On one side stood Dr Constance Hughes; behind her was that very general practitioner and ancient rival— Joseph Harford. It was the lady who replied.

"As to where you are, you're in my house. And you've come back to your senses just in time to let us know if you would like your leg cut off."

"My leg?"

"I said your leg. At present it's a question of that only. It may be necessary to proceed further later on."

"What do you mean?"

Bruce Palliser was conscious that his right leg was subjecting him to so much agony that beads of sweat stood on his brow.

"Compound fracture. Tibia and peroneal both broken. Mr Harford is of opinion that the only thing is to amputate at once."

"Is he? I'm much obliged."

"I say no."

"Do you?"

"I do. I say they can be set, being of opinion that it's worth while risking something on the off chance of being able to save your leg, since it's better to go about with two than one."

Mr Harford shook his head.

"I've had my say; having done so I wash my hands of all responsibility. If we amputate at once your life will not be endangered. If there is any postponement we may not be able to operate at all; you may lose your life and your leg."

"That is your opinion?"

"It is—emphatically."

"Then I'll keep my leg. Set it." He closed his eyes, he had to, the pain just then was so exquisite. Presently he opened them again to address the lady pointedly. "*You* set it."

"I intend to. Would you like an anæsthetic? It won't be pleasant."

"No."

"Then grit your teeth. I'll be as quick as I can; but I'm afraid you'll have a pretty bad time."

He gritted his teeth, and he had a pretty bad time. But through it all he recognised that the work was being done by a workman, with skill and judgment, with as much delicacy also as the thing permitted. He had not thought that such a slip of a girl could have had such strength or courage. When the task was over she gave what sounded like a gratified sigh.

"That's done. You've behaved like a man."

"And you're a surgeon born."

That was all he could mutter. Then he swooned, unconsciousness supervened; he had come to the end of his tether.

The bad time continued longer than he cared to count. The days slipped by, and still he lay in that bed. One morning he asked her,—

"How's it going?"

"As well as can be expected; better perhaps. But this is not going to be a five minutes' job—you know better than that?"

"I ought to have let old Harford cut it off; I should have made a quicker recovery."

"Nonsense. In that case you would never, in the real sense of the word, have recovered at all. Now there's every probability of your being as sound as ever. You only want time. There's no inflammation; the wound keeps perfectly sweet. You've a fine physique; you've lived cleanly. I counted upon these things when I took the chances."

Two days afterwards he broached another matter.

"You know I can't stop here. I'm putting you to tremendous expense, and no end of inconvenience. The idea's monstrous. I'm ashamed of myself for having stopped so long. You must have me put into the ambulance at once and carted home."

"You will stay where you are. I'm in charge of this case. I decline to allow you to be moved."

"But—!"

"But me no buts. As your medical adviser I refuse to permit of any interference. In such a matter you of all persons ought to set a good example."

He was silent. Not only was he helpless and too weak for argument, but there was in her manner an air of peremptory authority before which he positively quailed. Yet, the next day, he returned to the attack.

"I don't want there to be any misunderstanding between us, so please realise that I'm quite aware that the accident was entirely my fault, that you were in no way to blame, and that therefore you are not in any sense responsible for my present position."

"I know that as well as you do. You ought to have had a bell; no bicyclist ought to be without a bell, especially at night. I did not hear you coming, but you heard me; yet you ran right into me although you heard."

"I lost my head."

"You lost something.

"Therefore I wish to emphasise the fact that I have not the slightest right to encroach upon your hospitality, or your time, or your services."

"Does that mean that you would rather dispense with the latter? Or are you merely again trying to display a refractory spirit?"

"I'm not doing anything of the kind. I simply don't wish to take advantage of your—your generosity."

"Generosity? My good sir, you are mistaken. Yours is an interesting case. I flatter myself that not everybody could have saved that leg of yours. You know how seldom one gets an interesting case at Market Hinton; I mean to make the best of this one now I've got it. You'll regard this as a hospital. And you'll stay in it, as patiently as your nature permits, until, in due course, you receive your discharge."

There was silence. He watched her while she adjusted fresh bandages. He thought that he had never seen work of the kind more deftly done. As she bent over him he noticed what a dainty profile she had, and what beautiful hands. Presently he spoke again.

"Miss Hughes—"

"Dr Hughes, if you please. I didn't proceed to my M.D. degree for nothing."

"I beg your pardon. Dr Hughes, what has become of my patients while I've been lying here?"

"I've been taking them. Do you object?"

"Object! Indeed, no; only—I'm afraid—"

He stopped.

"Yes? What are you afraid of?"

"Nothing; that is—I hardly know how you'll take it."

"What are you afraid of?"

"Only that, when they've once tried you, they won't care to return to me."

"That's it, is it? I thought so. Do you take me to be that kind of person? I'm extremely obliged."

"You're quite mistaken. I didn't mean it in that way at all, as you know. I meant it for a clumsy compliment."

"It's a kind of clumsy compliment I don't care about, thank you very much."

"But, professionally, you are infinitely cleverer than I am."

"Professionally, I am nothing of the kind. It's not fair of you to laugh at me. Wherever I go people tell me how skilful you are, especially those who know. Besides, you need have no fear of illegitimate competition. It is not likely that I shall remain in Market Hinton."

He started.

"You are not going away?"

"I am, most probably. I only came here as an experiment; from my point of view it is an experiment which has failed."

He was still, to speak again after another interval. A more serious note was in his speech.

"Dr Hughes, when that man in the omnibus said I had stolen your purse, did you believe him?"

"I did not."

"Not for an instant?"

"Not for a single instant. And that for the best of reasons; my purse had not been stolen. I could have bitten my tongue off directly I had allowed myself to hint that it might have been; because it instantly occurred to me that it was well within the range of possibility that I had left it behind me at a shop at which I had been making some purchases. I drove straight back to the shop, and there it was."

"Why didn't you allow me to explain?"

"There was nothing for you to explain. As a matter of fact the explanation would have had to come from me, and I was in too bad a temper for that. Women have a reputation for making spectacles of themselves in that particular fashion; it didn't please me to think that I'd fallen in line with my sisters." She added, after a pause: "You've no notion what a vile temper I have."

"I doubt if it's such a very bad one."

"You doubt? You don't! You, of all people, ought to know what kind of temper I've got."

He smiled enigmatically.

"I do."

It was some time afterwards, when he had advanced to the dignity of an easy-chair and a leg-rest, that some of the points of that conversation were touched on again. It was he who began.

"Dr Hughes."

"*Doctor* Palliser?"

The emphasis which she laid upon the "Doctor" was most pronounced.

"Pardon me, I am not a doctor, I am a mere F.R.C.S."

"Is it necessary that you should always 'Doctor' me?"

"Pardon me again. I remember an occasion when you went a little out of your way to make it plain to me that you had not proceeded to your M.D. degree for nothing."

"You needn't always flaunt that in my face."

"I won't, since you appear to have changed your mind—until you change it again." She looked at him, with a gleam in her eyes which was half laughter, half something else. He went on: "At the same time, since what I have to say to you is strictly professional, I don't think that, on this occasion, the 'Doctor' Hughes will be out of place. You once said to me that you had some vague intention of not remaining in Market Hinton."

"It wasn't a vague intention then; it is less vague now. I am going."

"That is a pity."

"Why? It will be all the better for you; one competitor less."

"I am afraid I don't see it altogether in that light. You see, I was thinking of taking a partner."

"A partner?"

"Exactly, a partner. The practice was getting a little beyond me. When I am able to move about again, as I soon shall be, thanks to you, it may get beyond me again. Now what would you say to taking a partner?"

"I! What! Bring another woman here?"

"No, I was not thinking of that. Indeed, I was not thinking of a woman at all. I was thinking of a man."

"A man!"

"I was thinking of myself."

"You! Mr Palliser!"

"Why shouldn't we—you and I—be partners? Miss Hughes—Dr Constance"—suddenly, as he went on she looked down—"don't you think that it is possible that we might work together? That an arrangement might be made which—would be agreeable to us both?"

"Of course—there is always a possibility."

"Don't you think that, in this instance, there's a probability?"

"There might be."

"Don't you feel that such an arrangement would be, from all possible points of view, a desirable one? I do; I feel it strongly."

"Do you?"

"Don't you?" She was silent; so he continued, "I'd give all I have in the world, all I hope to have, to hear you say that you'd like us to be partners."

She looked up at him.

"I'd like to have—you for a partner," she said.

REWARDED

I

"Am I altered?"

She was, and yet was not. In one sense, not so much as he had expected. In another sense, more. Or was the alteration in himself? Mr Ferguson was conscious of a curious qualm as he recognised that at least the thing was possible.

He had told himself, over and over again, not only that he was not a romantic man, but that there was no romance about the story. He had loved Helen Sinclair when he was scarcely more than a boy, and when she was, certainly, nothing but a girl. Sir Matthew Griswold had come her way, and—well—she had married him. How much her mother had had to do with the match, and how much she herself had had to do with it, was a matter Mr Ferguson never could determine. Griswold was scarcely more than half an Englishman. His mother had left him large estates in South America. To those estates he had departed with his wife. On those estates for eighteen—or was it nineteen?—years Lady Griswold had practically resided.

If Mr Ferguson was broken-hearted when his love forsook him, he concealed the fact with admirable ability. Indeed, it is an open question whether, very soon, he did not tell himself that it was just as well. A poor wife, possibly any sort of wife, might have proved a drag on his career. For he had a career. And, in a certain way, he had succeeded in that career to quite a remarkable extent. He was M.P. for the Culmshire Boroughs. He had made a name in literature. Literature, that is, of a kind. Not light and fanciful, but matter-of-fact and solid. He was, in fact, that wholly indescribable personage, a promising politician. He was beginning to feel, and possibly others were beginning to feel as well, that there was only one thing needed to enable him to turn the promise into fulfilment. That thing was money. He was not, in a positive sense, a poor man. In a relative sense, he was. He was very far from being as rich as he felt that he ought to be if he was ever to occupy that position in politics which he would like to occupy.

Helen Sinclair had sent him a little note when her marriage with Sir

Matthew was finally arranged. Mr Ferguson had not replied to it. She had particularly desired that he would not reply. After that there had been no communication between them for years. Mr Ferguson, of course, was aware that Lady Griswold was still alive. The Griswolds were sufficiently important personages in English society to be heard of now and then, even from that remote portion of the world, from an English social point of view, in which they chose to dwell.

One day a certain young friend of Mr Ferguson's made up his mind to travel in South America. He came and asked Mr Ferguson if he could make him known to any persons "over there." The request was, geographically, rather vaguely worded, but Mr Ferguson, smiling to himself as he wrote, gave him a note of introduction to Lady Griswold, in case he should get, say, within a hundred miles of her. That young man got within a hundred miles of her. He made a long sojourn with the Griswolds. They made much of him. Lady Griswold even went so far as to write and thank Mr Ferguson for having thought of her. Mr Ferguson replied to her letter. The lady replied again. And so, between them, there grew up a curious correspondence, a correspondence which, if they had only known it, was in its way pathetic. Perhaps, after a fashion of their own, they did recognise the pathos of the thing. Then Sir Matthew died. He was thirty years older than his wife. The widow, in her distress, wrote to Ronald—Mr Ferguson was once more "Ronald" to her—in her grief. And, in soothing her sorrow, Mr Ferguson had dropped a hint. When he wrote again he dropped another hint. And then another, and another, and another. By degrees the widow began to take the hints. The end of it was, that, after many years of exile, Lady Griswold had come home.

Mr Ferguson understood quite well that it was because of those hints which he had dropped that Lady Griswold had come home. He had not written one plain word. Nothing which she would be able to fasten on and say, "Did you not write this, or that, and so deceive me?" His political training had tended to develop the bump of caution which he had originally possessed. "Non-committal" was the watchword for him. He was unwilling to commit himself to any person, in any way, on any subject whatsoever. Experience had taught him, or had seemed to teach him, that that was the safest policy. But he certainly had dropped those hints. And, as it appeared to him, with cause.

It is true enough that, since he was left forlorn, he had never thought of marriage. Never once, until Sir Matthew died. He had discovered, with an old sensation of surprise, that he had still a tenderness for his boyhood's love. Though until he saw Lady Griswold's handwriting—she wrote the same hand which she had written as a girl—he had been unaware of the fact during all these years. That young man had sent Mr Ferguson a glowing account of his sojourn with the Griswolds. According to him, Lady Griswold was the most charming woman in the world. And so young. The traveller protested that she scarcely looked as if she were more than twenty. Even allowing for the natural exaggeration of grateful youth, this sounded well. In her letters Lady Griswold had herself declared that she felt young. She only had one child, a girl. That young man scarcely spoke of the girl. Lady Griswold alluded to her rarely. When Mr Ferguson heard that Sir Matthew had divided his vast possessions equally between his wife and his daughter, and that the widow was free to do with her portion exactly what she pleased, his heart actually throbbed a little faster in his breast. Here was the wealth he needed to make his standing sure. It was then he dropped a more decisive hint than any other of the hints which he had dropped, the hint which had induced Lady Griswold to come home.

She had told him that he was not to meet her on her arrival in her native land. She would let him know when he was to call on her in town. She had let him know. He had waited on her command. He had been conscious of a slight internal fluttering as he came up the stairs. Now he held her by the hand.

"Am I altered?"

It was when she asked that question that Mr Ferguson had been made aware of that curious qualm. She had not altered anything like so much as might reasonably have been expected. She showed not the slightest sign of having lived in such a very trying climate. She was, perhaps, a little filled out. Perhaps a little more stately. There was about her the certain something which so distinctly divides the woman from the girl. But there was not a wrinkle on her face. Not a line of sorrow or of care. She looked at him, too, with the eyes of a girl; she certainly looked very much more like twenty-six than thirty-six. And yet!—

And yet, what? It is rather difficult to put the matter into words. The truth is, that as he stood in front of her, holding her hand in his, looking into her eyes, he felt an absolute conviction that this was not the sort of woman that he cared for. That this was not the sort of woman that he ever could care for now. But he could not tell her so. Just as little could he leave her inquiry unanswered.

"No, I do not think that you have altered."

Her womanly perception was not to be deceived.

"You are saying that to please me. I see you do think that I have altered."

"I think that you have grown younger."

"Ronald!"

She dropped her eyes, as a young girl might drop her eyes on receiving her first compliment. The blood showed through her cheeks. He felt that she expected him to say something else. But he could not say it.

"And me—what do you think of the changes which have taken place in me?"

She looked up at him shyly, with a shyness which he found curiously embarrassing.

"You are just what I expected you would be. See here."

Taking him by the hand she led him to a table. On the table lay a photographic album. The album was of considerable size. It seemed to be full of photographs. She opened it.

"See," she said, "I have them all. At least, I think I have them all."

The album contained nothing but photographs of Mr Ferguson. He filled it from cover to cover. When he perceived this was so, he was tongue-tied. He felt, almost, as if he were some guilty thing. She went on,—

"I made arrangements with someone over here—he is in a news agency, or something. I told him to find out whenever you were photographed and to send me copies. So you see that I have been able to follow the changes which have taken place in you from year to year."

He said nothing. He could say nothing. He could only turn over the leaves of that photographic album.

"But I not only have your photographs, I have every speech you ever made. I have read them over and over again. I believe I know some of them by heart. I have everything you ever wrote. I have records of you which will surprise you, one day, when you see them, Ronald." She paused. Then added, half beneath her breath: "And you? Did you take any interest in me?"

"Were not my letters proofs of that?"

"Yes, indeed! Ah, Ronald, if it had not been for you I should never have come home."

He was startled.

"But what was there to keep you out of England now?"

"Nothing, only you. I always told myself that I never would come back unless you wrote and said you wished me to."

He was silent for a second, oddly silent. It was with an effort that he seemed to speak.

"You take my breath away."

"Do I?" she laughed. "Ronald, instead of being eighteen years, it does not seem to me as if it were eighteen days since we were parted." Not eighteen days! It seemed to him as if it had been eighteen hundred years and more. "I want to tell you all about it. I always said to myself that I would tell you all about it the very first time I saw you, if I had to tell you on my bended knees."

"What is there to tell?"

"What is there not to tell! Now sit down and listen."

He had to sit beside her on a couch, and he had to listen. He did not know how to help it. He would have given something to have known. He felt that between himself and this woman there was a great gulf fixed. While she—she seemed to be so happy in his presence as to be unconscious that anything was wrong. She seemed to be unconscious that there was a single jarring note which marred the perfect harmony.

"Ronald, do you remember Major Pettifer?"

Pettifer! The mere mention of the name brought back to him the long passage of the years. Why, Pettifer had been dead these dozen years and more. He told her so.

"Has he? Well, it was owing to Major Pettifer that I married Sir Matthew Griswold."

"Owing to Pettifer? How do you mean?"

"He came down with you one day to mother's. At that time mother was worrying me to marry Sir Matthew, and Sir Matthew himself was worrying me even worse than mother. Between them I was nearly driven out of my mind. I chanced to be passing an open window when I overheard a remark which Major Pettifer addressed to you. 'To you,' he said, 'marrying a poor girl means ruin.' 'Well,' you answered, 'it shall mean ruin.' Your words struck me as with a sudden light of revelation. I made up my mind upon the instant. I told myself that if marrying a poor girl did mean ruin, then a poor girl you should not marry. Sir Matthew seemed even older than he was. My mother had told me, with her own lips, that it was quite possible that he would not live a year. I knew all through that you never would marry anyone but me. I knew you, Ronald! Even supposing Sir Matthew lived two years—then I should not be poor. You would not be ruined by mating yourself with poverty."

She was silent. And he was silent. This was far worse than he could possibly have expected.

"Do you mean to say that you married Griswold because of some chance words which you heard Pettifer address to me, a mere fragment of a conversation to which you did not even possess the key?"

"I do. I simply made up my mind that you should not be ruined by marrying me, even though, for love of me, you courted ruin. I resolved that when I became your wife, in every possible sense of the word I would bring you fortune."

"But during eighteen years of married life have you had no sort of compensation?"

"I have had the compensation of looking forward, the compensation of expecting this."

What *could* he say to her? He vowed that never again would he commit himself even to the extent of dropping a hint. He ought to have better learnt the lesson which had been taught him on many and many a platform.

"You have had children."

"One child—a girl."

"Was she no compensation?"

"Really, I can hardly tell you. I seem to have seen so little of her; though, of course, she has been with me nearly all the time. But, somehow, to myself, I never seem yet to have become a mother."

"How old is she?"

"Let me see, she was born the year that I was married, so she must be nearly eighteen. Frankly, Inez is so different to me in all respects that she never seems to me to be my daughter. Here she is." If Lady Griswold did not welcome the opening door, which was possible, she allowed no sign of annoyance to escape her. "Inez, this is Mr Ferguson."

Mr Ferguson stood staring, as if spellbound, at the girl who had entered the room. He felt more than half inclined to rub his eyes. It was an extraordinary thing. This big-eyed girl, who was so unlike the fair and stately Lady Griswold that she might almost have belonged to a different race of human beings, he seemed to have seen many and many a time in his dreams. He who flattered himself that he was no dreamer. Her appearance was so familiar to him that he could have drawn her likeness even before she entered the room. It was odd. It was even preposterous. Yet it was so. She advanced with outstretched hand. Even her soft, musical voice, with its faint suggestion of a foreign accent, seemed familiar to him.

"Mr Ferguson, I have seen you before."

"You have seen me, Miss Griswold? Where?"

"In my dreams."

Her mother interposed.

"In your dreams? Inez, don't be so silly! What do you mean?"

"I mean what I say." She turned to Mr Ferguson. "In your dreams, have you not seen me?"

Mr Ferguson hardly knew what to make of her, or of himself.

"It is an extraordinary thing, but I do seem to have seen you in my dreams, many and many a time."

"It was not seeming. It was reality. We have seen each other in our dreams."

"Inez! Mr Ferguson, let me show you some photographs of our home in South America." She led Mr Ferguson towards a table on which there was a large portfolio. As they went, she whispered, "Ronald, I sometimes really think that Inez is a little mad."

Mr Ferguson answered her never a word. For in an instant of time, in the flashing of an eye, something seemed to have come into his life which had never come into it before. For one thing, there had come into his life the real presence of the ideal woman of his dreams.

II

"I think that I have earned him, Marian!"

Mrs Glover, putting up her glasses, surveyed Lady Griswold through them quizzically.

"Earned him? You have earned him, over and over again, a hundred thousand times, my dear."

Lady Griswold positively blushed with pleasure.

"Do you really think so? Do you really think that he will think so too? To look at me you would not think I was romantic, but I suppose I am."

"If there is a more romantic creature at present existing in the world I should like to meet her, or rather, I am almost tempted to say I shouldn't. Are you sure that after all your romance will end well?"

"Sure?" Lady Griswold seemed surprised. "How do you mean?"

"Are you sure that this Mr Ferguson of yours will adequately reward you for your eighteen years of—what shall I say?—servitude or waiting?"

Lady Griswold dropped her eyes in that girlish way she had. Her fingers trifled with a fold in the skirt of her dress.

"You do not know him."

"I fancied that I did. I assure you I hear enough of him from Mr Glover. Mr Glover seems to think that some fine day Mr Ferguson is going to save the country."

"I have no doubt that he will, when there is need of him. I mean that you do not know him as—I know him. He will adequately reward me for—oh, for more than I have done."

"Indeed." There was an odd smile about the visitor's lips. "He seems to be very much struck with that girl of yours."

"With Inez? He is good to her for my sake. I know what he suffers, because, you see, she is so different from me in all respects. But it is like him, to suffer for me."

"Frankly, Helen, is there a definite engagement between you?"

"Well, Marian, you are trying to dig deeper into my secrets than I quite bargained for. But I don't mind telling you that it was he who asked me to come home."

"He asked you to come home, did he? Did he ask you to come home to be his wife?"

Lady Griswold's cheeks went flaming red.

"Marian, I will tell you nothing else than this, that I am the happiest woman in the world."

There was an odd smile about the visitor's lips.

"You are at least the funniest woman in the world, my dear. It appears to me that you have devoted one portion of your life to the pursuit of one chimera. I only hope that you are not going to devote the remaining portion to the pursuit of another."

"A chimera! Do you call Ronald a chimera?" Lady Griswold laughed. "I will tell Ronald that you called him a chimera."

Mrs Glover rose to go.

"You may tell him that I called him what you please. I don't think he is likely to care for what I may call him. He has been called too many things in his time to be super-sensitive. Mr Ferguson was born hard. The life he has lived has made him one of the hardest men I know. I am not saying it at all as a reproach, my dear; it seems to me that coming statesmen have to be hard, but it is so."

"My dear Marian, you don't know Ronald. He may seem hard outwardly. Inwardly, it only requires a touch to turn him into a naming fiery furnace."

Lady Griswold stated the truth more exactly than, for an instant, she imagined. Mrs Glover would not allow that it was the truth.

"You really are the funniest woman, my dear Helen. If Mr Ferguson's temperature ever gets to summer heat he will be in danger of—well, cracking. But never mind that. All's well that ends well. I only hope that it will all end well with you, my dear."

"All end well!" Lady Griswold told herself, when her visitor had gone. "She only hopes that it will all end well with me. As though it could end any other way but well! Foolish Marian! These women of the world have not, in their keeping, all the wisdom. Their besetting weakness is that they are so apt to measure other people's corn with their own bushels."

There was a photograph frame, fastened with a clasp, on the table at which she was standing. She unclasped it. It contained the usual photograph of Mr Ferguson, the very latest.

"Ronald, she does not know you, she says that you are hard. My Ronald!" She pressed her lips against the pictured lips in the pictured face. "How often I have kissed your effigy! When—" she was actually trembling—"when shall I kiss your living lips instead?" Laying the photograph down upon the table, she covered her face with her hands. "When, when? How often have I cried for you in the dead of the night, and—and yearned to hold you in my arms!"

She seemed to be positively crying. She was crying, there was not a doubt of it. Removing her hands from before her flaming face, with her handkerchief she dried the tears which stood in her smarting eyes.

"I think, as Marian says, that I have earned you. I have waited for you eighteen years. You must not make me wait much longer. I will not let you, Ronald. When one has loved, for eighteen years, as I have loved, one's love— one's love becomes—too much for one." She looked down as if, although she was alone, she was ashamed. "I wonder if it was the climate, or whether it is I. I think—I think that it is I. Love with me is not, I think, an affair of climate." She stretched out her arms in front of her with a strange gesture of strange passion. "I think that I am made for love! Ronald, I am made for love! That day of which, almost in my madness, I have dreamed, that day for which I have waited eighteen years, that day when you shall take me in your arms, I shall go mad—with joy—that joy which follows after waiting. Ronald! Ronald!"

Again she put her hands before her face. She trembled as with fever. She began to pace, feverishly, about the room.

"I wonder what he is waiting for? I wonder if he thinks it is too soon? Too soon! Too soon! If he thinks it is too soon, I, even I, I myself, will show him if it is too soon. Ronald! Ronald!"

Even while the name was still upon her lips a servant was standing with the handle of the open door in his hand, announcing,—

"Mr Ferguson!"

And Mr Ferguson came in.

As Lady Griswold turned to greet him, one could not but feel that she was beautiful. Beautiful with the beauty which is the crowning beauty of all beauty in the eyes of many men. The beauty of the beautiful woman who is in the full, rich, ripe glory of her summer's prime. She advanced to him with both her hands held out.

"Ronald!"

There was a look of welcome on her face, and in her eyes and about her lips, and, as it seemed, in every curve and outline of her body, for which some men, to have had it appear for them, would nave given a good slice of their possessions. But Mr Ferguson seemed, positively, as if he would rather that it had not been there.

He seemed reluctant, even, to yield her one of his hands in exchange for both of hers.

"Lady Griswold—"

"Lady Griswold! Why do you call me Lady Griswold? Call me Helen! Am I not Helen?"

He was silent. To himself he said,—

"It is going to be more difficult even than I fancied. After all, I almost wish that I had written. Bah! I am a coward! Better to face it once and for all."

Then, to her, "Lady Griswold, who *once* was Helen." Before she could interpose, he added, "There is something I wish particularly to say to you."

"To me?" She caught her breath. "Ronald! What is it?"

He saw she caught her breath. It made him awkward. He began to blunder,—

"I trust that what I am about to say to you will not—cause you to feel annoyed."

"Annoyed! As though anything which you could say to me could cause me to feel annoyed! Ronald, how little you know me after all."

He wished to Heaven that she knew him better.

"I can only hope that, when you have heard me out, you will not think that I have, in any way, misled you."

"Misled me! As though you had misled me, as though you could mislead me—Ronald."

Mr Ferguson was a cool and a courageous man. But his courage almost failed him then. He felt that he was face to face with the most difficult and the most delicate task that he had ever had to face in all his life. The look which was in this woman's eyes, which was on her face, which was, so to speak, all over her, was, to him, nothing less than terrible. He would rather have encountered a look of the deadliest hatred than the love-light which was in her eyes. As a rule, in his way he was a diplomatist. Now, his diplomacy wholly failed him. He struggled from blunder on to blunder.

"I feel that—that, in this matter, I may not, myself, have been wholly free from blame—"

"Blame? You have not been free from blame? I will not have you say that you have been to blame in anything, I will not let you say it, Ronald."

"But—"

"But me no buts! If there has been blame, then it has been wholly mine. But, Ronald, you will not blame me—now?"

"If you will permit me to explain—"

"Oh, yes, I will permit you to explain. Will you do it standing up? I would rather, since you ask my permission, that you make your explanation sitting at my side. I would rather, Ronald, have it so?"

It was maddening. Did she mean to compel him to play the brute?

"Lady Griswold, I—I must really beg you to hear me, without interruption, to an end."

"Ronald! Is that your House of Commons manner when the Opposition won't be still?"

He was a man whom it was notoriously, exceedingly difficult to irritate. But he was beginning then to be conscious of an unwonted feeling of irritation.

"I am simply here, Lady Griswold, to inform you that I propose to marry."

"Propose to marry! Is that the way in which you speak of it? And you do really think that it is news to me—after all your letters? Ronald! Ronald!"

It was inconceivable that a woman could be such a fool. Yet it was so. There was a rapturous suggestion in her voice which, literally, frightened him. The devil fly away with those letters of his! If ever he even dropped so much as a shadow of a hint again! She actually began to woo him. She came to him, she took both his hands in hers, she looked into his eyes—how she looked into his eyes! And he—he almost wished that he had no eyes to look into.

"Ronald! Ronald!" With what an unspoken eloquence of meaning she pronounced his name. "News to me? Rather—I will say it, after all these years—tidings of great joy. News to me! I will make you my confession, sir, in full." Why did he not nip her confession in the bud? Why did he stand there as if spellbound? He was speechless. A bolt seemed to have come out of the blue, and to have struck him dumb. And she went on,—

"For eighteen years, my lord, I have dreamed of this—this one hour. I cannot tell whether I am a wicked woman, or whether I am not. I tell you just how it has been with me. I have done what seemed to me to be my duty, from day to day, from month to month, yes, from year to year, and I do not think that anyone has ever heard me once repine. But all the time it has seemed that I, my own self, have been far away, and I watched and waited till I could join my own self—where you were. I knew that this day would come. I knew it, with a sure and a certain knowledge, all along. You see, Ronald, I knew you. I think it is that knowledge which kept me young. For I am young. I still am young, Ronald, in every sense. Indeed, I have sometimes feared that I am too young to be a fitting mate for a leader among men. Ronald, love of my life, speak to me, my dear."

He was looking away—down at the floor. He was standing in front of her, wearing the hang-dog air of a convicted criminal. He spoke to her.

"It is Inez." That is what he said.

She did not catch his meaning. Perhaps she did not distinctly catch his words. "Inez? What is Inez? Inez has nothing to do with us, my dear."

"Whom I am going to marry."

She looked at him as if she were dimly trying to realise what, by any possibility, could be his meaning. She seemed almost to think that great joy had caused him to lose his mental equilibrium, as it most certainly had caused her to lose hers. She put out her hands, as if he were a child, and advanced them towards his face.

"Ronald—kiss me,—after all these years."

Then the man blazed up. He seized her wrists just as her fingers touched his cheeks. He broke into a fury. "Don't."

She looked at him askance.

"Ronald—won't you kiss me?"

Still he could not tell it to her, not face to face. He roughly dropped her hands. He turned away. She looked at him in wondering amazement.

"Ronald, what do you mean?"

Then he turned to her. On his face there was that expression of resolution with which, in certain of his moods, the House of Commons was beginning to be very well acquainted.

"Lady Griswold, the purpose of my visit was to inform you that, with your permission, I propose to do myself the honour of marrying your daughter Inez."

Still she did not understand him.

"Ronald, what—what do you mean?"

She compelled him to be brutal, or, at least, it seemed to him that she compelled him.

"Lady Griswold, you must forgive my saying that you have made what I had hoped would be the happiest hour of my life one of the bitterest. If you had permitted me to speak at first you would have spared us both much pain. It would be absurd for me to pretend that I do not understand your meaning. You seem to take it for granted that things are to be with us as they were before the war. You appear to be wholly oblivious of the fact that eighteen— or is it nineteen?—years ago you jilted me."

"Jilted you? I—Ronald—I—I jilted you?"

"It is always my desire to use the most courteous and the gentlest language which will adequately convey my meaning. I know not how you may gloze it to yourself. To me it seems simply that—you promised to marry me, and you married Sir Matthew Griswold."

"But—Ronald—I—I have explained—just—how it was."

"Madam, did I require your explanation?"

She shrunk away, cowering as if she were some wild, frightened thing.

"But—but you wrote and asked me to come home."

"Lady Griswold, if you will refer to the letters of mine to which you are alluding, you will perceive that I merely suggested that it was possible that you might find more congenial surroundings in England than in Mexico."

"You—you meant more than that. And, Ronald—Ronald, I haven't ceased to love you all the time!"

"Lady Griswold, you compel me to use what may seem to be the language of discourtesy. How was I to know that, married to one man, you loved another? When you married him you died to me. I thought that, for me, all love was dead. But when I saw your daughter Inez—I have a constitutional objection to use the language of violence, or of passion. It is a plain statement of the naked truth that, when I saw your daughter Inez, that instant I knew that for me all love was not yet dead. It may appear to you that I have known her but a short time. Too short a time for knowledge. But I will say to you what I would not say to all the world. I seem to have known her—yes, certainly for years. I must certainly have known her in my dreams. I could have drawn her portrait, which would have been her very duplicate, instinct with all but life before she came into this room."

"Indeed. Is—is that so, Ronald?"

"I must have loved her in the spirit before I met her in the flesh. I must have done. And the strangest part of it all is that she seems, also, to have loved me."

"I do not think that that is strange, though the whole affair is, perhaps, a little strange."

"So, Lady Griswold, I have come to crave your permission to make your child my wife."

"I see. You want to marry Inez. Now—now I understand. Well, Ronald, I think I have known you long enough to be able to trust you with my child." The door opened to admit Miss Griswold. "Inez, the strangest thing has happened, which I am sure will overwhelm you with surprise. Mr Ferguson actually tells me that he loves you."

How we can smile, some of us, both men and women, when our very hearts are weeping gouts of blood. It is a curious illustration of the dual personality which is in each of us.

"My dear mother, that is no news. I know he loves me!"

"And what is even stranger, he tells me that you love him."

"That thing is less strange even than the other. I have loved him—oh, for years. Really, since the hour I was born. I believe that I was predestined to love him when I still was in the womb of time. I certainly have loved him for eighteen years, dear mother."

"For eighteen years? How odd! Well, Mr Ferguson, you will make her happy—always happy—won't you? And, Inez, you will be a good wife to—to Ronald? And so may every happiness be yours, you foolish pair!"

And before they suspected her intention, Lady Griswold had departed deftly.

ON THE RIVER

AN IDYLL OF A BEANFEAST

I

THE PLEASURES OF THE PEOPLE

Yes, I went on the river. I thought it would give me a chance to blow off steam—and it did.

I ran down to Richmond, and I got a craft from Messum, and I turned her nose up stream, and I started to scull for Molesey, but I never got there.

It was a lovely day. There was a cloudless sky. A twittering breeze, springing into being when least expected and most desired, plashed against one's cheeks with cooling kisses, It was a day when the glamour of the waters, the magic of the stream, the poetry of the river, should have been at its best. And it was. There had been an extensive beanfeast.

And the beanfeasters had been beanfeasting.

I afterwards became acquainted with the name of the firm which had beanfeasted. It was one which stands high in the commercial aristocracy of this country. Its products are known, and respected, and bought, and eaten, and liked! the wide world over. It is understood to treat its employees well. Undoubtedly that day it had treated them well—uncommonly well—or somebody had. If there was any male person who could have been adequately described as perfectly sober, I did not see him, while there were as many as several who would have been most inadequately described as quite another kind of thing.

It was between four and five when I got afloat, an hour at which, I have since been informed, the average beanfeast begins to be beanfeasty, a point to be borne in mind. There were about five thousand beanfeasters—the statistics are pure guess-work—of whom four thousand nine hundred and ninety-nine were on the river. If there were any who had been on it before they hid themselves away in nooks and crannies, and dissembled, for I am willing to assert, and even bet sixpence, that if any of those I saw had handled a scull on a previous occasion, it was in the days of their innocence, and that since then they had become hazy as to which end of it ought to be put in the water.

When I was clear of the bank I started to take my jacket off. Immediately I was the object of remarks which, by a slight effort of the imagination, might almost have been described as personal.

"He's undressing! I say, Jim, 'ere's a bloke undressing! Now, you girls, turn yer 'eads away!"

"Excuse me, sir, but do you 'appen to 'ave observed as there's lydies present?"

"If you're a-goin' to bythe don't you do it. Git be'ind a tree. It ain't to be allard. Where's them coppers?"

"Can't yer let the gentleman alone? 'E's a-goin' to wash 'isself! Ain't no one got a kyke of soap to lend 'im?"

"Gar on! 'E's Beckwith's brother, that's who 'e is. 'E's goin' to give a little entertainment. Now then, 'and the 'at round, you'll 'ave to mike it thirteenpence before 'e's goin' to begin!"

These remarks were made in tones which were distinctly something more than audible. It was gratifying to find that the advent of an inoffensive and sober stranger could be an occasion of so much public interest. If the mere removing of my coat caused such comment, what would happen if I turned up my shirt sleeves? I am bound to admit that the large majority of the other oarsmen kept their coats on, either in the interests of decency or something else, and their hats too—which if the same were not "billy-cocks" then they were "toppers." The sight of an amateur sculler with a black coat buttoned tightly across his chest, and a billy-cock hat set on his brow at an angle of seventy-five degrees, digging the handle of his scull into the back of his friend in front of him in his efforts to keep out of time, always pleases.

Steering I found a trifle difficult. There were boats to the left and boats to the right of me, boats in the front and boats at the back of me, and as few of them seemed to have any real notion as to which direction they were going, the question became involved. I had not got properly under way before I found this out.

"Now, then, where are yer goin' to?"

This question was put to me by a gentleman in a check suit and a top hat, who was tugging at a pair of sculls as if he was having an argument with them, two male friends being fore and three females aft. Two of the ladies had, in a playful manner, each hold of a rudder string, and as one jerked against the other the movements of the boat were of the teetotum order.

I replied to the inquiry with the courtesy which I felt that the occasion required.

"Where am I going to? Shortly, sir, I expect to go into the river, when you have finally decided to send me there."

This courtesy of mine the gentleman in the check coat and the top hat mistook for humour.

"Funny, ain't yer?"

"I shall be when they fish me out. Not a doubt of it."

"I shouldn't be surprised but what you fancies yourself."

"Should you not be surprised? Indeed. Think of that now!"

This remark of mine seemed to rouse the gentleman's ire. I do not know why. He became personal.

"I've seen better blokes nor you sold down our street two for three ha'pence, with a plate o' whelks thrown in—long-faced lardy!"

"Go a'ead, Bill, never mind 'im!"

"'Is mother don't know 'e's out!"

This from his two friends in the bow. Bill went "a'ead." He thrust his sculls into the stream, or meant to, and pulled with all his might, and caught a crab, and went backwards on to the twain in the prow. It was a marvel the craft did not go over. The ladies screamed, the gentlemen struggled, but there is a providence which attends on fools, and the last I saw of them, Bill, having another row with the sculls, was starting in pursuit of his top hat, which floated on the shining waters.

This sort of thing was doing me good. Ordinarily I should have resented Richmond emulating Hampstead Heath on a Bank Holiday; but, things being as they were, the position gave my nervous system just that fillip it required. I felt that if I could only have a row royal with some half-dozen of those beanfeasters—a good old-fashioned shindy—they would enjoy themselves and I should, and I should go back to dream dreams with a sound mind in a sound body, even though the latter was ornamented by a bruise or two.

I had that trifling argument, dear me, yes. Shades of my sires! what displays of oarsmanship I saw that afternoon.

"I say, matey, give us 'old of that there oar!"

The request came from an individual who formed one of a crew of four, with the usual eight or ten passengers, and who was looking with a certain amount of longing at a scull which was drifting on the stream towards me.

"How did you happen to lose it?" I inquired, as I drew it towards me.

"It was my friend as done it; 'e 'it it out of my 'and."

This was an allusion to the rower in front of him, which the rower resented.

"'Ow do yer make that out? Didn't you clout me in the middle of the back with it, and ain't you been clouting me with it all the way along, and didn't I say to you, "Enery, if you keeps on a-doing that something'll 'appen'?"

The gentleman who had been deprived of his scull dissented.

"If you knocks your back against my oar what's that got to do with me?"

"Why, you crackpot, don't you know better than that? If you was to 'old your oar as you ought to, I shouldn't come agin it, should I?"

"It's easy talking!"

"Ain't I sittin' in front of yer?"

"Course you are."

"Then why don't you keep your eye on the middle of my back?"

"So I do."

"Then why don't you move when I move?"

"'Ow can I? 'Ow am I to know when you're goin' to move? Sometimes you never move at all."

"You're a pretty sort to come out rowin' with, you don't know no more about a boat than a baby. 'Ere, put me ashore! I've 'ad enough of bein' mucked about by the likes o' you. I should enjoy myself more if I was lookin' on from the land."

The last speaker was, I believe, the most sensible man on the river that afternoon.

On a sudden I found myself in the middle of a race. I was lazying past the Island. I had long since given up all thoughts of Molesey, and was taking my ease, anticipating what might happen, when three boats which I had just passed all at once went mad. There was a single and a double skiff, and a four-oared tub. With one accord they started racing. I was only a yard or two in front, and though I might have pulled clear, on the other hand I might not;

and, anyhow, it was their business not to run me down, a fact which they did not seem to be aware of. On they came, shouting and splashing, the steering, in particular, being something frightful to behold. In a minute we were all four in a heap. They yelled at me, passengers and crews, with an unanimity which was amazing.

"Why don't yer get out of the way?"

"Pardon me, ladies and gentlemen, but, really, how could I?"

"If yer don't know 'ow to row what d'yer want to get into a boat for?"

"That, curiously enough, was an inquiry which I was about to address to you."

The stroke of the four diverted public attention from me by falling foul of the lady who was supposed—it was the purest supposition—to be acting as coxswain.

"Don't pull both strings at once! Pull this 'and, now pull the other! Don't I tell you not to pull both strings at once! What d'yer think yer doin'?"

"Fust you says pull this 'and, then you says pull that 'and, 'ow am I to know?"

A gentleman in the double skiff interposed.

"That's right, my little dear, don't you tyke none of 'is lip. You jump inter the water and swim to me, I'll look arter yer!"

Apparently this gentleman had forgotten that there was somebody else whom it was his duty to look after, a fact of which he was suddenly reminded.

"I'm sure if the lydy'd like to chynge places with me, I'm willin'; it don't myke no manner o' odds to me. If this is your idea of lookin' arter a lydy, it ain't mine, that's all I sye."

When I at last drew clear they still were wrangling. I have a faint recollection that the ladies were threatening to "mark" each other, or anybody else who wanted it. It seemed clear that their ideas of pleasure were inseparably associated with words of a kind.

II

THE ROMANCE OF THE LADY IN THE BOAT

As I was abreast of Ham House my attention was caught by the proceedings of the occupants of a boat upon my left. These were two gentlemen and a lady. The gentlemen were not only having "words;" quite evidently they were passing from "language" to something else. I thought for a second or two that they were going to fight it out in the boat, in which case I should quite certainly have enjoyed an opportunity of earning the Royal Humane Society's medal, but, apparently yielding to the urgent entreaties of the attendant lady, they changed their minds.

"Don't fight 'ere!" she exclaimed. "You're a pretty sort to come for a holiday with, upon my word!"

They undoubtedly were, on anybody's word. With the possible intention of meeting her views to the best of their ability, they began to pull to the shore as hard as they could, each keeping severely to a time of his own. Before the boat was really close to land the gentleman in the bow sprang up, jumped overboard, and splashed through the foot or two of water to the bank. Declining to be left behind in an enterprise so excellent, his companion was after him like a shot, and in less than no time they were going it like anything upon the sandy slope. In their ardour it had possibly escaped their attention that the result of their manœuvres would be to leave their fair associate in what, all things considered, might be described as a somewhat awkward situation. There was the boat drifting into the middle of the stream, the oars, which the enthusiastic friends had left in the rowlocks, threatening every moment to part company, while the lady called upon heaven and earth to witness her condition.

Pulling alongside, I took off my cap.

"Pardon me, madam, but since your natural protectors appear to have deserted you, might I hope to enjoy the extreme felicity of your presence in my boat?"

She stared at me, askance.

"Who would yer think ye're talking to?"

"You, my dear madam. Do me the pleasure of sharing my craft."

She smiled bewitchingly.

"I don't mind if I do. It'll just about serve 'em right, the—!"

Then she used words. And she hopped into my boat and I thought that we were over. But there is a providence which watches over us, so we only shipped about a bucketful. I began to row her over the sunlit ripples, and made conversation as we went.

"Your friends appear to have had a little difference of opinion."

"Couple of bloomin' fools, that's what I call 'em, straight! Tom 'e says Joe splashes 'im, then 'e splashes Joe, then Joe splashes 'im, then they gets to words, then they wants to fight it out in the middle of the river. Nice I should 'ave looked if I'd a let 'em!"

"You would."

"What do you think? silly softs! No, what I says is if two blokes wants to fight, let 'em do it on dry land, or else let 'em put me on dry land before they does it in a boat."

"Your sentiments do you credit."

"All I 'opes is they'll give theirselves a fair old doin'. I'd like to see 'em knock the stuffin' clean out of theirselves, straight, I would."

"So should I. They appear, however, to have decided not to. They seem to have had their attention diverted by the discovery that you are missing."

My impression was, and is, that they had been made acquainted of my abduction of the lady by persistent shouts of interfering friends upon the river. They left off fighting, and, instead, took to running along the bank and yelling at us.

"Eliza, what are you doing in there? Come out of it!"

This question and command, shouted by the shorter of the two, a sandy-haired young ruffian, with a voice like a brass trumpet, seemed, under the circumstances, to be singularly out of place. The observations of his companion were more to the point.

"All right, guv'nor, you wait a bit! you wait till I get a 'old on yer! If I don't play a toon on yer, I'll give yer leave to call me names!"

The lady comforted me.

"Don't you mind what they say."

"I don't."

But presently someone came upon the scene whose remarks I decided to mind, in a way. An unwieldy tub bore down upon us, containing perhaps twelve or fourteen people. A stalwart young fellow, standing up in the bow, addressed himself to me.

"Excuse me, guv'nor, but might I ask what you're doin' along of that young lady?"

"Pardon me, sir, in my turn, but might I inquire what business that is of yours?"

"I don't want none of your sauce! Just you tell me what's your little game."

This struck me as being tolerably cool, sauce being evidently at least as much in his line as in mine.

"My little game, sir, is a saunter on the stream. Good-bye."

And with that I pulled away. The stranger became almost inarticulate with rage.

"Set me alongside of 'im! put me aboard of 'im! I'll knock 'is somethinged 'ead off 'is somethinged shoulders!"

His friends yelled in chorus. One shouted question caught my ear.

"What are you doing along of the bloke's wife?"

I looked at my companion.

"Is it possible that the gentleman is your husband?"

"Course 'e is. You put me into the boat 'long with 'im right away! Tom and Joe, they're friends of 'is, but you ain't no friend of 'is, nor yet of mine. I don't want to get into no trouble along o' you! Do you 'ear what I tell you, put me into 'is boat!"

"With the greatest possible pleasure."

But the thing was not so easy. The whole dozen were screaming at once, and, judging by the threats they used, it seemed tolerably plain that if I brought my craft within reach of theirs an attempt would be made to board me, and there would be every probability of an awkward spill. So, deeming discretion to be the better part of valour, I made for the Surrey shore, intending to there land my passenger and restore her to a—I trusted—fond, though excited, husband's arms. My intentions, however, were misconstrued; they supposed I was running away, proposing to save my skin from a drubbing instead of the lady's from a ducking, so they started hotly in pursuit, their shouts redoubling. What was worse, the lady thought so too, and commenced to give me a side of her tongue which I trust, for his sake, it was her wont to spare her husband.

I never was better abused; the bawling crew behind were good at the game, but the ungrateful virago I had snipped was easily first. I grew a trifle warm. If I was to be slanged I would be slanged for something. I decided to give the husband a chase and the wife a little excursion. It would have been easy enough to have shown a lead to the pursuing tub until the end of time. I bent to the oars and let her have it. You should have heard the hubbub. They saw that if I played that trick they would never catch me, and how they raved! The joke was that my lady passenger raved with the best of them—and her adjectives!

"Something, something, something you! If you don't put me into my husband's somethinged boat, I'll spill the somethinged show!"

"Spill it."

For a moment I thought she would. Then she hesitated, reflected that she not improbably might be left to drown, and didn't.

"I'll mark your face for you!" she screamed.

"If you move from your seat, my dear madam, I'll upset the show."

"Do!" she yelled. Then, as an afterthought, "'Elp! murder! police! 'E's a-goin' to drown me!"

It seemed absurd to exhaust oneself for the sake of giving a pleasant trip to a lady who would persist in shouting for the police in a voice loud enough to be heard a mile away, especially as people on the Twickenham shore evinced signs of misconstruing the situation. I resolved, by way of vengeance, to concede what she wanted, and let the pursuers catch us.

"My dear madam, as I have already informed you, nothing would give me greater pleasure than to put you on board your husband's boat—I will prove it."

Precisely what I expected happened. The lumbering tub came up. The husband, with half a dozen of his friends, tried to board us. The frail skiff careened. There was the crowd of us, including, thank goodness! the lady passenger, in the stream. I had taken the precaution to draw close into shore before staying my wild career, foreseeing the inevitable catastrophe, so that it was only an affair of wading, yet I do believe that I was the only one who really enjoyed the thing. I doubt if the lady did. She swooned, or pretended to, directly she reached dry land. As for her friends, the whole gallant gang would have set on to me at once. But I will do her husband the justice to admit that he was a man. He claimed the affair as his own, and he insisted on taking it on as his own, and he took me on with it.

I had wanted a row royal and I had got it. Beanfeasting had not knocked the fighting qualities out of him. If he was not a professional pugilist he was a near relation. I can use them a bit, but he gave me as good as I sent, and a trifle better. It was the difference between the amateur and the professional; at his own game the tradesman always wins. If we had fought to a finish I should have had enough, but we didn't. A policeman came across the stream and stopped us. I had escaped a black eye, but that was about all I had escaped. I had landed a few, but they had been returned with interest. Twice had I been fairly grassed, once with a tingler under the chin. I felt for a moment as if I had swallowed every tooth in my head. I had the devout satisfaction of knowing that my nervous system had received just that fillip which it stood in need of.

"I'll have a lesson or two," I told myself, "from someone who can kill me at sight, and the next time I meet my lady passenger's husband I will do the grassing."

There's nothing like argument *a priori* for clearing the air or cobwebs from the brain. Do not talk to me of arbitration. I am a physical force man. I returned to town feeling twice the man I left it.

A MEMBER OF THE ANTI-TOBACCO LEAGUE

I

THE SIX CIGARS

Sunday morning. A cold wind blowing, slush in the streets, sleet drizzling steadily down. For the moment the market was deserted. Not because of the weather, wretched though the weather was, but because of the excitement which was in the air.

A crowd buzzed about the entrance to the court. A crowd which grew every second larger. A crowd which overflowed from the street itself, so that its tributaries streamed into the network of lanes and of alleys. An excited, a noisy, a shouting crowd. An angry crowd. A crowd which gave utterance to its opinions at the top of its voice, in language which was plain-spoken to a fault.

Jim Slater caught sight of a friend. He twisted himself round to shout at him.

"Wot yer, Bill! That's another one he's done for—that makes seven!"

"It is true then? He 'as done it."

"Done it! I should think he 'as done it! Found the pore gal just as he left 'er, lying up agin the wall, with 'er clothes over 'er 'ead, and 'er inside, wot 'e'd cut out, lying alongside—a 'orrid sight!"

"I'd like to 'ave the 'andlin'? of 'im!"

"'Andling of 'im! My Gawd!" A volley of expletives from Jim. "If I 'ad the 'andling of 'im once I wouldn't want it twice. I'd cut the — up for cat's meat!"

There was a chorus of approval from those who had heard. A woman's voice rose above the hubbub; she shook her fist at the police who guarded the entrance to the court.

"What's the good of you p'lice? You lets a chap carve us women up as if we was cattle, and you never don't trouble yourselves to move a finger! I'd be ashamed."

She was supported by a lady friend, a woman with a shawl over her head, her hair streaming down her back; a woman who, evidently, had risen hastily from bed.

"You're right, Polly! If a pore bloke steals a 'aporth o' fried fish, they takes jolly good care, them slops, they runs him in, but a — can do for as many of us gals as he — well chooses, and they don't even trouble themselves to ketch 'im. Yah-h! I'd like to see him do for some of them, I would—straight!"

From the crowd another loud-voiced chorus of approval. Jim Slater formed a speaking-trumpet with his hands, and yelled,—

"Why don't yer ketch 'im?"

A hoarse, husky murmur from the throng, rapidly rising to a roar,—

"Yes, why don't yer?"

The inquiry was repeated over and over again, each time more angrily. The people began to surge forward, pressing towards the entrance of the court, where the police were standing. A sergeant was heard shouting, in staccato tones,—

"Now then! Stand back there! No pushing!"

Policeman YZ 001 spoke to the comrade at his side.

"We shall have to call some more of our chaps out. They look to me like meaning mischief."

"Now then, stand back there! What do you want to shove like that for?"

Then came back question for question.

"Why don't yer ketch 'im?"

But none of these things troubled the Rev. Simon Chasuble. His house was within a few minutes' walk of the scene of all the hubbub. It was a new house, newer, even, than the church which it adjoined. Both church and house stood in a side street, within a stone's throw of the great thoroughfare in which something like a riot seemed to be threatening.

As yet no whisper of the growing excitement seemed to have penetrated the sacred precincts of the clergyman's home. The Rev. Simon was in his study. A man of medium height, with iron-grey hair, shaven cheeks, and light blue eyes.

He appeared to have been engaged in what, considering all things, was a somewhat singular pursuit. He seemed to have been manufacturing cigars. On a table in front of him was tobacco, both in roll and in leaf, and some of the implements which are used, when pursuing their trade, by the makers of cigars. It seemed clear that some of these implements had been in recent use, for actually with his own fingers the Rev. Simon was putting finishing touches to six cigars.

For many reasons the thing seemed strange. It was Sunday morning. The Rev. Simon had, not very long since, returned from officiating at early celebration. The bell would soon be rung to announce the commencement of another of the multifarious services in which the soul of the reverend gentleman delighted. His surplice, his bands, his hood, his biretta were lying ready on a chair, so that, without loss of time, he might slip them on, hurry across the courtyard which divided the house from the church, and plunge at once *in medias res.*

It seemed an odd moment for a clergyman to select to engage in the manufacture of cigars! Especially bearing in mind the Rev. Simon's well-known and peculiar tenets. He was the leader, through all that district, of the Anti-Everythingites. "Down with every sort of Reasonable Enjoyment!" was the motto which, metaphorically, he had nailed to his banner. And, among the other varieties of reasonable enjoyment, especially "Down with Tobacco!" He was a member of the Anti-Tobacco League. He had spoken, preached, and written against the use of tobacco in any and all of its forms. Indeed, at that very moment, cheek by jowl with the tobacco itself, was a heap of anti-tobacco literature. That curious tract, in the form of a leaflet, "Is Tobacco Smoked in Heaven?" lay on the top of the pile.

There must have been some curious cause which had impelled the Rev. Simon Chasuble to engage, even on a small scale, in the manufacture of cigars. And, in fact, there was, and curious cigars they were which he was making.

As he covered, with a really credible dexterity, each cigar with an outer wrapper, he left the bottom of it open. After covering the six cigars he did some rather funny things. Unlocking a drawer in a cabinet, which stood against a wall, he took out an unusually large pair of plain glass goggles. He put them on. He stuffed two small corks, which seemed to have been shaped for the purpose, up his nostrils, as far as they would go. He tied an enormous, and peculiarly shaped, respirator over his mouth. After completing these preparations he produced, from a corner of the same drawer, a small metal box and a little instrument, fashioned something like the tiny spoon with which we serve ourselves to cayenne pepper. As very carefully he unscrewed the lid, it was seen that the interior of the box was of ingenious construction. It was divided into two halves. In one division was a colourless liquid, in the other a powder of a vivid violet hue. In the centre of each of the pieces of glass was a hole which was just large enough to allow of his inserting the delicate instrument which, at one extremity, was shaped something like a tiny spoon. With this he took out first a spoonful of the violet powder, which he dropped into the end of one of the cigars which he had purposely left open, the thin end; then a spoonful of the colourless liquid, which he dropped on to the powder. Without an instant's loss of time he re-screwed the lid on to the box and, with an almost simultaneous movement, completed the manufacture of the cigar, closing and shaping the end in a manner which, if it was his first attempt in that direction, was not a little to his credit.

He repeated the operation with each cigar, reopening and re-closing the box each time, and that with a degree of celerity which was not the least singular part of the whole performance. When he had finished his proceedings he removed the goggles, the plugs from his nostrils, the respirator from his mouth, and, together with the metal box, and the spoon-shaped instrument, he replaced them in the drawer.

With a smile of beaming satisfaction he turned to the result of his handiwork. There they lay, six very fair-looking cigars, not too pointed and not too stubby, all in a row in front of him upon the table.

"An old secret adapted to a new purpose. These cigars are likely to be more efficacious in repressing the nicotine habit than all the sermons that were ever preached, and all the books that were ever written."

The Rev. Simon chuckled, a startling chuckle it was. It distorted his whole countenance; made another man of him; turned a not ill-looking gentleman into a hideous thing. It was the chuckle of a lunatic. It came and went in, as it were, a twinkling of the eye; but the Rev. Simon Chasuble had only to indulge in that sinister chuckle in public once, and the incumbency of St Ursula's Church would there and then be vacant.

"I'll put them in the case."

He placed the cigars carefully, one by one, in a handsome case, which had been lying beside them on the table.

"How fortunate that the secret should have been in my possession; that it should have been given to me to adapt it to so rare an end! What a power for good the adaptation places in my hands! Given the opportunity it may be mine to remove the nicotine habit for ever from the world. One whiff and the slave is gone. And none shall know from whence the blow has come. It will seem as though it has fallen from on high."

Again that dreadful chuckle, coming and going in a second, as the Rev. Simon was in the act of making the sign of the cross.

Someone tried the handle of the door; then, finding it locked, rapped upon the panel.

"Papa! papa!"

The Rev. Simon turned towards the door, a sudden look of keen suspicion in his light blue eyes. But his voice was smooth and soft. "Helena?"

"Oh, papa, another of those poor women has been murdered!"

The Rev. Simon seemed to hesitate. The fashion of his countenance was changed. It became unrelenting, pitiless. His voice became harsh and measured.

"Do you mean that another of the inhabitants of Sodom has met with the reward of her misdeeds? Well? God has judged!"

"Oh, papa, don't talk like that! The poor creature has been almost cut to pieces, it is dreadful! The whole place is in excitement, we are afraid there'll be a riot. Do open the door!"

"Have you yet to learn that, under no circumstances, do I allow secular matters to interfere with the due performance of my spiritual duties on the Lord's own day? If the woman is dead, she is dead. I am no trafficker in horrors. To-morrow I shall hear all that I need to hear. Go. I am engaged."

The girl went. The Rev. Simon listened to her retreating footsteps. And, as she went, there was heard a sound which was very like the sound of a woman's sobbing.

The Incumbent of St Ursula's stood with his hands clasped in front of him, his eyes turned upwards. He quoted scripture.

"'The adulterers shall surely be put to death!' 'It is the day of the Lord's vengeance!' 'Vengeance is mine, I will repay, saith the Lord!' And am I not thy minister, O God, that Thou hast appointed to work Thy will?' The harlot's house is the way to hell, going down to the chambers of death!' Yea, O God, yea! 'So let the wicked perish!'"

The Rev. Simon took a crucifix, which dangled from the cord of his cassock, and held it in front of him. He crossed himself. He pressed the crucifix to his lips. He seemed, for some seconds, to be engaged in silent prayer. Then, very methodically, he removed the evidences of his having been engaged so recently in the manufacture of cigars. The cigars themselves, oddly enough, he slipped, case and all, into an inner pocket of his cassock.

All at once there was borne on some current of the air the distant murmur of a crowd. He stood and listened. The sound grew louder; it seemed to be coming nearer. The light faded from the Rev. Simon's eyes; every faculty was absorbed in the act of listening. The sound was approaching; it rose and fell; now dying away in a sullen murmur, now rising to a startling yell. His hand stole into his bosom. When it reappeared it held a knife, shaped something like a surgeon's scalpel.

"'The sword of the Lord and of Gideon.'"

Again that chuckle, the revelation of the lunatic.

Momentarily the noise increased. One began to individualise voices; to realise that the tumult was the product of a thousand different throats.

"Some riot, I suppose. One of their periodical differences with the police. What's that?"

II

THE CIGAR WHICH WAS SMOKED

"That" was the sound of heavy footsteps hastening towards the study door. The handle was turned; a fist was banged against the panel.

"Who's here?"

"I am here! Let me in!"

The voice was quick, sharp, abrupt, distinctly threatening. The Rev. Simon looked round the room with shifty, inquiring eyes. He whispered to himself.

"Philip Avalon? My sister's son? What does he want with me?" He felt, with his fingers, the edge of the knife which he was holding. He asked aloud, in a voice which was more than sufficiently stern, "What do you want with me, sir?"

"I want to speak to you. Do you hear? Be quick and let me in!"

The speaker's tone was even more threatening than before; it was as if he defied disobedience. The shifty look in the Rev. Simon's eyes increased. Again he whispered to himself.

"It is nothing, only some fresh insolence, some new bee he has in his bonnet."

Then aloud, "You speak with sufficient arrogance, sir, as if the house were your own."

For response there came a storm of blows upon the panels of the door.

"By —, if you don't open the door I'll break it in!"

Wheeling right round with a swift, crouching movement, the Rev. Simon ran towards the window. It seemed, for the moment, as if he meditated flight. He already had his hand upon the sash, to throw it open, when he changed his mind. He drew himself up, he thrust the knife back into his bosom; he strode towards the door with resolute, unflinching steps. With unfaltering hand, turning the key in the lock, he flung the door wide open. His voice rang out in tones of authority.

"Philip Avalon, how dare you conduct yourself in such a fashion? Do you forget what day this is, and that I suffer no bawling intrusion to divert my thoughts from my ministrations at the altar?"

The rejoinder which came from the young man who, regardless of the Rev. Simon's attempt to prevent his ingress, thrust his way into the room, was more forcible than civil.

"You villain! You damned villain!"

The Rev. Simon drew himself still straighter. His bearing, while it suggested horror and amazement, commanded reverence.

"Philip Avalon! I am the priest of God!"

"The priest of God!" In a fit of seemingly uncontrollable passion, the young man struck the elder to the ground. "Lie there, you hound!"

For some seconds the Rev. Simon lay where he had fallen.

The young man who had used him with such scant ceremony was tall and broad. He had a fair beard, and was about thirty years of age. His dress was careless. He stood glaring down upon the clergyman with gleaming eyes. He seemed mastered by irresistible excitement.

The Incumbent of St Ursula's raised himself sufficiently from the floor to enable him to glance up at his assailant.

"You have laid the hands of violence not only upon a much older man than yourself, and one who is your own flesh and blood, but also upon a priest of God. It completes the measure of your crimes. Coward! as well as sinner!"

For a moment the young man remained speechless. When he did speak the words came rushing from him in a torrent.

"If you continue to play the hypocrite and to adopt that tone with me I'll go and I'll stand upon your doorstep, and I'll shout to the people—you hear them? They are already beside themselves with rage!" As he spoke yells and execrations were borne from the street without into the room. "I'll shout to them, 'You want Tom the Tiger, the fiend in human shape who has butchered seven helpless women in your midst? He's in here! He's my uncle, Simon Chasuble, the Incumbent of St Ursula's! I deliver him into your hands! Come in and use him as you will!' And they'll come in, come swarming, yelling, rushing in—men, women, children—and they'll tear you limb from limb, and will mete out on your vile body the punishment which, after all, will be less than it deserves!"

As he paused the young man stood with clenched fists and flaming looks, as if it was as much as he could do to keep himself from a repetition, in a much more emphatic form, of his previous assault.

The Rev. Simon rose to his feet gingerly. He withdrew himself, with commendable prudence, further from where Philip Avalon was standing. The shifty look came back into his eyes. But his voice was firm.

"What wild words are these?"

"The words may be wild, but they are true ones. Since these hideous butcheries have been taking place in the surrounding slums and alleys a Vigilance Committee has been formed, with a view of assisting the police. I am a member. This morning I was out on my appointed beat. I saw someone coming down Rainbow Court. I drew back into the shadow, and I stood and I watched. It was you. You had on a rough black overcoat and a cloth cap, and though you were laughing to yourself you seemed desirous of avoiding observation. I wondered what you were doing there at that hour in such a guise. I hesitated a moment whether to follow you. Then I plunged into the court. Just where I had seen you standing I found a woman lying on the ground, dead—murdered—disembowelled; unmistakeably the handiwork of Tom the Tiger. I was so amazed, so horrified, so actually frightened, that for the life of me I could not think what I ought to do. I've been walking about London all night trying to make up my mind. And now I have come to ask you if there is in you sufficient of the man to give you courage to go at once and yield yourself to the police; if there isn't, I shall drag you."

"It's a lie!"

"What is a lie?"

"All that you have said is a lie. You always were a liar, Philip Avalon."

The nephew stared at his uncle. It seemed that he found it hard to believe that a man could be so shapen in iniquity.

"You can still speak to me like that, knowing that I know you. You certainly are, to me, a revelation of infinite possibilities in human nature. But I am not here to palter. Do you intend to surrender yourself, or am I to drag you to the police, or am I to call in the assistance of the people in the street? I give you a minute in which to decide."

The young man took out his watch. Layman and cleric eyed each other. As they did so the Rev. Simon's countenance was transfigured in a fashion which startled his nephew not a little. Before Philip Avalon had guessed his intention, the Incumbent of St Ursula's, hurrying past him, had locked the study door and pocketed the key. As he did so he broke into chuckling laughter. As his nephew surveyed him a glimmer of new light began to find its way into his brain.

"Man! what is the matter with you? What have you done?"

The Rev. Simon continued chuckling. Indeed, it seemed as if he would never stop. And there was something so unpleasant about his laughter that, considerably to his own surprise, Philip Avalon found himself giving way to shudder after shudder.

"Mad! stark mad!" he told himself. "And to think that none of us ever guessed it!"

Now that the fact was actually revealed he perceived, too late, what a lurid light it threw upon the puzzles of the past. As to the man's madness there could be no shred of doubt. He stood gibbering in front of him. And though Philip was very far from being, in any sense, an expert in mental pathology, he was acute enough to realise that an element of something horrible, of something altogether dangerous, differentiated this man's madness from that of the ordinary lunatic. As by the stroke of a magician's wand the clergyman had been transformed into a fiend. He held out his hand toward Philip, never ceasing to chuckle. Even his voice was changed; it had become an almost childish treble.

"Yes, I did it. I! I! Seven, Philip—seven harlots slain by my single hand! All England rings with it, yet no one guesses it was I!"

In the sudden horror of the situation the young man found it difficult to preserve his presence of mind. He endeavoured to collect his thoughts. He resolved to continue to speak with the voice of authority. With some recollection of stories which he had read, or heard, of the power of the sane man's eye, he did his best to unflinchingly meet the madman's glance.

"Give me the key of the door, at once!"

"The key? Of the door? Oh, yes! Here is the key of the door."

The Rev. Simon produced from the bosom of his cassock what looked to Philip Avalon very like a surgeon's scalpel. The weapon gleamed ominously in the madman's hand. Involuntarily the young man shrank back. His uncle noticed the gesture. His chuckling increased. He held out the knife.

"Yes, Philip, this is the key of the door. It is with this key that I unlocked the gates of the chambers of death for the seven harlots." The madman's voice sank to a whisper, a whisper of a peculiarly penetrating kind. "Philip, the Lord came to me in a dream one night, and bade me go out among the armies of the wicked and kill! kill! kill! And I arose and cried, O Lord, I will do as thou biddest me! And I have begun. The tares are ripe unto the harvest, and I have my hand upon the sickle, and I'll not stay until the whole of the harvest is reaped and cast into the fire which never shall be quenched!"

Philip Avalon found that his uncle's manner and conversation was beginning to have on him an effect which he had often heard described, but which he had never before experienced, the effect of making his blood run cold. What was he to do? It seemed to him that to attempt to grapple with a homicidal madman, while he was in the possession of such a weapon, was not an adventure to be recommended. A thought occurred to him. He moved across the room. The madman immediately moved after him.

"What are you going to do? Stand still!"

Philip turned.

"I was merely about to ring for a glass of water."

The madman's suspicions were at once on the alert.

"A glass of water? What do you want with a glass of water? No! You sha'n't ring! you sha'n't!"

He brandished his weapon in a fashion which induced his nephew to take temporary refuge behind an arm-chair.

"Take care, sir! You will do yourself a mischief."

The Rev. Simon proved that he was, at least, in certain directions, sufficiently keen of apprehension.

"No, Philip, it is not myself I shall do a mischief to, it is you. You would prevent a servant of the Lord from doing his master's will; it is meet, therefore, you should die."

Philip braced himself for the struggle which seemed to him to be inevitably impending. But, as he paused, a sudden idea seemed to come into the Rev. Simon's disordered brain. His chuckling redoubled.

"No! no! no!—a better way!—a better way! Philip, you're a smoker; smoke one of my cigars."

The Rev. Simon took a cigar case from an inner pocket in his cassock. Opening it, he held it out towards Philip Avalon. It contained six cigars. The young man's bewilderment grew more and more. That the Rev. Simon Chasuble, whose fulminations against what he was wont to speak of as the "nicotine habit," had always made him seem, to his nephew, to be more or less insane, should actually produce a case of cigars from a pocket in his cassock, and offer him one to smoke, to Philip Avalon the action seemed to paint the disorder of his uncle's brain in still more vivid hues.

In his bewilderment the young man refused his uncle's offer.

"Thank you, I do not care to smoke just now."

But the Rev. Simon was insistent.

"But I say you shall, you shall! You never smoked a cigar like mine before, and you never will again!"

Again that accentuation of the chuckle. Thinking that by humouring his uncle's whim he would at least be afforded breathing space, Philip took, from the proffered case, one of the six cigars. The Rev. Simon watched him with eager eyes.

"Cut off the tip! Quick, Philip, quick!"

"What does he think he's up to now?" inquired Philip of himself. He cut off, with his penknife, the point of the cigar, and as he did so an idea came also to him. "I'll strike a match and light up; then I'll drop the match into the fireplace, and that'll give me a chance to ring the bell."

Only the first part of this programme, however, was carried into effect. He struck a match, smiling in spite of himself at the eagerness with which he perceived that his uncle watched him. He applied the lighted match to his cigar. And as the slender whiff of smoke came from between his lips, as if struck by lightning, he fell to the floor stone dead.

The Rev. Simon Chasuble's experimental essay with his ingenious contrivance for the conversion of smokers had been a complete success. He knelt beside the silent figure. He kissed his crucifix; he crossed himself.

"I thought that it would be a better way. So shall all the enemies of the Lord perish from off the face of the earth! Shall I?"

He made, with his knife, a dreadful significant gesture over the region of the dead man's abdomen. As he did so the bell of the adjoining church was heard summoning the worshippers to service. On the Rev. Simon the sound had a marvellous effect. He rose to his feet. Every appearance of madness passed away from him. He seemed clothed again in his right mind. He glanced at the clock upon the mantelshelf. His manner became clerically stern.

"It is time for service to begin. I must suffer nothing to interfere with my ministrations at the altar." Going to the door, he unlocked it, and threw it open. He called, "Helena!"

A girl's voice replied, she thought he was calling her to church.

"Yes, papa, I'm coming! I am almost ready."

"Come here at once. Something has happened to Philip."

The girl came hurrying in, buttoning her gloves as she entered. She exclaimed at the sight of her cousin lying so still upon the floor.

"Oh, papa, what is the matter with him? Is he in a fit?"

Her father was rapidly donning his surplice, his stole, and his hood, surveying himself, as he did so, in a mirror.

"He is in something of the kind. As I was talking to him he fell suddenly to the ground. See that he receives every necessary attention. It is time for service to commence. I cannot stay."

The Incumbent of St Ursula's left the room. Directly afterwards he was seen, in his clerical vestments, hurrying across the courtyard towards the church.

THAT FOURSOME

"Come with me," said Hollis, "down to Littlestone."

Littlestone? Never heard of it. Didn't know there was such a place. Told him so.

"I cannot help your ignorance, my dear Short. I can only tell you that it is the spot for you." He looked me up and down. "For a man of your build the very spot." What he meant I hadn't the faintest notion. "If you do there what you ought to do, and what everyone does, it'll get seven pounds off you inside a week." I began to guess. "Such air, such breezes, and the finest links in England!"

"Links?" I glanced at him out of the corner of my eye, commencing to perceive that there was something at the back of this man's mind.

"Links, Short, which are links. Better than Sandwich. St Andrews are not to be compared with them. And as for Wimbledon, bah! You come down with me to Littlestone and I'll teach you how to play golf—golf, sir! The Royal and Ancient! The king of games! You'll feel yourself a different man from the moment your fingers close about a club."

I knew it was all nonsense. Was perfectly aware of it. Entirely conscious that it was mere flummery to talk about my being a different man from the moment my fingers closed about a club. But I'm one of the best-natured souls alive. If a man wanted me to go tobogganing with him down the icebergs round the North Pole—wanted me strongly enough—I do believe I should have to go. I should be positively unhappy if I let him go alone, though I should be a good deal unhappier if I didn't. There is nothing I dislike so much as cold. Unless it is tobogganing. I once tobogganed down a hill in Derbyshire. I wish to say no more except to mention that I am still alive. Though when part of me reached the bottom of the hill that was all there was to it. To this hour, when I touch certain portions of my frame I remember.

But I wish to harrow no one's feelings.

I went down to Littlestone. Found it was in a remote corner of Kent. Travelled by the South Eastern. Dismal, dirty, draughty carriage. Cold wind blowing. Tried every means of escaping it short of hiding underneath the seat. Stopped once at each station and twice between most of them. Changed whenever it occurred to the officials that they'd like a sort of game of "general post." Arrived at a shed which did duty as a station, chilled to the bone and feeling as if I had had the longest journey of my life. Was bumped along in a thing which I imagine was called an omnibus to Littlestone. Found Hollis awaiting me.

"Welcome to Littlestone, Short! You look another man already." I felt it. "I'd have come to the station only no one ever knows when those trains will get in." Mine had been about an hour and three-quarters late, at least, according to the time-table. "Did one of the best rounds of my life this afternoon; sixteenth hole in four; stroke under bogey."

A person who could talk of "rounds" and "bogey" when I felt as I felt then, I had no use for. I stood before the fire trying to get warm.

Had a pretty bad dinner. Heard more golf in half an hour than during the preceding ten years. Then more golf afterwards. In ordinary society one is not supposed to talk of one's own achievements, good, bad or indifferent. Unless my experience was singular, the people in that place talked of nothing else. Went to bed as early as possible to escape it. Dropped off to sleep wondering if the wind would leave anything of the house standing by the morning.

Forgot to lock the door. Roused by Hollis entering my bedroom. It was broad day. But it seemed to me that I had only just closed my eyes.

"Come out and have a swim. The water's like ice, brace you up. Strong current. Man drowned here last week."

"Thank you. I've no intention of being the man who's drowned here this week. I prefer a tub."

Had a tub. Went down to survey the scene. Never more surprised in my life. Road. Strip of rusty grass in front. Vast quantities of stones beyond. Then sea. Confronted by perhaps twenty houses. Cheap stuccoed structures of the doll's-house type of architecture. Beyond, on either side, desolation. A flat, rank, depressing, stony wilderness. Whether Nature or man was most to blame for making things as bad as they seemed under those leaden, before-breakfast skies, it would have needed an expert to determine.

No one was in sight. Until Hollis appeared I was the only idiot about. His teeth were chattering.

"Not a pretty place," I observed.

"No, it isn't."

"Neither the place nor its surroundings seem to have many claims in the direction of the picturesque."

"It's a beastly hole. That's what we want."

"You want it to be a—beastly hole?"

I looked at him askance. Wondering, for the moment, if he was joking. But he wasn't.

"Rather. Crowds of people would come if we made it attractive. Place'd be ruined."

"Ruined?"

"For golf. As it is the place is packed in summer. People come from all over the place. Can't play on our own links. Regular mob. Confound 'em, I say. Why, this last summer a man brought his wife with him. She rowed him like anything when she found out what sort of place it was. Had brought a lot of pretty dresses with her, and that sort of thing. Didn't see being left alone all day with nothing to do except sit on the beach and throw stones in the sea. That wasn't her idea of a holiday. We should have a lot of women of that sort about if we didn't take care."

Unreasonable some women are who do not golf. Especially when they are attached to men who do. So selfish on their part to even hint that they have ideas, or tastes, of their own.

At breakfast the great theme was broached. Hollis regarded me with what I was dimly conscious was a cold and a scornful eye. I had had no idea that he was the kind of man he really appeared to be. Or I should certainly never have come. In a manner of speaking our acquaintance, of some fifteen or sixteen years' standing, had been merely superficial. I was beginning to wish that it had continued on those lines.

"I believe you've never played."

"I've handled a club."

So I had. I had once been round some fields with six balls and a club. I brought the club back—that is, most of it; the man from whom I had borrowed it seemed to be tolerably satisfied, on the whole; though I had, as it were, scattered the balls about me as I went. Amazing the capacity those six golf balls had for losing themselves. I was without a caddie. Grass was long. Even when I managed to hit one, I seldom saw where it went. That is, with sufficient precision to be able to lay my hand upon it afterwards. With balls at a shilling apiece I concluded that golf might prove expensive.

Hollis read more meaning into my words than I actually intended.

"That's all right. I didn't know you'd gone as far as that." I did not propose to correct him; though without an adequate understanding of what it was that he might mean. "What's your handicap?"

"I can't say that I have one."

"I suppose you belong to a club."

"Well, not exactly."

"Not exactly? What do you mean? Either you do or you don't. Speak up, man, and say what you mean."

His manner was positively warm. I endeavoured to explain. It was not the last explanation I did endeavour to make.

"You see, it was this way. I thought of putting up for a club——"

"What club?"

"Oh, a little local one; nothing of any account; a sort of place where people in the neighbourhood go and mess about."

"Mess about?"

"I fancy the word adequately describes what takes place. They've knocked up a course of a kind on some local common-land, it's quite rudimentary. I don't think that any serious play takes place. It was that, in a measure, which actuated me."

"Weren't you elected?"

"Elected? I never put up. I'd no doubt that they'd have been delighted to have me, only I didn't go so far. I only thought of doing so." Something in the expression of his face induced me to hasten on. "My dear Hollis, you may take it for granted that in everything which concerns golf I'm a novice."

"There are novices and novices. I call a man with a handicap of eighteen a novice."

"You may certainly credit me with a handicap of eighteen. I would remind you that you asked me to come to Littlestone in order that you might teach me golf."

"I'll teach you, if the thing's to be done." He regarded me in a manner which I did not altogether like. I do not know why people are apt to look at me in a peculiar way when I propose to make myself proficient in some branch of athletics. "I have arranged a foursome with old Pickard. He has a friend who ought to be about your mark. I'm told that he's a perfect ass." I imagine that Mr Hollis perceived that there was something on my countenance which made it desirable to throw light upon words which distinctly needed it. "I mean, of course, in a golfing sense only. I daresay that in any other sense he's all that could be desired, as you are, old man."

Almost immediately after breakfast, Hollis and I started for the links, where we were to meet our antagonists. As we had but a short distance to go we walked, each of us carrying a bag full of clubs. After we had gone a few steps I became conscious that Hollis was regarding my bag with what I could not but feel was a considerable amount of interest.

"You seem to have a newish lot of clubs."

"They're brand new, all of them. I bought them on purpose to come down here."

During the interval of silence which followed, Hollis stroked his moustache. I had an idea that he was smiling; though I did not know what at. I was not aware that I had said anything humorous.

"You seem to have a goodish few."

"I told the assistant at the shop to let me have everything that was requisite. I must admit that he seems to have interpreted my intentions in a generous spirit. I appear to have more clubs than you do. I don't know if that's an advantage or not."

Rather to my surprise Hollis stood still and turned to me.

"I say, you know, that friend of Pickard's has played."

"So I gathered."

"He's not a regular idiot."

"I thought you said he was."

"Well, there are degrees even in idiots. And Pickard himself is a bit short-tempered."

"If he has a wife, if that is the case, I am sorry for her. Otherwise I don't see how the fact of his good or bad temper can concern me."

"No? Perhaps not. He can control himself. After all, a foursome has to give way for a twosome. I think I ought to tell you that we're lunching at two."

"At two? That's all right. Why, it's only just past ten."

There was that in Hollis's words and manner which I could not but regard as cryptic; though I did not feel disposed, at the moment, to point this out to him. Presently he asked a question.

"By the way, what club do you use for your tee-shot?"

"The tee-shot?" I had heard the expression. I have no doubt that, if I had had a little time for reflection, I should have recalled in what connection. As it was, feeling a trifle flustered, I—if I may put it in that way—hedged. "It depends upon the—eh—position of the ball and—so on. What club do you use?"

"I always use a putter."

"A putter? Do you? Indeed. I can't say that I invariably use—ah—a putter, not for a tee-shot. What are you laughing at?"

Hollis had burst into a loud, and so far as I could perceive, wholly unprovoked guffaw. The man was developing a keenness of scent for what was funny with which I had not credited him. I wondered if I had said anything which was unintentionally amusing. In my pocket was a little manual of terms used at golf. I was disposed to refer to it with a view of ascertaining exactly what a putter was; but I refrained.

"Short," continued Hollis, "I'll get you the smartest caddie obtainable. If you'll take my strong advice, you'll act on any hint he may happen to drop; and, in particular, you'll use each club as he hands it you without a word."

Again there was that something in Hollis's words and manner which I can only once more describe as cryptic. Indeed, I will go further and say that I found it a little disconcerting. We had but another hundred and fifty yards to go. While we were traversing that short distance I was almost moved to suggest that I was not feeling altogether inclined to play that morning; and that, therefore, if a substitute could be found to fill my place he had better find him. I wish I had suggested it. It was merely the desire not to spoil Hollis's game which stayed my hand. And a lamentable lack of gratitude, to speak of nothing else, he displayed. I have seldom had a more uncomfortable experience. To think that I had gone to that wretched place, out of the purest good-nature, simply and solely to allow myself to be subjected to such treatment. Nothing could have been more unexpected. To say not a word about the money which I had expended on that bagful of clubs. Quite a sum.

We came to a spot where three or four men were hanging about, and where one man was hitting at a ball.

"Is this where we start?" I asked.

"This is the first tee."

"The first tee? Oh! Indeed."

I wish to state here, before going further, that that was the first time I had ever been on a golf course in my life. The desire was borne in upon me very strongly to mention this to Hollis before any misunderstanding could possibly arise; because I foresaw, even then, that misunderstandings might arise, in consequence of which I might find myself in a false position. But, for one thing, I felt that Hollis might possibly think that the moment was ill-chosen to make such a communication; and then, striding up to the other men, he began talking to them as if he had known them all their lives; and so, since I could hardly interrupt him, the opportunity was lost. Which I have ever since regretted.

Presently I was aware that Hollis was calling the attention of one of the strangers to me.

"This is my friend Short. Short, this is Pickard. Pickard, Short's a dark horse; one of those unattached men who have no handicaps."

"I take it that you're a plus man, Mr Short."

I perceived at once that Mr Pickard was a Scotchman. I do not desire, in any illiberal spirit, to say that I object to Scotchmen as a nation; but I do not hesitate to affirm that I realised, on the instant, that this was the type of Scotchman with whom I was not likely to find myself in sympathy. He was six feet high and grey-bearded, and had a dry way of speaking which made it difficult to determine, especially for a stranger, what it was he really did mean, and a trick of looking at you from under his beetle brows, which was actually threatening. I did not know what a plus man was, but I supposed that he was endeavouring to perpetrate something in the way of a joke, so I made an effort to fall in with what I imagined to be his humour.

"Oh, yes, Mr Pickard, I'm a plus man." Directly I said it Mr Pickard looked at me a little oddly, and as the other men who were within hearing turned towards me as if I had said something surprising, not knowing what it was I really had said, I tried to pass it off, as it were, with a little joke of my own. "That's to say, I'm a surplus man."

Nobody laughed except myself, and I only did it with difficulty.

Hollis had walked off with my bagful of clubs. Just then I saw it advancing towards me slung across the back of a disreputable urchin of about twelve or thirteen years of age. Hollis had talked of getting me the smartest caddie procurable. If that little ragamuffin was his idea of smartness, I could only say we differed. Mr Pickard was not unnaturally struck by the incongruity of the association of my beautiful new clubs with that unwashed youngster.

"My gracious!" he exclaimed. "Here's some pretty things! And who might be the owner of these pretty things?"

"They're mine," I explained.

"Yours? Mr Short, have you had a fortune left you? To be sure they look as if they were all of them new."

"They are. I bought them yesterday."

"Did you, indeed? And what have you done with the old lot?"

"I left them behind me."

As a matter of plain fact, the clubs in that bag were the first I had possessed in my life. But in view of that old man's malicious glance, and with a suspicion flashing through my brain that some of the other men were grinning, I did not feel called upon to admit it. Mr Pickard continued,—

"I think, Mr Short, you said that you were a plus man. To a player of your calibre I take it that it doesn't matter how new a club is. Unfortunately, some of us weaklings can't touch a ball with one that isn't an old friend." He turned to a little slip of a man, with an eyeglass and a vacuous smile, and a pair of perfectly ridiculous stockings. "Let me introduce you to Mr Barstow, who is to be my partner in the thrashing you are about to give us."

Mr Barstow's smile expanded. I immediately perceived what Hollis had meant by speaking of him as a perfect ass; though why he had coupled him with me I did not understand.

"I suppose you and I are the duffers," he observed, which was an uncalled-for remark to make. One, moreover, which, so far as he could tell, was without a shadow of justification. "I hope," he added, "that you are a bigger duffer than I am."

"I can only trust that I am not," I retorted with what, I imagine, was some dignity.

The game was started. Mr Pickard hit off, his ball going what seemed to me a terrific distance. Hollis went next, his ball going as far as Mr Pickard's. Then Barstow went. He went through a series of acrobatic contortions which were simply ludicrous. Recorded by the cinematograph they would have been side-splitting. When he did play his ball did not go anything like so far as either of the others.

"Barstow, you've a pretty way of addressing a ball," remarked his partner.

"Yes," he said, "that's the best part of my game."

What Mr Pickard meant by "addressing a ball" I did not know. It appeared to me to be an absurd phrase to use. But I did not doubt that it conveyed a scathing comment on Barstow's performance. My turn followed. Remembering what Hollis had said, I took the club that young ruffian handed me without a word of remonstrance; though it seemed somewhat hard that, as the possessor of such a number—and such an expensive lot—of clubs I was not at liberty to select which one of them I chose; particularly as it seems only reasonable to assume that in such matters each man has his own ideas. However, my cue was to be docile, and to defer, so far as was possible, to the judgment of one whose knowledge of the game was, presumably, greater than mine. Though I did resent being dragooned by an unwashed urchin whose whole attire would have been dear at five shillings; especially as I had a kind of feeling that there was that in his bearing, and in the way in which, out of the corner of his eye, he kept looking at me, and at my clubs, which was positively impertinent.

I had noticed, with that quickness of observation for which I am peculiar, that each of the others had swung his club two or three times through the air before actually striking the ball. I did not know why they had done this. So far as I was able to judge there was no ostensible cause for such a proceeding.

But as it was apparently one of the formulas of the game, and I was desirous of avoiding anything approaching to irregularity, I followed their example.

Unfortunately I must have moved my arm before I was quite prepared; and also with more vigour than I had intended. Because, not only did I almost lose my own balance, but the end of the club, not travelling quite in the direction I had meant it should, struck the wretched boy who was carrying my clubs with what, I must admit, was considerable force. He gave a yell which must have been heard a mile off. He dropped to the ground with a degree of promptness which took me quite aback. I was commencing to explain that really the boy ought to have had sense enough to stand farther off, when Hollis cut me short with a brusqueness which was most embarrassing.

"If you hadn't hit him you'd have hit someone else. Haven't you sense enough to know that you ought to see that you're well clear of everyone before you start to swing? You'll be committing murder next."

I need hardly say that I did not like being addressed, in public, in that way, by one who called himself my friend. Nor was my sensation of annoyance lessened when it was discovered, as of course it was discovered, that the boy had been scarcely touched. Presently, getting up, through his grimy tears he expressed his willingness to continue to carry my clubs, though, so far as I was concerned, I was quite ready to let someone else carry them. Under the circumstances, the way in which Hollis spoke to him was unnecessary.

"You're a well-plucked lad," he said. "Never mind, bear up! If you've luck you'll get round without being killed."

If Hollis's words were unnecessary, which, I hold, they were, Mr Pickard's interposition was monstrous.

"That ought to cost you five shillings, Mr Short. I shouldn't like you to hit me a crack like that for a good deal more than twice the money."

In pecuniary matters the stinginess of Scotchmen is proverbial; which was perhaps the reason why he was disposed to make so free with other people's money. I said nothing. One had only to glance at my bagful of clubs to perceive that it was going to cost me enough to play golf as it was. If I had to pay five shillings, or anything like five shillings, every time some clumsy boy chose to place himself where I did not expect him to be, and where, therefore, he ought not to be, golf, as a game, would be placed out of my reach on the mere ground of expense only.

In silence I approached the little heap of sand on the summit of which my too-obvious caddie had planted my ball. I prepared to hit it. Before doing so I glanced round in order to make sure that, this time, no one was within reach;

and was gratified to find that, taking, as it were, the hint, everyone had withdrawn to a respectful distance; though I could not see why they need have moved either so fast or so far.

"We're giving you plenty of room, old chap," said Hollis.

Since there was no one within perhaps twenty yards of me I could see that for myself, so that that was another unnecessary remark which he thought it worth his while to make. Then I made my stroke.

There is more in hitting a golf ball than some might imagine. There is more, even, in swinging a club—with anything, that is, approximate to ease. It is not so easy to do either as it seems to be when you watch other people doing it. When I saw Hollis and Pickard hitting their balls, what struck me most was the simplicity of the thing. Barstow's comparative failure to hit his had caused me to regard him almost with contempt. To begin with, it was only when I got the club into my own hands, and was making ready to strike with it, that I realised how long it was, how uncomfortably long. I had to put myself into quite an ungainly attitude in order to swing it clear of the ground. After what had already occurred I did not wish to say anything; but had I been left to myself, I should have gone carefully through that bag of clubs, and selected one the mere handling of which did not fill me with a feeling of comparative helplessness.

Then again, it was only when I stood in front of it that it was brought home to my sense of perception how small the ball was, how unreasonably small. The two things seemed so out of proportion; the long, unwieldy club, the minute ball. It was difficult to make up one's mind just where to stand in order to reach it to the best advantage. If you stood straight over it you not only could not see it, but you had to hold the club half-way down the butt in order to strike with it at all. If, on the other hand, you stood at a little distance, it seemed to me not easy, owing to the size of the ball, and its peculiar situation, to make sure of hitting anything but the vacant air.

I own that, actuated by these considerations, I tried first one position and then another, and then, possibly, a third, and soon, in order to ascertain by actual experience, which would suit me best; but my legitimate anxiety did not afford Hollis a ghost of an excuse for still one more of his unnecessary remarks.

"Make up your mind what you are going to do, Short. I think I told you lunch was at two."

Without another moment's hesitation I made my stroke, in what I may almost speak of as an access of temper. I closed my eyes and let fly. Quite what had become of the ball I could not say, but I was conscious of having hit

146

it; and when I opened my eyes again I found that everyone was gazing to the right of where I was standing with what was evidently a considerable amount of interest.

"That was a fine drive!" exclaimed Mr Pickard. "It must have had a carry of a couple of hundred yards."

"It's about that distance off the line," said Hollis.

What he meant I could not tell. I was finding myself at a continual disadvantage in not being acquainted with the technical terms of the game; but from a certain sourness in his tone I suspected him of being jealous of a more generous player's commendation. He and Pickard and Barstow started off, each with a caddie in attendance; while, apparently ignoring their movements, my wretched boy started off in quite a different direction. I heard Hollis's coarse laugh, and Pickard's Scotch chuckle, and Barstow's vacuous snigger. Wondering what was amusing them, I called after my caddie, who was walking away, totally oblivious of the fact that I was standing still.

"Boy, where are you going to?"

Without troubling himself to stop, or even to glance in my direction, he answered me over his shoulder as if, instead of being his employer, I was not a person of the least importance.

"I'm going after your ball. Don't you want it?"

The youngster's impertinence was so marked that a stranger who was standing beside me was moved to nearly uncontrollable merriment. When I turned and stared at him he offered what he possibly meant for an explanation.

"I fancy you'll find your caddie's right, sir; you sent your ball in that direction."

Refraining from a reply—the man was beneath my notice—I strode on after the boy. On and on we went, and the farther we went the farther we were from Hollis and the others.

"It must have been a tremendous hit," I observed, "if the ball came all this way."

"The hole's not over here," was all that boy condescended to say. Then he added, as if by way of an afterthought, "You might as well have hit it behind you. Now you'd better drive it back to the sandbox, if you can do it. It's the shortest road to the green—and the easiest."

When at last we reached the ball we found that it was in a wholly inaccessible position, amid uneven ground, at the bottom of a small hole, surrounded by grass and weeds, principally thistles, which were almost breast-high.

"It is unfortunate that it should have stopped just here," I remarked.

That boy said nothing. He looked at me. He handed me a club, which was rather shorter than the one I had used at first, and had a piece of metal at the lower end, with an air which was partly sulky and partly something worse. Then, with a sort of hop, skip and jump, which was grotesque in the extreme, he withdrew himself ten or twelve feet from where I was, and waited in the apparent expectation that, with that ridiculous implement, I was going to strike the ball just where it was. As this was evidently a boy who needed keeping in his place, I addressed him with a certain degree of sternness, holding out the club which he had given me.

"What do you call this thing?"

"That's your lofting iron."

"It might have been of some use if you had given it me when I made my first shot—"

"You can't drive with a lofting iron."

"Can't I! I don't know how it is that you are in a position to say what I can or what I can't do. You have never seen me play before."

"No, that I never have."

He said this with an emphasis which was in itself an impertinence. I eyed him with an even greater sternness than at first.

"It occurs to me, my boy, that you're not the sort of lad I should have chosen for a caddie had I myself had a voice in the matter. Let me give you fair warning that I am not a person whom it is safe to trifle with, so be careful. Lift that ball—at once, and place it in a position where it will be more convenient for me to strike it."

"Lift the ball!"

His eyes and mouth opened wide. I might have said something amazing.

"I told you to lift the ball; and I added, at once."

"Lift the ball!" he echoed, with parrot-like stupidity. "If I was to do it they might never let me on the links again."

"Don't talk nonsense. And don't attempt to take advantage of my inexperience. I am not so simple as you may imagine, as you will shortly learn. Do you suppose that I, or anyone else, with a thing like this, can hit a ball out of a hole like that?"

"You have only to give it a bit of a twist and it'll come flying out."

"Will it? Indeed. That is your opinion, it isn't mine. However, since I emphatically do not wish to bandy words with a mere child like you, I will give you a practical demonstration of the truth of what I assert."

I gave him one, which, as I expected, was entirely successful. I made at least a dozen attempts to get the ball out of that hole, while he stood looking on, with feelings which I do not attempt to depict. Really serious attempts, which increased in vigour as they multiplied. I struck at it with all the force of which I was capable, repeatedly, again and again. But so far from it "flying out," to adopt that ignorant lad's ignorant phrase, I doubt if I moved it so much as an inch. I sent the sand and dust "flying," but I sent nothing else. It was not for want of perseverance, because I kept on hitting until I not only became hot, but until I realised that, if I persisted in my futile efforts much longer, I, a man of the world, of ripened years, of good social and commercial position, might run the risk of becoming a ridiculous spectacle in the eyes of that soapless little vagabond. So, snatching up the ball out of its preposterous position, with it in one hand, and the useless implement which that boy had given me in the other, I started at a good round pace towards where Hollis and the others were waiting for me at a distance of a quarter of a mile.

I need scarcely mention that, by the time I reached them, I was hotter than ever; hot, also, in more senses than one. It was very present to my mind that I had not gone to Littlestone for that kind of thing. I had gone to play golf, and not with the intention of performing a series of monkey-like antics in front of a dirty little ragamuffin who—to all intents and purposes—had been thrust upon me against my will. Such being my dominant sensation it will easily be believed that I was not inclined for badinage, whatever shape it might take. However, with complete indifference to what my feelings might be, Hollis began practically as soon as I was within shouting range.

"I hope we haven't hurried you, Short. I think I told you lunch was at two."

Even under difficult circumstances I was dignified.

"I hope, gentlemen, that I have not kept you waiting."

"We're blocking the course, but we will devoutly trust that that doesn't matter. Two men who passed us just now—after waiting, they declared, a quarter of an hour—seemed disposed to think strong thoughts, but some men are like that. We were afraid we'd seen the last of you. You went with your ball for a trip into the country, and you seemed disposed to stay there. What's happened? Have you holed out in two?"

Completely ignoring the singularity of Hollis's manner I did my best to make clear how the delay had been caused.

"I am a stranger here, so it is far from my wish to make any complaint; so I will only say that the lad who is supposed to act as my caddie has totally disregarded my instructions, and thus much time has been lost."

"What is it that the young rascal wouldn't do? We noticed that you seemed to be enjoying a little discussion; we wondered how long it was going to last."

I explained, or rather, I had better put it that I endeavoured to, because after events proved that I endeavoured in vain.

"My ball was lying in a position in which it was perfectly impossible for anyone to hit it; yet when I asked him to place it somewhere where it would be more get-at-able, I won't say he refused, but he certainly didn't do it."

"Do you mean to say he wouldn't put your ball somewhere where you could get an easy whack at it?"

"At least he didn't. As a consequence I have been pounding away at it in the most ridiculous manner, so that, finally, rather than lose any more time I picked up the ball myself, and I've brought it with me."

The three men looked at each other in a way which was significant of something, though I was not able positively to decide of what. There was a momentary silence. Then Hollis remarked, with an air of gravity which was almost too portentous to be real,—

"So you brought it with you, and that is it in your hand; I see. Perhaps you adopted the shortest way of getting it here. Short, you're a more remarkable player than I suspected. Pickard, I think we'll give you this hole. We may have better fortune with the next—that is, if Short is lucky."

We all marched forward in a body. Not a word was spoken. For some reason no one seemed to be in a conversational mood. Beginning to feel the silence almost irksome, I was trying to think of some appropriate remark with which to start the ball of conversation rolling, when, without the slightest warning, one of the caddies—not my caddie, but one of the others—stopped short, and began to emit yell after yell of laughter. What had caused him to behave in that unseemly way I could not even guess. I was amazed. I stared at him.

"What is the matter with him?" I asked.

Directly I did so Mr Pickard clapped his hands to his sides and began to yell even louder than the caddie. And Mr Barstow joined him. And the other caddies, even my own. There they were, all of them, doubled up—positively doubled up—by uncontrollable mirth, caused goodness alone knew by what. Hollis and I were the only persons who preserved our gravity; and, as I glanced at Hollis, I noticed that his features seemed to be distorted by pain.

"Don't—don't!" he gasped, waving his hands feebly in the air. "You'll put me off my game!"

"What's the matter with them? What's the joke?" I inquired with, I am sure, the most exemplary mildness.

Hollis's reply wasextraordinary.

"Don't speak to me like that, Short—don't—or the consequences may be serious! My suffering's internal."

What he meant I had not a notion. Few things are more annoying than to feel that individuals in whose society you are are revelling in a joke the entire identity of which is hidden from you. In my judgment, in such a situation, it is someone's plain duty to drop some sort of a hint as to where the jest comes in. However, once more, I refrained from comment.

We reached the starting-place for the second hole. They wanted me to commence, but I declined. So they had their strokes, and then my turn came. I had very carefully noticed how they managed, so that I approached the ball feeling that I had picked up several more or less valuable hints, of which I promised myself that I would not be slow to take advantage. And I have little doubt that I should have done very well had not Hollis chosen that moment to make some more, to say the least of it, unnecessary remarks.

"Let me point out to you, Short, that the second hole lies over there, and that therefore you should drive your ball neither to the right nor the left, but as straight in front of you as you can, because the straighter you drive, the nearer to the hole your ball will be, and the object is to reach the hole in as few strokes as possible. And I may take this opportunity to observe that it is not one of a caddie's duties to place a player's ball in the exact position in which the player would like it to be placed."

Again someone laughed. I fancy more than one, but I did not look to see who. I began to suspect that this was a case of actual bad manners.

"I can't play with this thing!" I exclaimed, eyeing the club which that impudent boy had given me.

"What's wrong with it? The gentleman whom you requested to provide you with every requisite for the game has supplied you with a liberal assortment of drivers; you ought to have no difficulty in finding one to suit you."

I myself chose a club from those in the bag.

"That's a niblick. You can hardly drive with a niblick."

"Why not? Is it an essential condition of the game that you should play a certain stroke with a particular club?"

"Not that I'm aware of. Still, I cannot but think that you will hardly do yourself justice if you drive with a niblick. If you are in search of a little variety why not drive with a putter? These are the clubs with which one generally drives."

He gripped half a dozen clubs, all of them more or less like the one with which I had played my first shot.

"But they are so long—and so unwieldy."

"That you should be of that opinion is unfortunate. Still, one generally drives with them. However, as you please. Drive with what you jolly well like. Only drive. Not only is lunch at two, but we are still blocking the course."

As it happened, two other men had come up, with their caddies. One of them said,—

"If you gentlemen are not in a hurry perhaps you won't mind our going on."

"Not in the least. Time is of no object to us. We are here for the day. You will probably find us still here when you come round again, should you propose to do a second round. Go on, please."

While they went on I examined the clubs which Hollis had suggested; finally deciding on one, though it was not at all to my taste.

"Mind you, this is much too long for me."

"It does not look as if it were the kind of club to which you're accustomed. Perhaps you would prefer a hockey-stick. Should I send for one while we're waiting?"

"I thought," growled Pickard, "that we'd come here to play golf."

With that I let fly. I did not propose to wait for the repetition of such an insinuation as that; emanating, moreover, from a complete stranger. I did not pause to consider, to take aim, for anything. Scarcely were the words out of that unmannerly Scotchman's lips than I made my stroke. Owing, no doubt, to the haste to which I was impelled, I hit nothing but the vacant air, though I had used such force that I myself almost tumbled to the ground.

"That would have been a good shot," commented Hollis, "if you had hit the ball. It's a pity you missed it. Have another go."

I immediately repeated my stroke, hardly giving myself time to recover my equilibrium. Not at all to my surprise, in view of the excessive length of the club, I struck the end of it against the earth so violently as to break it clean in two, to say nothing of the jarring sensation which went right up to my shoulder.

"You hit something that time," murmured Hollis, "though it wasn't the ball. Have another club. There are plenty more where that came from."

I took another club from that impudent lad. I was hot—more, I was indignant. It galled me to be compelled to suspect that it could be possible that I was providing unintentional amusement for a number of persons, not one of whom, under ordinary circumstances, I should have thought worthy of my serious attention. Again I made my stroke. And this time I not only hit the ball, but, in consequence, I presume, of the almost frenzy with which I was actuated, the club itself slipped from my hand, and went careering through the air.

"You hit the ball that time," admitted Hollis. "But—you are a remarkable golfer, Short, and it's an extraordinary fact that your club should have gone farther than the ball."

"We'll give you this match, Hollis," growled Mr Pickard, with an air which I could only call uncouth. "I'm off."

"My good Pickard, we'll give it you. Or—should we postpone it to a day on which we can all get up early, say at sunrise, so that we can have the whole day before us, and the links to ourselves?"

"No thank you, I've had enough."

"I am sorry, gentlemen," I observed, "if I have spoilt your game."

No statement, as coming from me, could have been handsomer, bearing in mind that I was the principal sufferer. But Mr Pickard was incapable of saying anything handsome.

"I didn't know we'd had a game."

"Come, Pickard," suggested the vacuous Barstow, "it hasn't been so bad as that. I've enjoyed it—as far as it's gone, thanks to Mr Short. I'm sorry, Mr Short, that I'm not staying down here long enough to enable us to finish it."

I said nothing. I was not disposed to cross swords in what he might imagine to be a duel of repartee with a man like Barstow. The two men marched off with their caddies without another word. I walked off with

Hollis.

Seldom have I had a more disagreeable walk than that was. Not that, so far as Hollis was concerned, it lasted for any considerable distance; though it was longer than I desired. In the course of a very few minutes he showed me the kind of man he was; and, in so doing, revealed a side of his character of whose existence I had not even dreamed. Scarcely had we left the golf links behind than he remarked—until that moment he had not uttered a single word, nor had I,—

"If you're going by the 12.48 I'll see you off."

"Twelve-forty-eight!" I cried. "I thought you said that lunch was at two."

"I had forgotten that I have an engagement for lunch with a man which I shall be compelled to keep. You needn't stay. There's nothing here but golf."

He looked at me in a manner which I resented with every fibre of my being.

"Allow me to remind you, Hollis, that I came here at your express invitation, on the understanding that you were to teach me golf."

"Did you? I'm sorry. I shall be happy to refund any expenses to which you have been put. But, if you take my strong advice, after your exhibition of this morning you will not stay here any longer than you can help. You might not find it agreeable. As I say, if you are going by the 12.48 I will see you off."

"Will you? I am obliged. You needn't. Nor need you come with me another step. Indeed, I would rather you did not. I will wish you good-morning here— and good-bye."

"Good-bye," he echoed.

Without uttering another syllable he swung round on his heels and strode back towards the golf-links, leaving me to pursue my way alone. My sensations I will not attempt to depict. What a discovery I had made! What a character had been revealed, as it were, by a flash of lightning! I had regarded this man as an acquaintance, almost as a friend, and yet had never known him till that moment.

I did not travel by the 12.48. I went up by the afternoon train to town. I lunched alone; and, in that place, could not have had better society. I am of a buoyant disposition. By the time I reached London I had, practically, wiped the whole regrettable incident off the tablets of my mind. And I had arrived at a decision. I had resolved to hire a field, or an open piece of ground, and engage the services of an expert golf player, a professional, to coach me in the rudiments of the game. And the next time I play a foursome I will undertake to surprise certain persons whose names I do not care to mention.

AN EPISCOPAL SCANDAL

It had been an eloquent sermon; the Bishop had been at his best. That was the general feeling. At the informal meeting which was held in the Dean's parlour, the morning after, this feeling was strongly expressed.

"If," said Mr Dean, "words can make men temperate, then surely the words which we were privileged to hear proceeding from the pulpit in our beloved cathedral yesterday afternoon must have carried conviction to many an erring soul."

So said all of them. Canon Gorse, in particular, felt bound to say that he had heard many temperance sermons in his time, but never one which had impressed him more strongly than the one which the Bishop had delivered yesterday to the clerical and lay workers in the cause of total abstinence. When the Canon made this outspoken declaration, every parson in the room —and every man of them had preached temperance sermons in his time, so they ought to have been good judges—exclaimed, "Hear, hear!"

Perhaps the enthusiasm was rendered greater by the fact that, until quite lately, the Bishop had scarcely been a stalwart. Always on the side of temperance—oh, yes, certainly that—but on the question, the vital question, of total abstinence his views had scarcely been so pronounced as some of his admirers, both clerical and lay, would have wished. Indeed, it was understood that the Bishop himself favoured a good glass of wine at times. In fact, it was reported that he was even esteemed a connoisseur in the matter of certain Spanish wines which are nowadays esteemed old-fashioned. That this should have been so was, in a degree, unfortunate; because how could teetotalism, as a propaganda, assume those dimensions which were in every way desirable in a diocese, the bishop of which, as it was well known, himself looked with a by no means unloving eye on the wine when it is red! When, therefore, it was announced that, if only for example's sake, the Bishop would henceforward shun the spirit which is man's universal curse, it was felt, and rightly felt, that a victory had been won. That victory had, so to speak, been consummated by the Bishop's sermon in the cathedral yesterday, in which he had declared himself a teetotaller, on the side of the teetotallers, and willing, nay, anxious, to stand in their forefront and to lead the van.

"One thing," observed Canon Gorse, "seems plain—that is, that we now shall be on safe ground in refusing to renew the lease of 'The Rose and Crown.' For that, thank goodness!"

Again the reverend Canon seemed but to give voice to the opinion of all who heard him. This question of "The Rose and Crown" had been as a thorn in the side of the cathedral chapter. "The Rose and Crown" was an inn which actually faced the door by means of which the choir and officiating clergy were wont to gain admittance to the sacred edifice. Sad tales were told of it: of how quarts of stout, and such like obnoxious fluids, had been sent in from "The Rose and Crown" to the choirmen while they had actually been engaged in practice, and other dreadful stories. The lease of the inn was running out. The landlord—one George Boulter—desired its renewal. The house, and the ground upon which it stood, was the property of the cathedral chapter. Mr Boulter had already been privately notified that, in all probability, his lease would not be renewed. It was the desire of the chapter that the house should be transformed into a Church institute. The only factor which might upon this point breed dissension had hitherto been the Bishop. But now, as the Bishop himself had signed the pledge, it seemed plain that, as Canon Gorse had observed, the scandal of a number of clergymen owning a public-house would be put an end to.

The Canon had scarcely uttered his remark when the library door opened, and a servant, entering, advanced to Mr Dean.

"Mr Boulter, sir, says he wishes to see you most particular."

"Mr Boulter!" exclaimed the Dean. The man himself, the landlord of "The Rose and Crown." The Dean reflected. He rubbed his nose with his glasses. "What is it that Mr Boulter can wish to say to me? However, I will see him. Tell him so." The servant vanished. The Dean turned to the assembled clergymen. "It is, perhaps, just as well that I should see the man at once, and let him know clearly what our position is."

"Exactly," said Canon Gorse. "Let him understand that plainly. It will not only be fair to ourselves, but it will also be fair to the man."

Mr Boulter was a portly person: his countenance was ruddy; in manner he was affable. He was, all over, Mine Host of the Inn; a type of Boniface which, if we may believe the chroniclers, used to abound, but which, under the present advance of the teetotal forces, is, we will say fortunately, becoming extinct. He reverenced a gentleman, but above all things he reverenced the cloth. His motto as a boy had been "Church and Crown"; but in these latter days he had begun to fear that both Church and Crown were on the side of the enemy.

"Mr Boulter," observed the Dean, as he entered the room in which that gentleman was waiting, "I am pressed for time. Indeed, I have a meeting in the library. I must therefore ask you to tell me in as few words as possible what it is you wish to say."

Mr Boulter turned the brim of his hat round and round in his hands.

"It is about the lease, Mr Dean."

"I thought so. I may as well be brief with you, and clear. You may take my word for it that the lease will not be renewed, and that, in short, 'The Rose and Crown' will cease to be an inn."

"I think not, Mr Dean."

"You think not, Mr Boulter! May I ask what you mean?"

There was something in the tone in which Mr Boulter said that he thought not which the Dean did not understand. He stared at Mr Boulter with dignified surprise. Mr Boulter actually smiled.

"I think that 'The Rose and Crown' will continue to be an inn. That is what I meant, Mr Dean."

The Dean shrugged his shoulders.

"If you choose to persist in thinking so, in spite of my assurance to the contrary, that is your affair, not mine."

The Dean turned to go, as if the interview were already at an end. Mr Boulter coughed behind his hand.

"I should like to have one word with you before you go." The Dean faced round. "Then am I to tell my tale?"

"Your tale? What tale?"

"About the Bishop, Mr Dean."

"About the Bishop?" The Dean looked the innkeeper up and down. A vague suspicion crossed his mind. Already, at this hour of the morning, could the man be drunk? There was nothing in the fellow's bearing to denote anything of the kind. And, indeed, it was matter of common notoriety that, personally, the landlord of "The Rose and Crown" was an abstemious man. But, none the less, there was at that particular moment something about Mr Boulter's manner which the Dean was at a loss to understand. "What do you mean by your tale about the Bishop, sir?"

For a moment or two Mr Boulter continued to turn his hat round and round in his hands, as if he found some difficulty in choosing the exact words in which to frame what he wished to say.

"I understand," he began at last, "that yesterday the Bishop preached a sermon upon temperance."

"You understand quite rightly. It would have done you good, Mr Boulter, to have heard that sermon. Had you done so, you would understand how strong would be the Bishop's opposition to any renewal of the lease of 'The Rose and Crown.'"

"Indeed!" Mr Boulter's tone was dry. "I am not so sure of that."

The Dean stared. The man's manner was so very odd.

"Be so good, Mr Boulter, as to say plainly what it is you mean."

"I don't know what you think, sir, of a bishop who comes straight from preaching a sermon on temperance into my public-house."

"Mr Boulter!"

"It's no good you're looking at me like that, sir. I was surprised, I don't mind owning it. But just let me tell my tale."

The Dean let him tell his tale.

"Yesterday afternoon I was standing at my private door, looking out into the street. It was getting dusk. The service in the cathedral was over, and I thought that everyone had gone. All of a sudden I saw the little door open which we call the Dean's door, and which you know is right in front of my house. Someone came out and walked quickly across the street towards my place. I drew back and went inside. When I got inside the bar I saw that there was some one in a little compartment which only holds about two comfortably, and which I call a private wine-bar. I heard him ask Miss Parkins, one of my young ladies, if we had such a thing as a glass of good sound port."

The Dean shuddered—he scarcely knew why. The fact is that port was the liquid of which the Bishop, in his less stalwart days, had been esteemed such an excellent judge.

"The compartment in which he was is meant for parties who wish to keep themselves quite private. It's boarded up on either side, and in front of it, facing the bar, is a panel of glazed glass set in a mahogany frame, with just enough room between it and the counter to pass, say, a glass of wine. If the party inside wants to keep himself to himself, it's next to impossible to see his face unless you go round by the door in the front. I couldn't see this party's face, but I could see enough of him to see he was a parson. He was short and stout"—the Bishop was short and stout—"and though he had the collar of his coat turned up, it wasn't turned up enough to hide the collar of his shirt. Seeing that I had seen him come out of the Dean's own door in the cathedral, and that he was a parson, things seemed a little queer. So I asked Miss

Parkins, on the quiet, if she knew who it was. I could see she couldn't altogether make it out. She said, although she hadn't seen his face, she seemed to know his voice. Well, he liked my port. I heard him say so; and I heard him tell Miss Parkins that he was considered as good a judge of port wine as any man in England." Again the Dean was conscious of a shiver. "Anyhow, he drank a bottle of it before he went."

"A bottle, Mr Boulter?"

"Yes, sir, a bottle, and one glass over. Directly he had gone my potman went into the private wine-bar for something or other, and as soon as he got inside he called out, 'Hallo! the gentleman's left his bag behind.' And he handed a little leather bag across the bar. Any gentleman who had put away a bottle of port wine in the time that gentleman had done might forget a trifle of a bag like that. It was a beautiful little bag. I had never seen one quite like it before. It had got some initials and a crest stamped on one side. I opened it to see if there was anything inside by means of which I could identify it, and return it to the owner. There was something inside—a sermon. I never saw anything more beautifully written than that sermon—it was like copperplate." Once more the Dean was conscious of a shudder travelling down his spine. The Bishop's beautiful caligraphy was famous—a fair handwriting is nowadays too rare. "On the front page was written the Bishop's name and address in full, and in the top left-hand corner was written: 'Preached in the cathedral on the afternoon of the 13th of November, 189—.' That's yesterday afternoon, sir. I've brought that bag with me. You'll find the sermon still inside. Perhaps you know whose bag that is, sir."

Mr Boulter picked up a small leather bag which had been lying, hitherto unnoticed, upon a chair, and handed it to the astonished Dean. The Dean *did* know whose bag it was—he knew too well. There was no mistaking those initials and that crest. There was no necessity to examine the sermon which Mr Boulter assured him was inside. The Dean gazed at that excellent example of fine workmanship in leather bags as if he realised that he had all at once become an actor in what might turn out to be a tragedy. Words proceeded from his stammering lips.

"You are, I am sure, too reasonable a man, Mr Boulter, to jump at impossible conclusions from imperfect premisses."

"I don't know what you call 'imperfect premisses.' Directly I saw the name and address which was written on the front page of that sermon, Miss Parkins cried out, 'Why, it was the Bishop's voice!' She stared at me as if she was going to have a fit—and well she might. Miss Parkins is a good girl, as all my young ladies are, and, indeed, everybody else about my place, although I say it." Mr Boulter glared at the Dean with eyes which were full of meaning. "She never misses a chance of hearing the Bishop preach when she can get one, and if there's anyone who ought to know the Bishop's voice it's her. It seems to me, begging your pardon, sir, that I ought to have a reward for bringing that leather bag back safe and sound."

"Certainly, Mr Boulter. Any sum in reason you like to mention."

"The reward I want is the renewal of my lease."

"That, as I have already told you, is—"

"Excuse me just one moment, sir. You see that?" Taking an envelope out of an inner pocket of his coat, Mr Boulter flourished it in the Dean's face. "I've a boy who lives in London, and writes for the papers; a smart chap he is, and well respected in his trade. I've written an account of how the Bishop preached a sermon on temperance in the cathedral—a fine sermon it was, I'm told by those who heard it—and of how he then walked straight out of the cathedral into my public-house, and put away a bottle of old port, and got so drunk that he forgot his bag and left it behind him, with the sermon which he had just been preaching on temperance inside of it. That account's in this envelope. I'm going to send it to my boy, and I'm going to tell him to turn it into money; and I'll lay you what odds you please—although I'm no more a betting man than you are—that, before a week is over, the tale will be told in every paper in England, ah! and known all the world over. You're going to take away my living. My grandfather kept 'The Rose and Crown' decent, my father kept it decent, and I've kept it decent; there's never been even so much as a shadow of a complaint made against me by the police, nor by no one. And yet you cathedral gentlemen have taken a sudden fad into your heads, and you're going to ruin me. Very well, ruin me! You think you're going to do good to the cause of temperance by shutting up 'The Rose and Crown.' What harm do you suppose will be done to the cause of temperance by that tale being told, as they do tell that sort of tale nowadays, in all the newspapers of the world? I guess the cause of temperance will not get over that tale for years —it will be always being told. At the very least, if I do have to go I will take care that somebody else goes with me. Now which is it to be—am I to have my lease renewed, or am I to post this envelope?"

The Dean hesitated.

"In any case, as you must be aware, Mr Boulter, the matter is not one which can be decided on the spur of the moment; the decision is not with me."

"Understand me, sir. If I go away from here without a promise of renewal, I post this letter. I know as well as you know that in the whole business your voice will be the ruling voice. You give me a bit of writing in which you undertake to do your best to get my lease renewed, and I will give you this envelope, with what's inside. And I will give you my promise never to breathe a word that the Bishop ever so much as came near my place. As for Miss Parkins, I know she won't speak unless she's forced. She's a religious girl; she thinks a lot of the Bishop, and she's too much shocked at the whole affair. I never saw a girl so upset. Now which is it to be?"

The Dean still hesitated—with sufficient cause.

"What term of renewal would you require?"

"The last lease was for ninety-nine years, and I want this lease to be for ninety-nine."

"Ninety-nine years, Mr Boulter?"

Mr Boulter did not get a promise of renewal for ninety-nine years, or anything like it, but he did get "a bit of writing." With that "bit of writing" in a secure division of his plethoric pocket-book he went away. The Dean was left to his reflections. The leather bag he held in one hand, the envelope which the landlord of "The Rose and Crown" had given him he held in the other. Putting down the bag, he tore the envelope into halves, then into quarters, and crossing the room he dropped the fragments in the fire which burned brightly in the grate.

"Terrible! terrible!" This he said as he watched the pieces of paper being consumed by the flames. Then he seemed to endeavour to pull himself together. "Well, I shall have to tell them. I must give reasons for the thing which I have done. The tale will have to travel so far, but"—the Dean pressed his lips together; few men's countenances were capable of assuming a severer aspect than Dean Pettifer's—"I will make it my especial business to see that it goes no farther." He still seemed to hesitate before returning to the apartment in which his colleagues were awaiting him. "I must say that I never thought it of him. I have been always conscious that in his latitudinarianism there was a certain element of danger. But I never dreamed that he was capable of such a thing as this—no, never!"

It was with a distinctly unsatisfactory look upon his face that he made his reappearance in the little impromptu meeting. The criminatory leather bag he carried in his left hand. It is not impossible that those who were present became immediately conscious that with the Dean, since they had seen him last, all things had not gone well. The buzz of conversation, which had been audible as he opened the door, ceased upon his entrance, as though something in his bearing acted as a damper.

The somewhat awkward silence was broken by Canon Gorse.

"Well, was Boulter troublesome?"

The Dean laid the bag in front of him upon the table.

"He was." The Dean carefully wiped his glasses. There was a suggestion of curious expectation in the eyes which were fixed upon him. Their owners already perceived that there was something in the air. Was it possible that the landlord of "The Rose and Crown" had behaved in the manner which, in the estimation of some persons, is a natural characteristic of individuals of his class, and had been guilty of actual violence in the sacred precincts of the Deanery? "He was troublesome in a sense for which, on this occasion, I will simply say that I was unprepared; and to such a degree that I have given him what amounts to a virtual undertaking that his lease shall be renewed."

This was evidently not the sort of thing for which his listeners had been waiting—one could see it by their faces. Some of them changed colour, and some of their jaws dropped open. Canon Gorse stared at the speaker, as if he found it difficult to believe that his own ears were capable of fulfilling their normal functions.

"Pettifer, impossible!" Perceiving that the word might seem too strong, he amended it. "That is to say, how do you mean?"

The Dean leaned over the table. His attitude, indeed his whole manner, suggested severity tempered by sorrow.

"Before I say anything further I wish to have an understanding with all of you that not one word of what I am about to utter will be breathed by any one of you to any creature living—and by that I mean neither to your wives, nor to your daughters, nor to any member of your households—that it will be received as though it came to you under the seal of the confessional." There was silence. "If anyone feels himself, for any cause whatever, unable to give such a pledge, then I must respectfully ask that person at once to withdraw."

No one did withdraw. No one said either Ay or Nay. So it may be supposed that the pledge which the Dean required was unanimously given. That the Dean understood that to be the case was evident. He held up the little leather bag in front of him as if it were some dreadful thing.

"This bag is the Bishop's—our beloved Bishop's bag. I know it, of my own knowledge, to be the bag which he had with him in the cathedral yesterday afternoon. It still contains the MS. of the sermon which the Bishop preached, and which we all rejoiced to hear. This bag has just been brought to me by the landlord of 'The Rose and Crown.' It was left, unintentionally left, on his premises by a person who, at the close of yesterday afternoon's service, went out of the Dean's door of the cathedral into one of Mr Boulter's private bars, and there and then consumed a bottle of port wine."

The Dean ceased. There again was silence—there well might be. The Dean again went on,—

"A son of Mr Boulter's is engaged on one of those scurrilous journals which are called society papers. Mr Boulter proposed to send this story up to his son to print. On the understanding that the matter shall be confined to his own breast, I have deemed it wisdom to give him, as I have said, what virtually amounts to an undertaking that his lease shall be renewed. That is all I have to say. You will feel with me that it is too much. May I ask you not to speak of this matter even among yourselves, but, as I shall do, to do your best to blot it from your minds? Let us, if we can, forget that this thing has ever been. And now, with your permission, I will wish you all good-day."

They went like a flock of sheep, although there was almost a suspicion of pathos in the manner of their parting. When they were gone the Dean set himself to perform a task of the exceeding delicacy of which, to say the least, he was fully conscious. He was not a man to palter with what he deemed his duty. He was certainly not a man to shrink from doing a thing merely because the thing was disagreeable. Therefore, scarcely had the last of his colleagues turned his back on the Deanery than he put the little leather bag into a larger bag, and, with that larger bag grasped firmly in his hand, he strode off to the Palace.

He was going to make it his business to see that without any further unnecessary loss of time the Bishop came into what was, undoubtedly, his own again.

He found his lordship in the library. The Bishop was dictating to his secretary, the Rev. John Budgen. The secretary was seated at a table; the Bishop took his ease in a capacious arm-chair. As the Dean entered, his lordship greeted him with that genial heartiness for which the Bishop of Boundersville is famed. Not a trace of guilty consciousness about him anywhere—not a trace! It was with a sort of shock that the Dean noticed that there was nothing of the kind.

"How do, Pettifer? I'm doing what I call my morning task of stone-breaking—writing letters, by proxy, to a lot of people who have more time on their hands than they know what to do with, and who, therefore, insist upon wasting mine. Anything particular to say to me?"

The Dean was, perhaps, too refined—the thing is possible. He was not only a fine scholar, he was a fine gentleman. He was of opinion that dignitaries, and particularly all dignitaries of the Church, should have the standard of manners which was peculiarly his own. The Bishop's heartiness, his rough-and-ready methods of expression, had always grated on his high-strung sensibilities; especially did they grate just then.

"I am bound to state, my lord, that what I have to say to you is of the first importance."

The Bishop looked at him a little quizzically. Possibly the Dean's exaggerated preciseness appealed to a sense which there is no reason why even a bishop should be without.

"Excuse me, Budgen; I'll ring when I'm ready." The secretary withdrew. "Now, Pettifer, fire away. Who killed the cat, and which cat's been killed?"

Such a fashion of speech was actually offensive to the Dean. Perhaps the spirit of mischief still lingered in the Bishop's breast; perhaps, at times, the Bishop found the Dean almost as trying as the Dean found him. Under the circumstances such a bearing on the part of the Bishop shocked the Dean almost into speechlessness. He gazed at his spiritual superior in a manner which, unless he was mistaken, made his lordship wince. "Has your lordship not missed your lordship's sermon-bag?"

At the question his lordship plainly started.

"My sermon-bag, Pettifer? What do you mean?"

"My lord, I mean what I say."

The Bishop was perturbed. Rising from his chair, he began to fidget about the room. "Why do you ask?"

"Because it has been returned to me."

"Returned to you—no!"

"Yes, my lord; I have it here." The Dean produced the little bag from inside the larger one. He held it up in front of him as he had held it up in front of him at the impromptu meeting at the Deanery. "I will not ask how it came to stray from your lordship's keeping."

The Bishop looked at the Dean; the Dean looked straight at him. It was evident that his lordship was not completely at his ease.

"I perceive that you have heard the story."

"I regret, my lord, to say that I have."

The Bishop plainly flushed; perhaps he found the Dean's tone and manner slightly galling.

"Perhaps it was not quite the thing to do, but"—his lordship shrugged his shoulders—"what does it matter?"

The Dean, in his turn, winced.

"What does it matter, my lord? Surely your lordship knows that it matters."

"How did the bag come into your possession, Pettifer?"

"It was brought to me by Mr Boulter, the landlord of 'The Rose and Crown.'"

"Boulter!—'The Rose and Crown!'—No, by George!"

His lordship said "By George!" and as he said it the Dean shrunk back as if he had received a blow.

"Mr Boulter, as the price of his silence, extracted from me a promise that his lease should be renewed."

The Bishop woke up. He showed more alertness than he had hitherto displayed.

"You promised him that his lease should be renewed—the lease of 'The Rose and Crown'?"

"I did. I thought it better that I should do so than that such a story should be told."

"Story? What story?"

The Dean, before he answered, indulged himself with a pause for consideration.

"My lord, if any word which I may utter seems lacking in respect, as coming from me to you, I entreat your pardon. My lord, when I heard that, after preaching a sermon, and so grand a sermon, upon total abstinence, you passed straight from the cathedral pulpit to the bar of a common public-house, and there drank so large a quantity of wine that, in the temporary forgetfulness which it occasioned, you left the sermon itself behind you in the bar, I felt that it were better that I should promise almost anything than that such a story should be told."

As he listened the Bishop's countenance underwent a variety of changes. When the Dean had finished the Bishop dropped into a chair, and—laughed. Not a genteel simper, but a loud and a long guffaw. The Dean felt that he could not endure such levity even from a bishop—his own bishop, too.

"My lord, in such a matter you may see occasion for merriment, but if you could have seen, at the Deanery, the faces of the cathedral clergy as I told to them the story—"

"Pettifer, what do you mean?"

Springing to his feet, the Bishop grasped the speaker by the arm. The Dean was startled.

"I say, if you could only have seen their faces—"

"Do you mean to say that you have told this story to anyone?"

"I was constrained to state my reasons for giving such a promise to the landlord of 'The Rose and Crown.'"

"I hardly know if I ought not to strike you, Arthur Pettifer."

"My lord!"

"I hardly know if I ought not to pillory you in the market-place, and so compel you to do penance for your slanderous tongue. I have long been conscious of a certain pharisaical narrowness in your mental and in your moral outlook. I have seen in you what has seemed to me a hideous tendency to think the worst both of women and of men. But I never thought you capable of such gross obliquity of judgment as you yourself appear now to own to. Is it possible that you believed that such a story as you have told me could be true?"

The Dean had turned quite pale. He seemed to speak beneath his breath.

"Is it possible that Boulter lied?"

"Is it possible, Arthur Pettifer, that you could believe that I—I, Ralph Ingall, with whose life's history you are as well acquainted almost as myself —could so perjure myself that, as God's minister, in God's house, I could pledge myself never again to let alcohol pass my lips in any shape or form, and that then, with that pledge still warm upon my lips, I could pass straight into a pot-house and stupefy myself with wine?"

"Was it—was it Budgen, then?"

"Budgen? Budgen? Pettifer, this is worse and worse! You know that Budgen has never touched a drop of alcoholic stimulant since the day that he was born. I will tell you the story of that bag so far as I know it myself. And I will see that your promise to the man Boulter is kept both in the spirit and the letter. I will place it upon you, as an enduring penance, that for the continued existence of his drink-shop you, and you alone, shall be responsible."

The Dean was silent. He seemed to totter as a man who received a crushing blow. The Bishop paced up and down the room. Like an accusing spirit—possessed of a tolerable corporation—he poured out upon the Dean a curious, correct, and circumstantial history of the adventures of his sermon-bag.

"There was a man at my college whose name I need not mention. We were ordained together. I will put it gently, and will say that he did not take full advantage of his opportunities. I believe that, for some time now, he has ceased to exercise his clerical office. He has become a reporter for the '—'"— the Bishop named a paper which all good Churchmen are supposed to read —"and he came to me yesterday afternoon, into the vestry, after I had done my sermon. Possibly you may have seen him there. He told me that he had come down from town specially to report my sermon. According to him the train had been late, and he only arrived in time to hear a part. He asked me if I would let him see my notes. On the spur of the moment I handed him my bag, with the sermon in it. I told him that he might make, what he expressed a desire to make, a verbatim copy, and that he was then to return to me my property. I felt immediately afterwards that I had, perhaps, not done the wisest possible thing. But it was then too late. After the story you have told me, what he did with bag and sermon I can guess."

While the Bishop was still speaking a servant appeared at the door.

"My lord, a person—I believe a clergyman—desires me to inform your lordship that he wishes to see you at once upon very pressing business."

"Yes, my lord; that is so."

The scandalised servant turned to find that the person alluded to had, uninvited, found his way into the Bishop's presence. The Bishop recognised his visitor; he signified the same to the servant who had *not* shown him in.

The visitor in question was an individual of somewhat doubtful appearance. He looked half cleric, half layman. He was short and stout, and so far resembled the Bishop, but the resemblance went no farther. The Bishop, taking possession of the little leather bag which the Dean still retained, held it out to the newcomer.

"Well, sir, have you come to make another copy of my sermon? As you perceive, it has been returned to me, but not by you."

The stranger wiped his brow. He seemed more than a trifle embarrassed.

"I regret to say that I have not yet taken a copy of it, my lord. The fact is, my lord, that, as I told you yesterday, I left town without having lunched, and after leaving your lordship in the cathedral I felt so exhausted that I just stepped across the road to take a glass of wine—"

"Quite so, sir. I understand too well. Since my sermon upon temperance has once been returned by the landlord of a tavern, I do not think that I care to run the risk of its reaching me by means of a similar channel a second time. So far as you are concerned, sir, my sermon must go unreported." The Bishop rang the bell. The servant reappeared. "Dawes, show this gentleman out."

The gentleman was shown out, though it seemed, from his manner, that there still was something which he would have wished to say.

When he had gone the Bishop placed the little leather bag upon a table. He turned to the Dean. He looked at him, and he said, more in sorrow than in anger,—

"Pettifer, how long does it take you to know a man?"

MR BLOXAM AND THE BRITISH CONSTITUTION

I say that the British constitution is in a shameful condition. I say that any system of legislation which breeds matrimonial discord and sets a husband against his wife, or, what is much worse, a wife against her husband, is a disgrace to civilisation. I say it without hesitation. I have said it before, and I say it again.

Look at me and Mrs Bloxam. From the first I have had difficulties with that woman. She has never properly perceived the inevitable and natural superiority of the husband over the wife. No, not once. I can prove it out of the mouths of a cloud of witnesses. But when it comes to making the husband the laughing-stock of his native land, not to speak of his own parish, and an object of derision in the low columns of a ribald press, then I assert, emphatically, that something must be done. And it will have to be done, too, and that before very long. I've had enough of it, I do know that. The time has come to throw aside the entangled folds of the cloak of dignity, and to wave the impassioned arms of a threatening Nemesis. Let her beware. And her aiders and abettors, let them beware also.

I had a difference with our rector. I do not deny that the Reverend George Crookenden has his good points. Every man has. Although Mr Crookenden failed to see that I have mine. Therefore, when it was pointed out that the parish of Copstone was in a state of educational inefficiency, I threw my weight into the scale of intelligence. It was shown that the Church school was a failure. So I said, "Let there be a School Board." And there was a School Board. And what is more, I was put forward as a candidate. I admit that, at first, I was unwilling. I declare, positively, that I refused five distinct and separate times. But at last I was overpersuaded. I stood. And now I wish to goodness that I hadn't. But who can foresee the march of events as they trickle through the convoluted waterways of an impenetrable thicket?

Mrs Bloxam has always been an enemy to the intellectual advance of the age.

"Bother your books and things!" she would say. "I want a girl with some knowledge of housework. Is she going to get it out of them?"

"Certainly, if she looks for it in the proper quarter."

"And pray, what do you call the proper quarter?" Mrs Bloxam looked at me in a way I particularly dislike, as if I were an inferior animal. "You are yourself such an omnivorous reader that no doubt you will be able to throw light upon the subject."

I knew what she meant, but I declined to let her see it.

"It is true that I do not read trashy novels, or sickly love tales, which present a false picture of the stern realities of life. I confine my attention to works of a higher class."

"There are not many of them published, are there?"

"What do you mean?"

"Because I have never seen you read anything but newspapers since we were married, and I doubt if you ever read a whole book through in your life."

The assertion took my breath away. But I declined to argue. I always do decline when circumstances permit. They did most clearly then. Though, when I considered the matter afterwards, I perceived that, had I chosen, I might have overwhelmed her with the force of my reasoning. In my opinion, reading is a finite process. I read a great deal when I was a lad, though I do not quite remember what. There the matter ended. Life is, as it were, divided into sections. Each section should be devoted to a different object. For me the section devoted to reading is passed.

The bombshell fell while we were at dinner, and while Jane was still in the room.

"What rubbish is this I hear about your being a candidate for this tuppenny-hapenny School Board which is going to plague the unfortunate people?"

"My dear, I am not responsible for all the rubbish you may hear."

"Then you admit that it is a rubbishing idea?"

"I do nothing of the kind; at least, so far as my standing is concerned. On the contrary, I am standing in deference to the earnestly-expressed wish of the more intelligent portion of the inhabitants of this parish."

"Meaning Broadbridge the cobbler, Tyler the blacksmith and their friends, who never attend any place of worship, but spend most of their time at the 'Fox and Hounds' instead. They know that you have been silly enough to quarrel with Mr Crookenden and propose to use you as a catspaw."

"I traverse the whole of your assertion, but decline to dwell on so delicate a subject. Any discussion had better be postponed to when we are alone."

"Jane, leave the room."

I did not wish Jane to leave the room. Not at all. On the contrary, I wished her to stay. I had yet occasion for her services. But, on the other hand, I did not desire to humiliate Mrs Bloxam by forbidding the girl to carry out her mistress's commands. So Jane went. And then Mrs Bloxam expressed herself on the subject of my candidature with a fluency which I found it difficult to curtail. As usual, she allowed her language to become stronger than the occasion required. But when it came to her "positively prohibiting"—her own words—me to go to the poll, I put my foot down. I pointed out, with irresistible clearness of reasoning, that I was pledged to represent the conscience of a well-defined section of our neighbours, and by that pledge my sense of honour constrained me to stand. And, in fact, that I would stand by it. Nothing she could say would turn me from my purpose. Not of such weak materials was I made. The sooner she understood that the better. And, at last, she did understand—in a measure.

"Then all I can say is that your quarrel with Mr Crookenden will be life-long. Which will be nice for me, and for all of us. So the sooner you sell this place and go to live elsewhere, the better it will be."

"Henrietta, I am ready to forgive Crookenden at any moment of any day. He has only to ask me; he will find me quite prepared. Do you mean to say that he is so dead to the beauty and the sweetness of a united parish that he is unwilling to allow to others that freedom of conscience which he claims for himself."

"It is unfortunate, Augustus, that when there are two ways between which to choose, you should always prefer the silliest. Still I feel that it is rather your misfortune than your fault, since it is in that way you are constituted. I can only hope that, on this occasion, you will yourself see your folly before it is too late."

There the discussion ended. I was not disposed to bandy personalities with Mrs Bloxam. I never am.

At the same time I am prepared to confess that I was not altogether satisfied with the persons who were bracketed with me as associates in my candidature. There were to be seven members of the Board, so there were seven of us. We found it rather difficult to complete the tale, but it was done. We called ourselves Progressives. We stood for intellectual advance. Our motto was "Brain Emancipation. Unchaining of the Intellect. Cultivation of the Mind." It was of my own composition, and was generally found to be pregnant with suggestion. As someone, I forget who it was, himself pointed out to me, "The more you look at it, the more you understand what it means." That I felt myself to be the case.

Unfortunately, my colleagues were hardly up to the standard to which this motto pointed, as a whole. Nor to be quite correct, even in part. There was Broadbridge, who undoubtedly does mend shoes, and who also, it is equally certain, drinks. He is the person I dislike most in the whole country side. Ever since this School Board business has been in the air he has endeavoured to borrow small sums of money from me, and has been in a state of almost continual intoxication. Tyler, the proprietor of the smithy on Wayman's Hill, calls himself a Red Republican, and is the most ignorant, argumentative and I may add, quarrelsome person I ever encountered. We three were the actual candidates. The other four were dummies, dragged in by the head and heels to make up the tale of the seven. One of them, Isaac Harding, who styles himself an "odd man," and who is in reality a loafing, able-bodied vagabond, who makes his wife support him by taking in washing, told me that his name had been used without his authority, and that he "didn't know nothing at all about it." Which I thought extremely probable. It is not easy to find seven Progressive candidates in a parish like Copstone.

Not the least of our misfortunes, from my point of view, was the fact that we were compelled to hold our meetings at the "Fox and Hounds." The parish room is practically under the control of the rector, and even had I been willing to ask his permission, which I was not, I doubt if he would have allowed us to have them there. So we were driven to what they call the "large room" at the "Fox and Hounds." I liked our quarters none the more because they were so exactly suited to the tastes of my associates. They loved the place; had they had their own way I believe they would have lived there altogether; the proximity of the bar was, to them, an unqualified, unceasing delight. I do not know what is the state of the law on the subject of treating at School Board elections; but if there is no clause objecting to candidates treating each other, then there ought to be. I never, at any hour of the day or night, met my colleagues without their suggesting something to drink, which, if I wished to avoid unpleasant observations, I had to pay for. It was most unsatisfactory. I found myself on the high road to being held up as an inciter to drink and an encourager of drunkenness. It was a decidedly undesirable condition of affairs.

But I could have borne it all. I could have put up with being seen with Broadbridge when he had to cling to my neck to prevent himself reclining in the gutter. I could have swallowed my feelings at being coupled with Tyler in his idiotic denunciations of all that is decent and respectable in my native land. It was to suffer in the cause of truth and progress, it was to show Mr Crookenden that there are persons who will not be trampled on rough-shod, and that he is not the only creature in the parish who dare call his soul his own. But there was something which I could not endure. And it was that which came soon. It was that which has caused that epoch in my life to become branded with indelible letters of flaming fire.

When I say that the first intimation was received from a third party, I say more than enough to show what was the state of affairs which obtained in my domestic circle. I was driving up Wayman's Hill, when, as I was passing his smithy, Tyler, coming out, called to me to stop. He was in his shirt-sleeves; had his hammer in his hand; and I could see that he was shoeing Mr Rudd's brown mare. As usual, he did without a preface.

"I don't know if you call this the proper way in which to treat us, Mr Bloxam, because, if you do, I don't. I thought that in this election business you were with us heart and soul. We're standing by you like men, why don't you stand by us?"

"What on earth do you mean?"

I wondered if, at that hour of the day, he had already been drinking.

He took a printed paper out of his pocket, smoothed it open with his dirty hand and passed it to me. It was the election address of the opposition candidates.

"That's an advance copy which I got from Briggs the printer on the quiet. Perhaps you'll let me know what explanation you have to offer."

There had been some mystery as to who Crookenden's supporters were to be. Now it seemed that the names were out. But what did the fellow mean by asking me for an explanation? What had I to do with Mr Crookenden's puppets? I glanced at the list. The first name was Crookenden's. Of course, it always would be first, where he had a voice in the matter. The second was "Ada Kate Laughton." It seemed incredible. Actually Mrs Laughton. Well, if Laughton chose to let his wife make a public exhibition of herself, all I could say was that I was extremely sorry for him. Hadn't the woman any household duties to attend to? Everybody knew who was the grey mare in that establishment. Some men do not know how to rule their wives. Still, that such a woman as Mrs Laughton should take it upon herself to oppose me was—I will be mild and say surprising. The third name was—it was a hoax, a silly hoax. Tyler, or someone, was trying to make me a butt for a practical joke. But I was not to be so easily caught, the thing was too preposterous. Yet there it was, in all the dignity of print. "Bloxam, Henrietta." Address, "The Chestnuts." Description, "Married Woman." The letters danced before my eyes. I stared at them with unseeing gaze.

"What nonsense is this?" I muttered.

"That's what I want to know, what nonsense that is. That's what I thought

I'd ask you to explain, like a man."

I looked at Tyler. Tyler looked at me. There was something on his face which I did not relish; something which approximated to a grin, an unfriendly grin.

"Where did you get this paper from?"

"I tell you—from Briggs the printer. He's printing them. That's a private copy."

"It's a hoax. Someone's been having a joke with you."

"Don't you make any mistake. No one would play a joke off on me, not round these parts."

He grasped his hammer in an eminently suggestive way. What he said was probably correct. He had the reputation, a well-deserved one, of being a man with whom one would joke with difficulty and danger.

"All the same, Mr Tyler, the statement on this paper is ridiculously incorrect. Mrs Bloxam, my wife, is not a candidate; she has no intention of becoming a candidate; and, I may say at once, that under no circumstances would I permit her to do so. Especially in opposition to me, her husband. The idea is really too ridiculous for contemplation. I beg you will dismiss it at once and finally from your mind."

I prepared to start. He held my horse's head.

"But suppose she is a candidate, what then?"

"You don't flatter me, Mr Tyler. Should you allow your wife to act in direct antagonism to your wishes?"

"I reckon not." He grinned significantly. "Then shall you leather Mrs Bloxam if she tries any of her little games? I rather fancy you'll find you've put off leathering her too long. They want a lot of strap when you're first starting."

What did the fellow mean? How dare he talk to me like that? Really, this business was bringing me on terms of uncomfortable familiarity with the most curious characters. Leather Mrs Bloxam! I shivered at the thought. What did he take me for? And her? Henrietta is not the sort of person to whom it is necessary to do more than remotely hint at what are the channels in which the course of a wife's duty flows. And yet—

I wished the fellow had never shown me his wretched, nonsensical, trumpery paper, which he had apparently stolen from the imbecile Briggs. As though my mind was not already sufficiently occupied. If I had dreamt that this preposterous School-Board business would have been such a source of worry, so far as I was concerned Crookenden and his Church school might have gone on for ever. In my agitation—I am agitated, sometimes, by a very little—I touched Toby with the whip, so that, when I got him home, he was in quite a lather.

Mrs Bloxam was in her own sitting-room. I found her there. I had worked myself into something approaching a state of indignation. I produced Tyler's handbill with a sort of flourish.

"Henrietta, some scoundrel has been taking liberties with your name."

"Mr Bloxam!"

She was engaged on some needlework of a domestic character, from which she looked up at me with an air of apparent surprise.

"I shall cause immediate legal proceedings to be taken against the man who has acted in a manner calculated to bring you and myself into public contempt."

"To what man do you allude?"

"To the man who put your name on this."

I gave her Tyler's handbill. She looked it up and down, very carefully, as it seemed to me.

"I fail to see what there is here to which you have any reason to take objection."

"Nothing there! When the impertinent rascal has dared to put you forward as one of Crookenden's puppets."

"If he has done so, he is to blame, for I certainly am no one's puppet. I have merely availed myself of that of which you have so freely availed yourself, the right to call my soul my own."

"Henrietta! I don't understand what you mean."

"And yet it is simple enough. Ever since I have been able to think on such subjects at all, I have had my own views on the subject of education—true education as opposed to false. When I see such creatures as Broadbridge and Tyler endeavouring to promulgate their hideous notions and notorious malpractices in the place in which I live, I cannot refuse to listen to the call of duty which summons me, both as a Christian and a woman of education and refinement, to take my stand against them."

"Then am I to gather that that name—that your name—that my name—is there by your authority?"

"Your name, certainly not. My name, undoubtedly."

"But have you forgotten that I am myself a candidate?"

"So, I am sorry to say, I have been given to understand."

"I represent the cause of progress and advance."

"Both, I imagine, in the direction of the public-house. I am credibly informed that since your candidature there has been more drunkenness in Copstone than has ever been known before in the annals of the parish."

It was a monstrous thing to say. Yet I wished that my associates had been teetotallers, and that we could have had the use of the parish room.

"Henrietta, I will not characterise the statement which you have just now made. I content myself by taking up my position as head of this household to prohibit your pursuing any farther the dangerous pathways along which your feet have been induced to stray by the Jesuitical teachings of an insidious foe."

"Speak English, Augustus, if you please, at home. Rodomontade, if you choose, where nobody understands you, or wants to. Here say plainly what you mean."

"I forbid you to carry the farce of your candidature any farther."

"That I readily undertake to do. I promise you it shall be no farce."

"Farce or no farce, I command you to take your name from off that list." I regret to say that Henrietta snapped her fingers in the air. "Am I to understand that you snap your fingers at the expression of my wishes?"

"You have not even troubled yourself to do that. You have known all along what my wishes were, yet you have chosen to entirely ignore my most sacred aspirations."

"Henrietta, the husband is the head of the wife."

"Who says so? Your friend Tyler? It is notorious that he scoffs at the sanctity of the marriage tie."

"Don't call that man my friend."

"No? Do you authorise me to state in public that you repudiate his friendship?"

"I won't chop phrases with you. I will merely remind you that at the altar you promised me obedience."

"Suppose you were to instruct me to commit murder, would you consider it my duty to carry the promise even so far?"

"I am not instructing you to commit murder."

"You are requesting me to do something analogous, to murder all that is best and noblest in the parish of Copstone."

"That's an outrageous falsehood."

She stood up.

"Of course, if you accuse me of deliberate untruth—"

"You won't get out of it like that. I tell you, frankly, that if you are not careful I shall go straight to Crookenden and tell him with my own lips that I have forbidden you to stand."

"He knows already that you would forbid me. They all know it. It is because of that knowledge they have urged me to take up the position I have done, and to persist in it; in the hope that my action may do something to mitigate the evil example which you are setting to the parish."

"This is awful. When I stood beside you at the altar I never thought that you would speak and behave to me like this—never!"

"Nor I that I should be constrained to such a course. You may, however, easily make the situation more tolerable."

"How?"

"By withdrawing your candidature."

"Indeed! Now I see the point at which the whole thing's aimed. Crookenden has egged you on to make a public exhibition of yourself in order to drive me from the righteous stronghold which I have occupied. I see the Jesuit hand."

She shrugged her shoulders as calmly as if we were discussing the question of thick or clear soup for dinner.

"You see things which do not exist. It is a condition of a certain mental state. There is one thing I should like to say. I have been told that courtesy is the characteristic note of English politics. That men may sit on opposite sides of the House and yet be very good friends both in and out of it. I hope that may be the same with us. You have taken up the cry of 'Beer and the "Fox and Hounds,"' I that of the 'Bible and Clean Living.' Let each admit that the other may be actuated by conscientious motives. Then we shall still be good friends, though we may agree to differ."

It was no use talking to such a woman, not the slightest. We all have to bear our burdens, and I bore mine, though I never supposed that it would have taken the shape of being opposed by my own wife in an election for the School Board. As a matter of fact, it was unendurable—yet I bore it. Not only did she persist in her candidature, but she carried it on with a degree of activity which was little less than astounding. The contest afforded considerable entertainment to the parish. From the public interest point of view there might have been only two candidates—she and I. It was a subject of constant comment in the public prints. "Husband and wife oppose each other at a School-Board election. Amusing situation. Lively proceedings." That was the sort of headline which confronted me in I do not know how many papers.

Some of my colleagues actually chose to regard me as responsible for Mrs Bloxam's conduct. It is a painful moment when a man, of a naturally sensitive disposition, has to state in public that his wife is acting in direct defiance of his wishes. And the delicacy of his position is intensified when his hearers begin to criticise her conduct. It is in accordance with the fitness of things to abuse your opponent; but when your opponent is your own wife, it is an open question whether, even if you are entitled to abuse her yourself, your associates have a right to do so too. It is obviously a problem of an exceedingly complicated character, and one which, I believe, has never been properly thrashed out. I shall never forget my sensations when, at a meeting at the "Fox and Hounds," Tyler began to call Henrietta names. I had to stop him. Then he said I was a traitor. He certainly succeeded in creating a suspicion that I was in collusion with my own wife to cause him and myself to be defeated. I had to put great restraint upon myself to prevent a vulgar brawl.

One morning, as I was walking along Church Lane, I met Crookenden. I stopped him. There was no beating about the bush. I went straight to the point.

"I hope, Mr Crookenden, that you are able to reconcile it with your conscience that you have succeeded in sowing the seeds of discord between husband and wife."

"Pray how have I done that?"

"You know very well what I mean, sir. Have the goodness not to feign ignorance with me."

"You refer to your wife's action with reference to that pet scheme of yours, the School Board with which you are about to saddle the parish."

He actually laughed. That is the kind of man he is. No wonder that some say the Church of England totters to a fall! Just then Colonel Laughton came through the clapper gate. Crookenden turned to him.

"Ah, Mr Bloxam, here is the man you should assail. Laughton, Mr Bloxam wants to know who induced Mrs Bloxam to put herself forward in connection with that School Board of his."

"Why, Madge, of course." The Colonel addressed himself to me. "Mrs Laughton said to your wife, 'Here's Bloxam making an ass of himself'—"

"Sir!"

"I'm not implying that that's the exact word she used, but that's the sense of it. 'Let's do something to show that it's not always the women who are idiots. If you'll stand, I will.' But your wife wouldn't, so Madge kept on, and kept on at her, till she did; few people can hold out against Madge when she's made up her mind about a thing." Laughton put his feet apart, his stick under his arm, and his hands in his trouser pockets. "Why, you don't mean to say that you object to your wife standing. My wife is, and I don't mind."

"The cases are not identical. Mrs Laughton is not standing in opposition to you."

"No, I'm not a fool—at least, I'm not that kind. Now, look here, Bloxam, we all know what's the matter with you, and why you've gone out of your road to set the parish by the ears. Crookenden's rubbed you the wrong way, that's the beginning and the end of it. Now here is Crookenden, and I'm speaking for him when I say that he'll be delighted to shake hands with you and say 'As we were.' Then your wife'll withdraw her candidature in favour of yours, and be only too glad to get the chance of doing it."

Crookenden held out his hand.

"Whether Bloxam prefers to stand as an opposition candidate or not makes no difference to me. But I do trust that he won't allow a friendship of many years' standing to be interrupted by a little difference of opinion on the subject of education."

There was a twinkle in the rector's eyes which I did not altogether relish. But I believe I should have taken his hand if Tyler had not just then appeared in sight. I remembered what I had said to him, and in his hearing, and I refrained. I observed, with dignity,—

"I am afraid that there is more in question than a difference of opinion on the subject of education."

And I walked away.

Tyler fell in beside me as I went along the field-path, inquiring,—

"Well, have you finally decided to give us the chuck?"

"May I ask, Mr Tyler, what it is you mean?"

"Oh, it's plain enough. I always am plain, I am." He was, confound his impudence! "Have you arranged to back out in favour of Mrs Bloxam? That's what I want to know. So long as one of the family gets in, I dare say you don't care which it is. But that won't do for me." He laid his great, grimy hand upon my shoulder, and kept it there in spite of my effort at withdrawal. "You've been stirring us up, you've been worriting us till you've got us all alive about this here School Board, you've got us all to stand, and now it looks to me as if you was going to dish us and leave us to be laughed at; because, don't tell me that a man can't get his wife to do what he chooses—leastways, a man that is a man." He looked at me with his great black eyes in a way I did not like. "You mind me, Mr Bloxam, if after all that's passed I'm left out in the cold, for folks to snigger at, no matter by whom it is, man or woman, you'll be sorry—you hear that? you'll be sorry. I'm not the sort to play a joke on, as perhaps you'll find before you've done."

He slouched off without affording me an opportunity to give him a piece of my mind, even had I been disposed to do so, of which I am not sure. The fact is, he is such an impossible character, having been convicted several times of assaults with violence, that he is not at all the sort of person with whom I should condescend to remonstrate, beyond, that is, a certain clearly-defined limit.

Two days afterwards the poll was taken. Very thankful I was. Had it been postponed much longer I should have gone away for a change of air. My system was completely run down. I saw most plainly that for a person of my constitution public life was not desirable. I wished, very heartily, that I had never had anything to do with the business from the first.

My emotions cannot be pictured when the result was announced. Mrs Bloxam and I were bracketed together at the head of those who were elected. We had each received the same number of votes. And it is my belief that all the idiots in the country-side, of every shade of opinion, thought it would be a joke to plump for the pair of us. On no other hypothesis can I understand such an obvious coincidence. Crookenden came next. And, after him, came four of his nominees. I was the only one on our side who was returned.

There, at present, the situation remains. The first meeting of the Board has yet to take place. I need not point out how, in anticipation of that event, my situation is painful in the extreme. That solemn truth is only too obvious. I am one against six; and one of those six is Henrietta. It is dreadful to think that, in public matters, my wife should be in a position to trample on me whenever she pleases. How can a woman respect her husband when he is in such a humiliating minority? Situated as we are she has only to contradict me to prevail. What, then, becomes of marital authority? Such a condition of affairs is an unnatural one.

My recent colleagues, by some perversion of reasoning, choose to consider, as they put it, that I have "dished" them. I do not know how they make it out. I can safely affirm that my conduct defies criticism. Yet Tyler has already nearly assaulted me in the street; while in the presence of a large number of persons, Broadbridge has asked me if I call myself a gentleman. It seems to me that I could hardly be in a more uncomfortable position.

I say—I have said it more than once before, but I repeat it again—that the fact that such a state of things should be even possible, points to a radical defect in the fabric of the British constitution. One, moreover, which calls for instant and drastic remedy, if we are not to relapse into a condition of worse than savagery. To speak of nothing else, how can a woman give due and proper consideration to the Apostolic teaching, "Wives, obey your husbands," if she is not only in active and even organised opposition to her husband, but actually in a majority against him of six to one?

I ask the question without having the slightest doubt of what is the answer which I must receive. It is not in accordance with the Divine intention that a husband should be made to look like a fool. And what else can he do if he finds himself in such a situation?

FOR DEBT

Fourteen days for "contempt of court"—ominous phrase that between the commas. The county court judge has made an order that a certain debt shall be paid within a certain time. Circumstances have been too strong—compliance has been impossible. You are summoned to show cause why, in default, you should not be committed to prison. The hearing takes place in a distant town. Circumstances are, just then, so strong that you are unable to put in a personal appearance—being without the money with which to pay your fare. Shortly afterwards—you having, in the interim, received no sort of notice as to what has taken place at the distant court—the high bailiff of your district writes to tell you that he has received a warrant for your arrest. He has, he says, written of his own initiative to your creditors' solicitors, asking if they will allow him to suspend the execution of the warrant for a week—to give you a further opportunity to pay. They have complied with his request. He hopes—in his letter—that, within the week, the money will be paid. You go at once to see him. You tell him you would if you could—you only wish you could! You never have been able to pay since the debt was incurred—circumstances have been too strong. He is a kindly-hearted man—though a shrewd man of the world. He is convinced, of his own experience, that imprisonment for debt does no one any good, neither the man who owes, nor the man who is owed, nor the onlookers who have to contribute to the support of destitute debtors. In your case he will write again, asking still to be allowed to give you time. You return home, hoping that some miracle may happen so that you still may pay. Four days afterwards you admit a young man at your front door. He has come to enforce the warrant. Your creditors have, that morning, instructed the high bailiff to take his prisoner at once—they decline to concede another hour. You and your wife put a few things in a bag—your wife trying her best not to let you think that she will cry her eyes out directly you are gone. She wishes you to take four and threepence in your pocket. Argument, at such a moment, would mean hysterics—and a scene. Her breath comes in great sobs as she kisses you. You give way. You take the money—leaving her with just one shilling. A small payment is due to you upon the morrow; it is on that she is relying; you hope, with all your heart and soul, that it will come. You go with the bailiff—to gaol—because circumstances have been too strong.

The bailiff is a communicative youngster, kindly hearted, like his chief. You are only the third one he has "taken." He is paid by the job, he will receive five shillings for "taking" you. He considers it money easily earned—he would have received no more had you "dodged" him for days. The county gaol is two-and-twenty miles away, in a lovely country, on the side of a hill, on the edge of the downs. You reach it about half-past four on a glorious July afternoon. You and your custodian are admitted through a wicket in the huge doors. The bailiff shows his warrant. The gatekeeper tells you to go straight on. You go straight on, across an open space, up half a dozen steps, under a lofty arch, which has some architectural pretensions, to a room on the left. The room is a sort of office. In it are two warders, a policeman and a man from whose wrists the policeman is removing a pair of handcuffs. The bailiff delivers his warrant to one of the warders. Certain entries are made in a book. The bailiff obtains a receipt for you—and goes. It is only when he has gone that you realise you are a prisoner. One of the warders favours you with his attention.

"What's in that bag?"

"Only a change of clothing and my work. Can I not work while I am here?"

"Don't ask me questions. You oughtn't to have brought any bag in here—it's against orders. How much money have you got?" You hand him over four and twopence—on the way you have expended a penny on a bottle of ink. "Can you write? Then put your name here."

You affix your signature to a statement acknowledging that you have handed the warder the sum of four and twopence. Another warder enters—an older man. He addresses you,—

"What's your name?" You tell him. "Your age? your religion? your trade?" You allow that you are a poor devil of an author. He goes. The first warder favours you again.

"Take your boots off! Come here!" You step on to a weighing-machine. He registers your weight. "Put your boots on again. Come along with me, the two of you."

He snatches up your bag, you follow him, accompanied by the gentleman who wore the handcuffs. Unlocking a door, he leads the way down a flight of stone steps to cells which apparently are beneath the level of the ground. "In there!" Your companion goes into one of them. The door is banged upon him. "In here!" You go into another. The door is banged on you. You find yourself alone in a whitewashed cell which contains absolutely nothing but a sort of wooden frame which is raised, perhaps, twelve inches from the floor of red and black lozenge-shaped tiles. After some three or four minutes the door is opened to admit the older warder. He hands you some books—without a word. And, without a word, he goes out again and bangs the door. He has left you in possession of a Bible, a prayer book, hymn book, an ancient and ragged volume of the *Penny Post*—in its way a curiosity—and a copy of *Quentin Durward*—Routledge's three-and-sixpenny edition, almost as good as new. Presently the first warder reappears.

"What property have you got about you?"

You give him all you have, he returning your handkerchief. Having given him everything, he satisfies himself that you have nothing more by feeling in your pockets.

"Can't I have my work? It is in my bag. Can't I work while I am here?"

"Ask all questions when you see the governor to-morrow." He vanishes. Another five minutes, he appears again. "Come along. Bring your books!"

You go into the corridor. Another person is there—in a brick-coloured costume on which is stamped, at irregular intervals, the "broad arrow." You recognise the gentleman who wore the handcuffs.

"Here you are!" The warder hands you a distinctly dirty round tin, holding, as you afterwards learn, a pint, filled with something which is greyish brown in hue, and a small loaf, of a shape, size and colour the like of which you have never seen before. The warder observes that you are eyeing the contents of the tin distrustfully. "That's good oatmeal, though you mayn't like the look of it. But it isn't the body you've got to think about, it's the soul—that's everything."

He says this in a quick, cut-and-thrust fashion which suggests that, behind the official, there is marked individuality of character. With the gentleman in the brick-coloured costume, you follow him up the flight of steps you not very long ago descended. He unlocks the door. "Stand here." Your companion stands. "You come along with me!" He unlocks another door, you follow him down another flight of stone steps into a lofty ward, on one side of which are cells. He shows you into one. Being in, he bangs the door on you. You are in a cell which is own brother to the one which you have quitted, only that this one makes some pretence to being furnished. It is, perhaps, ten feet by eight feet. The roof is arched, rising, probably, to quite twelve feet. Walls and roofs are of whitewashed brick. The floor is tiled. Opposite to the door, about five feet from the ground, is a small window. Panes of ground glass about two inches square are set in a massive iron frame. The only thing you can see through the window are iron bars. If you get through the window, you will still have to reckon with the bars.

The furniture consists of a wooden frame about two feet by six. An attenuated mattress, which you afterwards learn is stuffed with coir. A pillow of the same ilk. A pair of clean sheets which, by the way, the warder gave you, and which you have brought into the cell. A pair of blankets which look as if they had not been washed for years. A coverlet which, in common with the rest of the bedding, is stamped with the "broad arrow." There is a heavy wooden stool. A table perhaps eighteen inches square. In one corner is a shelf. On it is a wooden soap-box, containing an ancient scrap of yellow soap, a wooden salt-box containing salt, a small comb and a round tin, very much like a publican's pint pot. On the floor are a tin washing-basin, a covered tin, which you find you are supposed to use for personal purposes, a home-made hand broom, an odd collection of rags, some whiting, by the aid of which latter articles you are required to keep your cell and your utensils clean and in good order.

While you are taking a mental inventory of your quarters a voice addresses you. Turning to the door you perceive that near the top of it is a "bull's eye" spy-hole, covered on the outside by a revolving flap. This flap has been raised, someone is looking at you from without.

"Where are you from?" You vouchsafe the information.

"How long have you got?" You again oblige. "Never say die! keep up your pecker, old chap!"

"Are they going to keep me locked in here?"

"Till you've seen the doctor in the morning, then they'll let you out. Cheer up!"

The speaker disappears, the flap descends. You try to cheer up, to act upon the advice received, though, to be frank, you find the thing a little difficult. You taste the stuff in the tin. It may, as the warder said, be good oatmeal, but to an unaccustomed palate it is not inviting. You try a morsel of the mahogany-coloured loaf. It is dry as sawdust, and sour. Opposite you, against the wall, hangs a printed card. It is headed, "Dietary for Destitute Debtors." You are a destitute debtor—for the next fourteen days this will be your bill of fare. For breakfast and for supper daily, a pint of gruel, six ounces of bread. For those two meals there does not seem to be a promise of much variety. For dinner, on Mondays and Fridays, you will receive six ounces of bread, eight ounces of potatoes and three ounces of cooked meat, without bone; or as a substitute for the meat, three-quarters of an ounce of fat bacon and eight ounces of beans—you wonder how they manage to weigh that three-quarters of an ounce. On Tuesdays, Thursdays and Saturdays, four ounces of bread, six ounces of potatoes and three quarters of a pint of soup. On Wednesdays and Sundays, four ounces of bread, six ounces of potatoes and six ounces of suet pudding.

Stretching out the mattress upon the wooden frame, you endeavour to digest the circumstances of your situation and the prospect of such a dietary. In the ill-lighted cell the shadows quickly deepen. There is a clock somewhere in the prison. It noisily clangs out the half-hours and the hours. Soon after it has announced that it is half-past seven there is a sound of hurrying footsteps, a clattering of keys, a banging of doors. All is still—curiously still. In your cell it is much too dark to read. You make your bed. Undressing, you get between the sheets—immediately discovering that they rival sandpaper for roughness. The bed is just wide enough to enable you to lie flat upon your back—if you turn, unless you are very careful, you either strike against the wall or fall upon the floor. Also, you are not long in learning that it contains other occupants besides yourself. You have heard and read a great deal about the cleanliness of prisons. However that may be, it is quite certain that cleanliness has no connection with that particular set of bedding. It is alive. All night you lie in agony—literally. The clanging clock makes darkness hideous—it seems to accentuate the all-prevailing silence. Your brain is in a whirl—thoughts are trampling on each other's heels. To mental discomfort is added physical. When the earliest glimpse of dawn peeps through the caricature of an honest window you rise and search. There is slaughter. Rest is out of the question. Putting on your clothes you pace the cell. Soon after six the door is opened, an officer thrusts in his head.

"All right?"

You answer "Yes "—what can you tell him? He disappears and bangs the door. At half-past seven there is a sound of the unlocking of locks and of footsteps. The warder, reappearing, hands you a tin and a loaf, own brother to those which you received last night.

"Can't I wash?"

"Haven't you any water?" He looks round your cell. "You haven't a water can. I'll bring you one."

He presently does—a round, open tin, painted a vivid blue, containing perhaps three quarts of water. You fill your basin and wash—the first pleasant thing you have done since you saw the gaol. Then you consider your breakfast. You are hungry, hungrier than you would have been at home—but you cannot manage the gruel, and the bread still less. Apart from the flavour, the gruel is in such a dirty tin that you cannot but suspect its contents of being dirty too. The bread is hard, dry and sour, bearing not the faintest resemblance to any of the numerous varieties of bread which you have tasted. Hungry as you are, you give up the attempt at eating. Sitting on the bed, you take up

187

Quentin Durward, which these many years you have almost known by heart. About half-past ten your door is thrown wide open.

"Stand up for the governor!" cries a warder.

You stand up. A short man is in front of you without a hat on, attired in civilian costume. Between fifty and sixty, with grey hair and beard, carrying a pair of glasses in his hand, quiet and unassuming—a gentleman, every inch of him. He puts to you the same sort of questions which have already been put to you by the officers at the gate.

"What are you here for? Where do you come from? Have you"—here was a variation—"anything to ask me?"

"Can I not work while I am here?"

"What are you?"

"An author. I have a commission for some work. If I cannot do it while I am here, I shall not be able to get it in in time."

"Did you bring anything with you?"

"I brought everything—paper, pens and ink."

"Certainly you can work, you are entitled to work at your trade. I will see that the things are sent to you."

He goes, leaving, somehow, an impression behind him that you are not entirely cut off from the world after all. Another half-hour passes; the officer who received you at the gate fetches you "to see the doctor!" "Seeing the doctor" entails the unlocking and locking of doors and quite a journey. You are finally shown into a room in which a young man sits writing at a table. He looks up. "Is this a debtor?" Then to you, "Is there anything the matter with you?"

You tell him that, to the best of your knowledge and belief, there is not. He looks down. You have seen the doctor and he has seen you; you are dismissed. The officer escorts you back to your ward.

"Now you've seen the doctor," he tells you, as he unlocks the door, "you needn't go back to your cell, if you don't like."

He lets you through, re-locks the door and vanishes. You go down the steps alone and at your leisure. You perceive that the ward is larger than you last night supposed. It is paved with flagstones. On one side there are two tiers of cells—one tier over yours. The upper tier is on a level with the door through which you have just come. An iron gallery runs down the front of it the whole length of the ward. Strolling along the flagstones, you find that an open door, almost opposite your cell, admits you into what, were the surroundings only different, would be quite a spacious and a pleasant garden. There is grass in the centre—in excellent condition—flower-beds all round. Between the grass and the beds is a narrow pathway of flagstones. Three or four men are walking on this pathway. At sight of you, with one accord, they come and offer greeting. It reminds you, in rather gruesome fashion, of your schooldays, of your first arrival at school—there is such a plethora of questions. You vouchsafe just so much information as you choose, eyeing the while your questioners. There are four of them—as doleful-looking a quartette as one would care to see. These men in prison because—they could pay, but wouldn't!—or can, but won't! Upon the face of it the idea is an absurdity. Apart from the fact that the clothes of all four would not, probably, fetch more than half a sovereign, there is about them an air of depression which suggests, not only that they are beaten by fortune, but that they are even more hopeless of the future than of the past. Yet they strive to wear an appearance of jollity. As to their personal histories, they are frankness itself. One of them is a little fellow about forty-five, a cabman. He is in for poor rates, £1, 12s. It seems funny that a man should be taken twenty miles to prison, to be kept there at the public expense, because he is too poor to pay his poor rates. Another is a hawker, a thin, grizzled, unhealthy-looking man about fifty; his attire complete would certainly not fetch eighteenpence. As he puts it, there is something of a mystery about his case—a moneylending job—two-and-twenty shillings.

"The worst of it is, I paid two instalments. The judge he ordered five shillings a month. I pays two months; then I has a slice of bad luck; then I gets here; and there's ten bob thrown clean away."

A third is an old man—he owns to sixty-six—unmistakably an agricultural labourer. He is the healthiest looking and the best dressed of the lot. He has evidently put on his best clothes to come to gaol, the chief feature of the said best clothes being a clean pair of corduroys. The story he tells is a queer one. He was away harvesting. His "old woman" bought a dress from a tallyman. She said nothing of her purchase to him, said nothing even when two months afterwards she died, aged sixty-eight—she must have been a dress-loving old lady! It was only after he had buried her that he learned what she had done. The tallyman presented a claim for eighteen shillings.

"This here dress wasn't no good to me; it were as good as new, so I says to this here chap, 'You can have it back again'; but this here chap he wouldn't have it, so here I be."

The fourth man appears to be the clearest-headed member of the party. He is a bricklayer's labourer, aged thirty-four. He is in for £1, 16s., an ancient baker's bill. His story also has elements of queerness. The bill was incurred nearly four years ago. He fell from a scaffold, was in hospital six months, his home was broken up; the baker, taking pity on his misfortunes, forgave the bill. Later on the baker himself was ruined. A speculator—you are destined to hear a good deal about this speculator; it seems that he sends a regular procession to the county gaol—bought up the baker's book debts. He immediately "went for" the bricklayer's labourer, who had the worst of it, and who, in consequence, is here. When in full work the labourer earns a pound a week. He was out of work for four weeks before he "came in." The day after he did "come in," his wife and six children went upon the parish. A pretty state of things.

I seems that there are four other prisoners for debt. But just now they are shut off in a room at the end of the ward, having an exercise-ground of their own; there is apt to be too much noise if the prisoners are all together.

Presently a warder appears, not only with your writing materials, but also with your bag, its contents left untouched, with all your property, indeed, except your watch, your tobacco, and your money. Almost simultaneously dinner appears, at noon. You are presented with two tins and a tiny loaf. The door leading to the exercise-ground is closed. With your dinner in your hand you troop up the stone steps with your companions. You discover that there is a large room at the end of the upper tier of cells, "First Class Misdemeanants" being painted on the panels of the door. There being, for the moment, no prisoner of that particular class, you have the use of it. It contains tables and stools, all sorts of things—among others, wooden spoons. Armed with a wooden spoon you investigate your tins. It is Wednesday. At the bottom of the large one, which is dirtier than ever, is a slab of suet pudding, brown in hue. With the aid of your spoon and your fingers you eat it; though lukewarm and sticky, it is grateful to your anxious stomach. In the smaller tin are two potatoes, in their jackets, said jackets having, apparently, never been washed. You eat the potatoes, too; but though you are hungrier than ever, the bread you cannot manage. On your mentioning that you could dispose neither of your supper nor of your breakfast, the labourer and the cabman tear off to your cell downstairs, immediately returning in possession of your despised food, which they eat with voracity. They assure you that you will be able to eat anything after you have been here a few days, even the tins. You learn that if you make your wants known to an officer, he will purchase whatever you choose to pay for. Your chief anxiety is to work. You know from experience that you cannot do good work upon an empty stomach. Slender though your resources are, you resolve that you will devote at least a portion of them to the purchase of something which you will be able to eat for breakfast and for supper.

In the afternoon, as you are working in your cell—with the door open—a warder enters the ward. You make known to him your wants. He says he will send you the officer whose duty it is to make purchases for prisoners. When the officer comes, you request him to lay out two shillings for you to the best advantage, and learn, to your dismay, that on the day on which you make a purchase you are supposed to be keeping yourself, and therefore receive none of the prison rations. It is too late to recede, so you tell the officer to make the best of your two shillings. You work till half-past four, then go into the exercise ground, which was opened again at two till five. At five it is closed for the night. Supper is served. You dispose of the greater portion of the gruel, this time you even dispose of some of the bread. Work in your cell till past seven, then stroll with the others up and down the ward. The room at the end of the lower ward has been unlocked. The prisoners are all together. The four you have not seen prove to be very like the four you have—two of them are here at the suit of the speculator in old and bad debts, who is responsible for the presence of the bricklayer's labourer; for poor rates another. A small calculation discloses the fact that a little over ten pounds would set all the eight men free. Shortly before eight you are locked in your cells till the morning. Another night of agony! When at half-past six the warder looks in to ask if you are all right, you answer "No"—you have not closed your eyes since entering the gaol—you have been eaten alive.

"I'll bring you a change of bedding." He does. "You'll find these all right, they've never been issued. You can't keep things clean this side—most of them wear their own clothes, you see, and they come in all alive, oh!"

You exchange your bedding for that which he brings, thankfully, wishing you had spoken before. About seven the same officer reappears. He brings your "things." There is a half-quartern loaf, two ounces of tea, quarter of a pound of butter, half a pound of cheese, tin of corned beef, couple of lemons; you never knew what good food was till you found yourself in possession of those supplies. Directly his back is turned, breaking a corner off the loaf, you rub it against the butter. If they would only allow you the use of a tin knife, what a godsend it would be! A kettle of boiling water is brought at breakfast time. Putting some tea in your pint pot, with a piece of lemon peel, you fill it from the kettle. Although you have to drink your tea from the teapot, you make a sumptuous meal.

At half-past eight you go with the other Church of England prisoners to chapel, a large room, which would probably seat five hundred, allowing to each person the same amount of space which he occupies outside. The debtors occupy the back seats. There is a gallery overhead. There are four raised seats on either side, against the walls; a warder sits in each of them. A pulpit is at the other end, an altar of rather a nondescript kind—which it need be, seeing that the Roman Catholic service is held here too—a couple of screens, more raised seats. A warder is standing before the altar; a door is at either side of him. Through these doors, so soon as the debtors are seated, begins to enter a stream of men, a space of several feet being between each. Those who are awaiting trial are the first to come. The prison costume of blue serge worn by the majority means that their own clothes are unfit to wear. So far as appearance goes, the four or five men in their own apparel would come within the scope of the immortal definition of a gentleman. You have heard about some of them in the debtors' ward. The slight, young fellow in black is a post-office clerk; he has to stand his trial for stealing a letter which contained a cheque. So soon as he reaches his place he falls upon his knees and prays. He wants all the help which prayer can bring him; in all human probability there is penal servitude ahead. The highly respectable-looking individual, with carefully-trimmed black hair and whiskers, who sits on the bench in front of you upon your right, is charged with stabbing his wife; luckily, she is not dead. The big, sandy-haired fellow upon his left, right in front of you, has rank murder to answer for. The story of his crime has been for weeks the talk of the countryside; a dramatic story, with glimpses of livid tragedy. He and his paramour, being shut out one night from the workhouse, took refuge on the hills under the shelter of an overhanging rock. In the night they quarrelled; he slew her with a stone. In the early morning a shepherd met him running across the hills, wet with her blood. Stopping, the man told the shepherd what he had done. Returning together they found the woman under the rock, dead, her head and face battered and broken, the stone beside her.

The trial men are followed by the convicted prisoners, in brick-coloured costumes; some with knickerbockers—those sentenced to penal servitude, who are waiting to be drafted to a convict station; some in trousers—those who are sentenced to not more than two years' imprisonment. The warders stand up as they enter, watching them as cats do mice. Each man is careful that he is a certain distance behind the man in front of him. They sit five on a bench which would comfortably accommodate twenty, in rows, each man exactly behind his fellow. While the procession continues, a woman passes behind one of the screens—a female warder. She commences to play a series of voluntaries on an unseen harmonium—"The Voice that Breathed o'er Eden," "There is a Green Hill"—airs which seem strange accompaniments to such a procession. The chaplain is away for his holidays. The schoolmaster reads the service—an abbreviated edition of Morning Prayer. He does not read badly. The congregation seems to listen with reverent attention, which is not to be wondered at, with the warders eyeing them like hawks. They join heartily in the responses, which is, again, not strange, considering that the only chance they have of hearing their own voice is in chapel. At the end a hymn is sung—"Thine for ever! God of love"—under the circumstance, an odd selection. The congregation sing with the full force of their lungs; perhaps strangely the result is not unpleasing. The female prisoners are in the gallery overhead. A woman's voice soars above the others, clear as a bell. You wonder who it is—officer or prisoner. After the hymn the schoolmaster pronounces the benediction. The service is over.

You work nearly all that day. How your companions manage without work is beyond your comprehension. This is an excellent school for the inculcation and encouragement of the Noble Art of Loafing. In the afternoon another prisoner is introduced. He calls himself a blacksmith, is about sixty, has scarcely a shirt to his back, and is here for poor rates! Later on, two more. One is in prison clothes, the other cowers in a corner of his cell, refusing to have intercourse with anyone. Presently the story goes that he is crying. The fellow in the prison clothes has been brought from a town more than thirty miles away, sentenced to fourteen days imprisonment, for a debt of twelve-and-sixpence.

When, shortly before five, ceasing work, you go into the exercise-ground for a breath of air, you find a warder with a bundle under his arm. In the corner is a brick erection with, fitted into the wall, a thermometer to register over 300° Fahrenheit. It is the oven in which they bake the prisoners' clothes. In the bundle under the warder's arm are the clothes of the twelve-and-sixpenny debtor. A debtor's clothes must be in an indescribable condition before they constrain him to wear the prison uniform. This man's rags—the warder, who is in a communicative mood, declares that you cannot call them clothes—are about as bad as they can be. It is only after the thermometer has continued for some minutes to register a temperature of over 230° that their unmentionable occupants are effectually destroyed.

You sleep better that night; the new bedding—from, at any rate, one point of view—is clean. The next day you come again upon prison rations, eked out, if you choose, with what is left of your own supplies. It is Friday. The Litany is read in the chapel. With what strenuousness do the members of the congregation announce that they are miserable sinners! After chapel you are beginning work when a warder calls your name.

"Put your things together—bring your sheets and towel—your discharge has come. Don't keep me waiting; come along!"

In a maze you ram your things into your bag. You follow the warder. He takes you to a room in which the governor is seated at a table. He addresses you.

"Your discharge has come." To the officer: "Get this man his discharge-note and such property as you may have of his."

Bewildered, you question the governor.

"But who has paid the money?"

"No one. You are discharged at the instance of your creditors. I will read you my instructions."

He does. They are to the effect that your creditors having made an application for your release, the registrar of the county court from which you were committed directs the governor of the gaol to discharge you from his custody forthwith. When he has finished reading, he hands you a letter which has come to you from your wife. Still at a loss to understand exactly what has happened, a few minutes later you find yourself outside the gates.

You have been a prisoner not three whole days. As you look around you—realising that you are once more your own man—you wonder what a man feels like, in his first moments of freedom, after he has been a prisoner three whole months. And years? Think of it!...

On reaching home you find that your wife has received a letter from your creditors. Somewhat late in the day they have been making inquiries into the truth of your statements. They have ascertained that it is a fact that circumstances have been too strong for you, that you have been unable to pay. That being the case, they tell your wife, being unwilling to keep you any longer in gaol, they have given instructions for your immediate release. So here you are. It seems strange, in these days of abolition of imprisonment for debt, that creditors should still have the power of sending their debtors to gaol when they please—and when they please, of letting them out again.

THE THIRTEEN CLUB

I

George Gardiner is a man whose ideas—when he has any—are beneath contempt. I always treated them as they deserved, save on one occasion. That I ever swerved, so far as he was concerned, from the paths of the scornful will, I fear, be the cause to me of lifelong regret.

He had been reading somewhere some nonsense about a number of weak-minded persons who had gathered themselves together in what they called a Thirteen Club. It had been the object of this preposterous association to trample on all sorts of popular superstitions. The members had made it their business to throw down the gage to Fortune, whenever, so to speak, opportunity offered. To challenge Luck, in and out of season, to come on and do its worst. Presumably they derived some sort of satisfaction from this course of conduct. Though, for my part, I cannot see what shape it can have taken.

It was at his own dinner-table he told us about what he had read. Having enlarged upon the subject at quite sufficient length he startled us all by suggesting that we should form a similar society on our own account. I was astounded. My own impression is that we all were. Though I am free to admit that we concealed the fact with a degree of success which, now that I look back, fills me with amazement.

There were eight of us present besides Gardiner. We were his guests. Some of us were sensible men. We must have been. Personally I have never heard so much as a hint breathed against the presumption that I am in possession of a considerable amount of commonsense. My mother has told me, times without number, that she always relies upon my strong commonsense—observe the adjective. If certain of my relatives have not treated me on all matters with that respect to which I consider myself entitled, I feel it is because Providence has seen fit to endow them but scantily with what I have in such abundance. By way of clinching the question I would remark that Miss Adeline Parkes—the young lady whom I trust one day to make Mrs Augustus Short—has more than once declared that the only fault she has to find with me is that I have too much sense. She has two or three times assured me—with the prettiest pout; there is a quality about Adeline's lips which gives charm even to a pout—that my point of view is always the sensible one, and that I do not make sufficient allowance for those whose strength in that direction is not so great as my own.

It would be ridiculous to assume that I was the only level-headed person among the eight individuals whom Gardiner had assembled in his dining-room. Indeed I have reason to believe that Ernest Bloxam is not entirely an idiot. And from the way Bob Waters has treated me I cannot but conclude that he has some notions of what is right and proper. Three of the men present were entire strangers to me. Though it would be wrong to set them down, merely on that account, as fools. Still I cannot forget that it was owing to one of these three, who told me his name was Finlayson, that I found myself involved in that cataclysm of events, my connection with which I shall continue to lament.

Gardiner waited till the cloth had been removed before he made his nefarious suggestion. I cannot but feel that he selected the moment with malicious intention, because at that period of the entertainment we had each of us already disposed of two or three glasses of champagne, and were engaged in the consumption of what I should describe as three or four more. Champagne is, to my mind, a most insidious liquid. It affects me before I really know what is happening. I am credibly informed that no sooner had Gardiner made his proposition than I seconded it with acclamation. I can only say that I am surprised. When I am further assured that I entered into the scheme with zest, and that some of the wildest proposals came from me, I can but turn to the pages of history and reflect, with a sigh, that even the greatest men have had their moments of weakness.

The outlines of the scheme which we drew up between us—I decline to allow for a single instant that I was the leading spirit; Gardiner was the instigator, and I have the clearest possible impression that the man Finlayson was his chief aider and abettor—were as follows. We were to form ourselves into a Thirteen Club. There were to be thirteen members, commencing with Gardiner and his eight guests, to whom four others were to be joined. We bound ourselves to act, under all possible circumstances, in opposition to the teachings of popular superstition. When we were told that a thing was unlucky we were at once to do it, and when lucky we were not to do it on any terms. For instance, we were always to look at a new moon through glass; always to walk under ladders; always to cross people on staircases; always to arrange for the most important events to occur on a Friday. On the other hand we were not to turn over the money in our pockets at the first glimpse of a new moon; not to make the sign of the cross when we met a person who squinted; not to salute a black cat; not to occupy a chair which was reputed lucky when engaged in a quiet hand at cards; not to pick up pins. The subscription was to be thirteen shillings. There was to be a dinner, which was to be a sort of glorification of our principles, at which all the members were to be present. The dinner ticket was to cost thirteen shillings, and thirteen shillings was to be spent in wine.

It was that Thirteen Club dinner which was the cause of all the trouble.

When, the following day, I was gradually recovering from the headache which had kept me in bed till afternoon, I was informed that Gardiner and the man Finlayson wished to see me. It was between three and four o'clock. Simply attired in a dressing-gown and slippers I was wondering whether it would or would not be advisable to venture on another seidlitz powder. I was trying to remember how many I had already taken. I had a notion that the box was full, or nearly full, in the morning, and as there were only two in it now it would seem as if I had taken nearly as many as were good for me. It will be seen that that was not a moment at which I would be likely to extend a warm welcome to the man who had caused me to spend the day in the society of a box of seidlitz powders. My instinct would have been to deny myself entirely, had I been afforded the opportunity, but I was not. Before I knew it they were showing themselves into my room.

Not the least irritating part of it was that they both of them seemed in the best of health and spirits. They glanced at me, then at each other. I am almost persuaded that I detected the man Finlayson in the act of winking.

"Hollo!" began Gardiner. "Got a cold?" I signified that I had something which perhaps might not be inaccurately diagnosed as being of the nature of a cold.

"Ah," remarked Finlayson, "there was a bad draught where you sat last night. What are you taking for it?" He perceived the box which was in front of me. "Seidlitz powders? Best thing possible for a cold—like yours."

I had not previously heard seidlitz powders spoken of as being of use in an affection of the kind. But I allowed the remark to go unanswered. I was not in a mood to chop straws with a person who was to all intents and purposes a stranger to me.

An observation, however, which Gardiner immediately made was productive of something very much like a shock to my system. Tapping the toes of his boots with his cane he said, in quite a casual tone of voice, as it seemed to me, *apropos* of nothing at all,—

197

"By the way, Short, it strikes me that we shall have some difficulty in arranging to have the tables shaped like coffins."

"Tables—shaped like coffins?" I stared at him. "What do you mean?"

"It was your idea, and not a bad one. As you said, we may as well be thorough. But, you see, it would involve our having the tables specially made for us, and that would come expensive."

While I was asking myself what Gardiner might be talking about, Finlayson struck in.

"We can manage about the skeletons as menu holders."

"And skulls and cross-bones as table ornaments."

"And a real live black cat for every guest; though it's doubtful if we shall be able to induce each waiter to carry one on his shoulders."

"You'll find that we shall have to confine them in wicker-work cages. If we left them free they'd make a bolt for the door. If we fastened them to the legs of the chairs there might be shindies. The waiters might object to being scratched. Not to speak of the guests. Some folks are so fussy."

I glanced from one to the other. I suspected them of a desire to amuse themselves at my expense. But, although their remarks were entirely beyond my comprehension, they appeared to be as serious as it was in their power to be.

"May I ask what it is you're talking about?"

My inquiry seemed to occasion Gardiner surprise.

"Why, about the inaugural dinner of the Thirteen Club, of course. I say, Short, has your cold caused you to lose your memory?"

It had. Actually. My mind was a blank page as regards what had taken place on the previous night bearing on that particular theme. When they favoured me with what they called a simple recital of what they stated had occurred I found it simply incredible. It was only when Gardiner produced a sheet of paper covered with my writing that I was compelled to belief. It was crowded with a number of memoranda on the subject of the rules and constitution of the proposed club. There was a list of the names of the first nine members, with my own in front. Notes having special reference to that ridiculous dinner. And, to crown all, a form of declaration by which each signatory had bound himself to do certain things, to which each person present had attached his name, with my own again, in front.

It is not too much to say that I gazed at this amazing document with eyes which almost refused to credit what they saw. The caligraphy was mine beyond a doubt, though here and there a trifle shaky. But in what condition I could have been when I penned such stuff as that I altogether failed to understand.

"I suppose," I observed tentatively, "that this is a joke."

"A joke?" echoed Gardiner. "Rather! It will be the best joke that ever was."

"Will be? What do you mean by will be?"

"Why, the whole thing will be. As for that dinner, if it's carried out on the lines which you laid down—and it sha'n't be our fault if it isn't—it will not only be the talk of London, but it will be a joke which we shall none of us forget as long as we live."

"Let us understand each other, Gardiner. I am not quite well to-day."

"You're not looking well."

"I'm not feeling well." There was something in his manner I resented. I desired that the tone of my reply should bring that home to him. "Something I had at your rooms last night has disagreed with me."

"Perhaps it was the oyster sauce."

This was Finlayson.

"I am not prepared to say exactly what it was."

"It couldn't have been the wine," Gardiner declared. "I was careful to see that every bottle was of the best."

"It might have been the olives," murmured Finlayson. "You never know."

"I repeat that I am not able to precisely locate the blame, but it certainly was something. I therefore beg you to understand that I am not in a condition to argue. So that when I ask you to forget, as I have done, what seems to have been a very poor jest, and when I tear this sheet of nonsense into shreds, as I now proceed to do—"

"Short!" Gardiner caught me by the wrist. "What are you up to? I had a clean copy made of that, and it's gone to the printer's. I felt that the original ought to be preserved."

"Gone to the printer's! Gardiner, what are you saying?"

"We left it at the printer's on the way to engage the room for the dinner."

"Engage the room for the dinner! Gardiner, are you in earnest?"

"Certainly, at the Coliseum Restaurant. We've settled the preliminaries. It's

199

to be on Friday week, the fifth Friday of the month, the unluckiest day of all, in accordance with your suggestion."

"Is it possible that you seriously suppose that I could allow myself to become associated with such a—such a travesty as this?"

I held up the sheet of paper.

"Allow yourself! Why, when you were unanimously elected president you spoke of the delight it would give you to serve."

"And you collected the subscriptions."

"Collected the subscriptions?"

"And deposited them in my tobacco jar, where, at the present moment, they repose. You appointed the first meeting for next Friday at my rooms, and promised you would occupy the chair."

"Gardiner, I have already alluded to the ill-health from which I am suffering—"

"Possibly," interrupted Finlayson, "it was the anchovy toast. You ate a plateful."

"I ate a plateful?" I looked at the speaker to see if he was gibing. He showed no signs of it. "If I ate anything like that quantity it probably was. But I do not wish to enter into that matter now. To show how constitutionally unfitted I am to become associated with such a scheme, I have only to point out that I am myself extremely superstitious in little things."

When I said that the man Finlayson broke into a gust of laughter, in which Gardiner immediately joined him. I observed their merriment with a growing sense of umbrage.

"I don't know what you see to laugh at in my plain statement of a plain fact. And to show you that it is a fact, I have only to inform you that with the fall of a great-aunt's portrait from its place against the wall I directly connect a long chain of disasters which presently followed."

On my volunteering that piece of information their screams of laughter increased to such an extent that I thought they would have done themselves an injury. It was some time before Gardiner was able to gasp out, between his guffaws, and with both hands held to his sides,—

"You're splendid! You're immense! Why, last night you suggested that each man should bring to the dinner a portrait of a relative; that the whole thirteen should be hung against the wall, and be sent, at intervals, toppling headlong to the floor."

"I suggested that—I?"

"Great Scott!" shouted Finlayson; and he actually slapped me on the back, as if he were the friend of a lifetime. "I thought last night you were the most amusing man I had ever met, but to-day, in that dressing-gown, and with that box of seidlitz powders in front of you, you'll be the death of me if you don't take care."

I never had been regarded as a humorist before. At least, so far as my recollection carries me. I do not know why, but such is the case. That these two persons should find me funny, especially as I felt in anything but a frivolous mood, was unexpected. They certainly persisted in their refusal to take me seriously. The graver I became the more they screamed with laughter. It was really disconcerting. And finally resulted in so destroying the mental equipoise on which I pride myself, not without reason, that I actually found myself indulging, without the slightest desire to do so, in those extravagances which they seemed so singularly disposed to relish.

With such completeness, indeed, was the balance of my mind destroyed, that when they went away they left me irrevocably committed to a scheme for which I felt the greatest possible natural distaste. My earnest desire was to contemn the very notion of a Thirteen Club. Instead of which I found myself in the position of president of such an association; regarded almost as its originator; certainly as one of its leading spirits. How it had come about I was at a loss to imagine. Moreover, I had undertaken to assist at a so-called dinner, which was to be an orgie of a character, the very thought of which sent cold shivers down my back.

During the next few days I felt most uncomfortable. As it were, as if I were under a ban. My life had hitherto been so regular. I had been so careful to observe the conventionalities; to do exactly what other people did, in exactly the same way, that I was ashamed to think of my connection with so extravagant a coterie. Not the least annoying part of the matter was that the very fact of my having joined a society which had undertaken to disregard all the trivialities of superstition seemed to compel me to treat them with more respect than ever before. The thing became quite an obsession. For example, someone had told me that in walking on the pavement one should be careful to place one's foot well in the centre of the flagstones, since it was unlucky to let it come in contact with one of the lines of union. This absurd remark came all at once to the forefront of my brain with such force that I more than once caught myself playing fantastic tricks in the open street in my desire to avoid the conjunction of the paving-stones. What opinion passers-by must have formed of my condition I do not care to think. Some equally weak-minded person had mentioned, at some period of my career, that it was a sure forerunner of misfortune if one walked through a street in which there were three black dogs. I had forgotten all about the nonsensical allegation till I joined the Thirteen Club. Then it came back to me in such a fashion that whenever I had to turn into a fresh street I would quite involuntarily pause to discover if anything could be seen in the shape of three black dogs. I am rather short-sighted, and am persuaded that in consequence I sometimes saw them when they were not there to be seen. But as a trampler on current superstitions I was not taking any risks. I must have walked unnecessary miles to avoid such an encounter. Not to speak of the money I lavished on cab fares.

Once, when walking with Adeline, as we were about to enter the park I saw a man leading three black poodles along the row. I started back, but Adeline addressed me in such a tone that I thought it prudent to pursue our original intention. So soon as we entered, the man with the poodles turned right round, and passed so close that one of his charges sniffed at me. I was conscious of a sense of vague discomfort. It is a curious commentary on the occurrence, that when I returned home I found that I had lost a five-pound note. It had been in my cigarette-case and I must have dropped it when taking out a cigarette. The accident did not tend to weaken my objection to three black dogs.

I was not reassured by the proceedings at the first meeting of the Thirteen Club which took place on the Friday in Gardiner's rooms. Several things were said and done to which I objected. Some of them, I regret to add, were said and done by me. The whole tone of the thing was most distasteful. A code of fines was drawn up which was monstrous. If you did not go out of your way to flout every credulous fancy you had to pay for it; sometimes a considerable sum. You were supposed to make open confession of your faults. But as I was conscious that the paving-stones and the black dogs between them might cost me a little fortune, in my case this was supposition only. For the future I would make a point of promenading up and down the thoroughfares which were ornamented by a trio of sooty-hued canine quadrupeds, and would persistently step on the seams in the pavement. But the past was past. It was not for me to resurrect it.

As the day appointed for that travesty of a dinner approached I became more and more alive to the unsatisfactory nature of my relations with Adeline. It had been my constant habit to tell her everything. There had been moments when she had seemed to hint that I had a tendency to tell her too much. As if my desire to make of her a confidante in the little matters of my daily life suggested a tendency in the direction of the egotistical. She even went so far as to assert that I was too fond of talking about myself. Which observation I felt to be uncalled for. For if a man may not talk to his future wife about himself what ought he to talk about?

I had this most uncalled-for insinuation in my mind when I refrained from mentioning to Adeline that I had become associated with the Thirteen Club. I own that I had a suspicion that she might not care for my having done so. But then I did not care for it myself. And in the delicate position in which I found myself placed my chief desire was to avoid unnecessary friction. Still as the fatal hour approached I did wish that I had been more open.

Especially in the light of a little conversation which took place during the usual afternoon call which I was paying her on the very day before.

"I see that some more ignorant and wicked persons have joined themselves in what they call a Thirteen Club."

She was looking at a newspaper, and I was thinking of Gardiner's obstinacy in insisting on having skeletons for menu holders. Her words, which were entirely unexpected, made me jump.

"Adeline, whoever told you that?"

"It's in the paper."

"In the paper!"

For an instant I felt as if I were in imminent danger of a paralytic stroke. Whoever could have put it in the paper? Had they dared to mention any names? Fortunately it appeared that they had not. Her next remark, however, added to my sense of discomfiture.

"It says in the paper that the whole thirteen of them are going to dine together to-morrow. To show, I suppose, how stupid people can be if they like. It will serve them right if they're all dead within the year."

"Adeline!"

Under the circumstances it was dreadful to hear her say such things. But she went on, wholly regardless of what I might be feeling.

"I've no patience with people who want to make fun of the most cherished beliefs of their ancestors."

"Surely, Adeline, you are not superstitious?"

"I am. All nice people are in their heart of hearts. I wouldn't walk under a ladder for anything, nor sit at a table on which the knives were crossed. And whenever I spill the salt I'm unhappy."

I was silent. I had myself driven up to the house because there seemed to be three black dogs in every street. What could I say?

When, the following evening, I went to that preposterous, and, I had almost begun to think, sacrilegious dinner, my heart was in my boots.

II

Somewhat to my surprise, just as I was about to start, Lawrence Jackson called. Jackson is an invertebrate, lymphatic creature, of whose mental equipment I have no opinion at all. How he ever brought himself to belong to such an organisation as the Thirteen Club was to me a mystery. I had not quite finished dressing when he arrived. When I entered the room I found him fidgeting in his usual purposeless way from chair to chair, and from table to table. I noticed at once that his shirt front was creased; a sure sign, in a man of his class, of cerebral disturbance. He rushed to me as I entered, gazing at me through his eyeglass.

"Now that I have come I don't know what to say to you, you are such an enthusiastic upholder of the club."

I was not so sure of that myself. Though I was aware that such an idea was current among certain of its members. To use what I believe is an Americanism—in my reply I sat on the fence.

"In its President what would you expect?"

"Quite so! quite so! I suppose it is all right?"

"All right? Jackson? What do you mean?"

"In going on as we are going on we're doing nothing wrong, running no unwise risks, or that kind of thing?" As I had been putting a similar inquiry to myself I was without an answer. When I turned away he broke out, in agitated accents, "Short, I've come to warn you!"

"To warn me, Jackson?"

"Whatever you do, don't ride in a cab drawn by a white horse."

"Why?"

"Don't ask me, but don't! Don't walk under a ladder when there's a red-haired woman looking on."

"What are you talking about?"

"Don't take the last piece of bread and butter off a plate."

"I never did such a thing in my life."

"Above all, don't sleep in a house in which there is a man with one leg shorter than the other."

"Jackson, occupying the position which I hold, which we both hold, I am surprised to hear you speak in such a strain."

"I knew you would be, but I can't help it. I suppose we're not allowed to believe in dreams?"

"Several of the rules are aimed at that particular form of foolish credulity."

"Foolish, is it? Then all I can say is, that the things I've dreamt about you during the last night or two have been enough to turn a man's brain. I've seen you in the most frightful situations, awful. Such dreams must mean something —they must. Anyhow, Mrs Jackson insisted on my giving you warning. She believes in everything."

"In a woman, Jackson, that sort of thing is excusable. We, as men, know better."

"If she knew that I was going to this—this flare-up I don't know what she would do. She'd expect to see me brought home dead on a shutter. I do hope no harm will come of it all."

"My dear Jackson, it is time to start. Suppose we have a glass of sherry before we go."

"It would brace us up."

I cannot say why he supposed that I required bracing up. Though his need was plain enough. As we drove to the Coliseum—I noticed, quite by accident, that the cab horse was not white—he entertained me with conversation of a kind to which I had a strong objection.

"I suppose that when thirteen people sit down to dinner, it's the one who rises first who dies within the year. Of course, as President you'll do that." Would I? we should see. "I have heard that if all rise together all are marked for death. I'll see that nothing of that sort happens, because I'll take particularly good care that I sit tight. I don't want to leave my wife a widow, and—and my children." His tone became lugubrious. "Not that I shall get much good by sitting tight, because I had an aunt who used to have it that it was the one who remained last at table who died. Mrs Jackson maintains that when thirteen people dine together the consequences are such that those who don't die within the year wish they could. Which is a cheerful way of looking at the thing."

It was. More than once during the drive I was on the point of informing Jackson that if he did not divert his conversation into different channels I should be moved to take the extreme step of throwing him out of the cab. By the time we reached the restaurant my depression had increased to what I felt must be a visible extent.

As the hansom drew up at the door the horse slipped. It was only by something in the shape of a miracle that the vehicle escaped being overturned. For a second I certainly thought that we were over. I was in a state of tremulous agitation.

"Ah," sighed Jackson, when at last we stood upon the pavement, "that's a precursor of what's to come. If we were sensible men we should act upon the warning, and go and have a chop together round the corner. I feel as if a grim, relentless fate was marching me to execution."

It was with no pleasurable anticipations that we approached the feast which had been prepared for us. My own impression is that if it had not been for the attendants we might have acted on Jackson's suggestion and dined upon a chop. A uniformed individual, advancing with what he possibly intended to be an ingratiating smile, murmured,—

"Thirteen Club, gentlemen?"

I do not know why he took it for granted that we belonged to an association of the kind. It is hardly probable that we bore the fact upon our faces. There were other persons coming to the establishment to dine to whom he did not address a similar inquiry; persons who looked quite as likely to belong to such an organisation as we did.

As we were being ushered up the stairs we encountered Boulter, Tom Boulter, who had apparently arrived just in front of us. He regarded me with what I felt to be a doubtful eye.

"Feeling peckish?" he cried.

"Well, I can't say that I do—very. Do you?"

The tone of his reply was decidedly emphatic.

"Not likely. Wish I hadn't come. I've a lot of delicate things on hand just now and want all the luck I can get, instead of fooling it away on a silly show of this kind."

Boulter is a member of the Stock Exchange. I understood him to be referring to speculations in which he was at that time engaged. The reference touched me on a tender spot. The shares of a company in which I was interested had fallen three-quarters that very morning. Suppose I discovered to-morrow that they had dropped another three-quarters, I should feel that the fall was of the nature of a visitation. If, by a sort of sympathetic consequence, all my investments were to become depressed, what would my emotions be?

We were shown into a room which was in partial darkness. Gardiner came forward and gripped me by the hand.

"What," I inquired, "is the matter with the light?"

"My dear Short, what a question. Evil fortune is supposed to lurk in shadows. It is our end and aim to laugh at all such fancies."

As I was about to observe that that was no reason why we should be driven to tread upon each other's toes, to my surprise he made quite a speech to the assembled company.

"Mr President and Gentlemen of the Thirteen Club,—We are all arrived and will now proceed to partake of that hilarious banquet which has been specially designed to enable us to express our scorn and contempt for those ridiculous superstitions which have bound our ancestors about as with swaddling clothes. We will show that we have risen superior to those foolish traditions, the fear of which haunted them by day and kept them awake at night. By way of making our position quite plain we will commence by doing something the mere thought of which would have made our great-grandmothers shiver and shake. A mirror will be handed to each of you. As you pass into the dining-room you will dash it to the ground with sufficient force to shatter it to fragments, exclaiming, as you do so, 'So much for the bad luck a broken mirror is supposed to bring!' It will be to begin as we intend to go on."

My own mother used to lay stress on the bad fortune which attends the fracturing of a mirror. It was with sensations almost amounting to dismay that I heard Gardiner's cold-blooded announcement of his determination to compel me, among others, to treat my mother's feelings with what was really equivalent to filial disrespect. Something of the kind, I am convinced, was nearly general, and would have found utterance, had not the man Finlayson stifled any attempt at remonstrance by bustling about and forcing each of us to take a small round mirror, which was without a frame. At the same time Gardiner, putting his hand upon my shoulder, actually impelled me towards a door leading to an inner room.

"I must protest—" I began.

But he cut me short, pretending to misunderstand what I was about to say.

"In one instant so you shall. You shall be the first to break your mirror, as you suggested."

"As I suggested!"

"Only give us time, and all your suggestions shall be acted on. You will find, my dear Short, if you will only have a little patience, that the whole affair has been planned on the lines which you yourself laid down. Gentlemen, Mr Augustus Short, as our President, will lead the way."

I do not know exactly what happened. I fancy that Gardiner jerked my arm, anyhow, the mirror slipped from my grasp, and although I certainly did not "dash" it to the ground, directly it touched the floor it was shivered into fragments with quite an extraordinary amount of noise. My conviction is that those mirrors were specially and artfully arranged to smash with a kind of explosion directly they came into contact with a resisting substance. I caught myself stammering, while I was still bewildered by the din the thing had made,—

"So much for the bad luck a broken mirror is supposed to bring!"

I have a vague idea that the others did as I had done, but my impressions were of such a variegated hue that for some seconds I hardly knew what was taking place. I found myself in an apartment the lights of which were shaded by globes of a peculiarly ghastly green. The walls were hung in black. Mottoes sprawled across them. I noted two, "The Thirteen Club laughs at luck." "Down with all Omens." There was a table in the centre shrouded in the same funereal shade. One presumed that it was laid for dinner. But the articles upon it were of such an unusual sort, and were arranged in such fantastic forms, that the thing was but presumption. Gardiner, however, did what I suppose he considered his best to make the matter clear.

"I think, Mr President and Gentlemen, you will agree with me that this is a fitting environment for such a function as the inaugural dinner of the Thirteen Club."

I, for one, disagreed with him entirely. But at that instant I found myself without the capacity to say so. To be frank, the look of the whole thing had surprised me into speechlessness. Gardiner went on in a tone of voice which suggested that he was enjoying himself immensely. If that were the case then I am convinced that he in his enjoyment was singular.

"We find ourselves surrounded by the proverbial attributes of gloom. The lighting is uncanny, it lends to us all the attributes of sick men. The walls and tables are decked with the traditional trappings of the tomb. The only ornaments upon the festive board are skeletons, cross-bones, and skulls. You will notice that the knives are crossed. The drinking cups are of funereal ebony. Beside each chair is a black cat in a black wicker cage."

That explained the peculiar sounds which were arising. Most of those cats were objecting to the position in which Gardiner had placed them.

"So far as we have been able, Mr Finlayson and I have spared no pains to provide a harmonious whole. Without self-conceit we are conscious that we have made just those arrangements for you which you would have wished to have made for yourselves. It only remains for the Thirteen Club to show that it can be gay and light-hearted even among surroundings the most forbidding. To your seats!" Gardiner bundled me to mine. "One little ceremony still has to be performed. Each will find in front of him a salt-cellar full of salt. Take it between your right finger and thumb and spill the contents on the board."

He forced what I perceived to be a salt-cellar between my fingers, then, giving my wrist a twist, he compelled me to upset it. I objected, strongly, to the unceremonious manner in which he persisted in making me behave as if I were an automaton. Moreover, I thought of Adeline's view on the subject of the spilling of salt.

"This is beyond a joke," I exclaimed.

"Beyond a joke!" he echoed. "I should think it was. It's a challenge from the Thirteen Club to the gnomes and goblins of Demon Fortune to come on and do their worst. One word as regards the waiters. We have been at some trouble to select notoriously bad characters, most of them with crime-stained hands. The costume is a little notion of my own. Waiters!"

There was a rustling behind us. From under the sombre hangings which screened the wall there appeared a number of the most forbidding-looking figures I ever beheld. They were enveloped from head to foot in some shiny material which was red as blood. Slits were cut for their eyes, nose, and mouth. Beyond that there was nothing to show that the creatures within were men. The sight of them made me positively uneasy. Especially after Gardiner's allusion to "notoriously bad characters" and "crime-stained hands." Had I anticipated anything of that sort I certainly should not have come.

"Another observation," he continued, in that strident voice which grated more and more upon my ears, "I would ask to be permitted to make before you fall to the feast with that appetite which, I am well aware, grows every instant sharper." Did it? That was decidedly not the case with mine. "Referring to the menu, I would beg of you to bestow on it a little careful study, and then to tell me if you are not of opinion that it is a masterpiece from the point of view of its suitability to this unique occasion. The conception, I hasten to add, is again my very own."

I glanced at the menu card which a small white skeleton thrust out towards me in its attenuated hand. This is what I read:—

MENU OF THE INAUGURAL DINNER
OF THE THIRTEEN CLUB.

Potages.
Consommé Tete de Mort.
Crème d'Entrepreneurs des Pompes Funebres;

Poissons.
Soles a la Pierre Tumulaire.
Saumon, Sauce Fossoyeur.

Entrees.
Ris de Veau au Jus Mortuaire.
Pajasky de Volaille en Cercueil.

Releves.
Quartier d'Agneau Roti, Sauce Cadavre.
Boeuf Braisé aux Revenants.

Legumes.
Pommes de Terre Meurtriere.
Petits Pois Nouveaux a la Suicide.

Rotis.
Canetons Rotis a la memoire de la Fin de Touts.
Salade des Espoirs Evanouis.

Entremets.
Savarin au Cimetiere.
Parfait Woking.
Gateaux Kensal Green.

My knowledge of French is, in a manner of speaking, limited. It was only after some moments' consideration that the monstrous nature of the thing began to dawn on me. Was it possible that we were supposed to eat food prepared in such fashions as the menu suggested? What connection could sweetbreads have with "mortuary juice," and potatoes with murder? What were "tombstone" soles, and "gravedigger" sauce? The allusions to "Woking" and "Kensal Green," at a dinner-table, in association with sweets, was enough to destroy one's appetite entirely. Was the intention to hint that the dishes so named would send us there? One shuddered at the thought.

I had not yet succeeded in realising the full horror of this final outrage when one of the gruesomely-attired figures which it had been Gardiner's humour to provide as waiters planted itself at my side. A voice issued from one of the slits in the scarlet envelope, deep, harsh, threatening, addressing me as if presenting a pistol at my head, and demanding my money or my life.

"Death's Head Soup, or Cream of Undertakers?"

The question so startled me that I nearly jumped out of my chair. What could the creature mean? A glance at the card which I was holding showed that the reference was to the first two dishes on the bill of fare. He was asking which of them I wished to have. I felt as if I were on the point of choking. The same inquiry, uttered, as it seemed to me, in the same sinister accents, came in a chorus from all round the table.

Silence followed. Then a voice was heard which I recognised as Tom Boulter's.

"Excuse me, Gardiner, but if you don't mind I think I'll slip round to a tripe shop I know and dine off a saveloy. I've heard a saveloy described as a 'bag of mystery'; but, anyhow, it can hardly be more mysterious than 'cream of undertakers.'"

"Personally I never eat a dish of which I know nothing—never. And it's outrageous—simply outrageous—that we should be expected to play tricks with our digestion by attempting to eat such—such extraordinary things."

This was James Rutherford, whose one hobby is what he calls "dieting" himself. What he would think of such a bill of fare I could dimly fancy. Lawrence Jackson spoke next. Judging from his tone he was on the verge of tears. He is a man who is easily moved in the direction of the melancholic.

"It isn't only what there is to eat. It's everything. Making us sit in a chamber of horrors, with a possible murderer behind your chair, and a green light always makes me ill. If I stay here much longer I shall have to be carried out, I know I shall. I was far from well when I came. Each second I'm growing worse. What my wife would say if she were here I do not dare to think."

"If this is a Thirteen Club dinner I'm off it. Stomach's turned."

I am thankful to say that this distinctly vulgar remark was made by a person who was a perfect stranger to me. A remark which was immediately afterwards made by the man Finlayson transfixed me with astonishment.

"I must own that I think our President's carried the whole thing a little too far."

I sprang to my feet.

"I carried the whole thing a little too far!"

"One cannot but feel that some of your ideas are a little morbid."

"My ideas!"

To my surprise, and also to my indignation, a chorus of voices rose from round the table, all, actually, condemning me.

"Certainly!"

"Beyond all reason!"

"Show a disordered imagination!"

"Monstrous that we should have to submit to them!"

"If we'd had the faintest notion of what you proposed to do we should none of us ever have come."

"Gentlemen," I shouted, "I protest that my ideas have not been carried out."

"Not in their entirety," the man Finlayson had the audacity to retort. "The notion that corpses should be scattered about the room, and that we should sit in coffins, and wear graveclothes, was a little—it really was a little, don't you think?"

"Mr Finlayson, do you dare to affirm that I—I—suggested that there should be corpses in the room, and coffins, and—and graveclothes? I have no hesitation in affirming that a more abominable insinuation I never heard."

The objectionable stranger to whom allusion has already been made rose from his chair.

"At last, Mr Short, I do agree with you. The business is an abominable one from beginning to end. As our President you have subjected us to a series of outrages against which it is our duty to protest in the most forcible manner."

"Hear! hear!" muttered someone. I do not know what ridiculous person it was.

"The most effective protest we can offer," continued the preposterous stranger, "is to at once leave the room. And that I for one shall instantly proceed to do. Those gentlemen who think with me will no doubt follow my example. You will be left to enjoy an orgie which a mentally, morally, and physically diseased imagination alone could have conceived."

Nearly every person present stood upon his feet. There were all sorts of exclamations.

"Hear! hear!"

"Bravo!"

"Excellently said!"

"Serve him right!"

One peculiarly offensive idiot observed,—

"Let him gorge himself upon his Death's Head Soup and his Cream of Undertakers!"

There was every symptom of a general stampede from the apartment. Just as the rush was beginning Gardiner's voice made itself audible above the din.

"Gentlemen, one moment, if you please. Am I to understand that the arrangements which have been made for you, as Members of the Thirteen Club, do not meet with your approval?"

"You are!"

"Then—they shall be changed!"

Precisely what took place I do not know. On a sudden the greenish coloured lights went out. The room was plunged into darkness. In the midst of the consequent confusion mysterious sounds were heard as of persons rushing hither and thither; of the swishing of draperies. People cannoned against me when I moved. That we were about to be the victims of some final, stranger outrage I greatly feared. Perhaps those miscreants whom Gardiner had engaged as waiters were preparing to dip their hands deeper still in crime. I endeavoured to retain my presence of mind, prepared to play the man, though expectant of the worst.

All in an instant, while I was straining my eyes to see what was happening in the darkness, the gloom was gone, the room flashed into radiant brightness. Not lit this time by greenish globes, but by a hundred incandescent lamps which starred the ceiling. And when by degrees our dazzled gaze became accustomed to the unexpected illumination, we recognised that a transformation scene had taken place. There were no funereal hangings, but gaily-frescoed walls. No sombre-looking board, fantastically disfigured, but an inviting-looking table, covered with snow-white drapery, decked with glittering glass and flashing silver. No blood-red figures suggestive of the assistants of the Holy Office, but a dozen smiling waiters, immaculately clad. And at the table's head stood Gardiner, who, with outstretched hand, invited us to take our seats. "Gentlemen, the Inaugural Dinner of the Thirteen Club is at an end, and with it the Club. A dinner of another sort is ready to be served.

I beg you will do me the honour of partaking of it as my guests."

III

Yes, George Gardiner and the man Finlayson had arranged it all between them. I am conscious that, in a fashion, they made of us their butts. They had their little joke at our expense. But, in the end, the laugh was on our side. So we forgave them easily, at least I know I did. I never yet sat down to a better dinner than Gardiner had had prepared for us that night, nor one as good. No doubt the reaction, the surprise, the laughter, provided a piquant sauce. For when we realised that that monstrous menu had been but a ghastly joke, and that a banquet calculated to tempt the jaded palate of an Epicurus was awaiting the favour of our consumption, we enjoyed the joke as heartily as its perpetrator could have himself desired.

As I departed homeward I purchased from an urchin for a shilling his last copy of the night's paper, and found that those shares in which I was interested had been firm, when the Stock Exchange had closed, at an advance of one and a half. Most satisfactory, really. On the following day, when I paid Adeline my usual call, I learned that a lately-deceased aunt had left her quite a snug little legacy. Nothing could have been more agreeable from every point of view. The foolish child assured me that she knew she was going to be visited by a stroke of good fortune since, only two days before, she had found a money spider on the brim of her hat. While I congratulated the dear girl I laughed at her credulity, pointing out that it is only the ignorant who believe in omens. In the present age of enlightenment and progress educated men and women treat them, as of course, with that indifference they deserve. I went on to explain that as articles of faith such trivial superstitions were only possible in the childhood of the world.

But whether or not she was in complete agreement with me I am not wholly sure.

THE END

CPSIA information can be obtained
at www.ICGtesting.com
Printed in the USA
LVHW111215280820
664156LV00004B/604